NOW YOU SEE HIM

BEN REHDER

For my favorite traveling companions...
Mike and Cynthia Smith
Rob and Toni Cordes
See you in August

ACKNOWLEDGMENTS

Much appreciation to Tommy Blackwell, Jim Lindeman, Becky Rehder, Helen Haught Fanick, Mary Summerall, Marsha Moyer, Stacia Hernstrom, Linda Biel, Leo Bricker, Kathy Carrasco, and Pam Headrick. Special thanks to Karen Hobbs and the Canyon Cruiser staff for helping me nail down some details. All errors are my own.

NOW YOU SEE HIM

A ROY BALLARD MYSTERY

BEN REHDER

1

The intruder could hear the heavy snoring of a person who'd had a lot to drink, and it calmed his nerves somewhat as he slipped into the bedroom in near-total darkness. He stopped for a moment and waited. Gave his eyes a chance to adjust. Helped a little. The bed was straight ahead, with the foot facing the bedroom door. To the left of the bed was a short, wide dresser. To the right, a nightstand. That's where the phone would be, if Harvey was like most people his age.

That was his name—Harvey. Harvey Selberg. Worked at a bank. Twenty-five years old. Like the rest of his group, Harvey had really cut loose the previous evening. Lots of shots. Lots of beer.

The air conditioner suddenly cut off and it became much quieter in the room—except for the snoring. Deep and regular. The dude was totally out.

The intruder's palms were moist and his heart was hammering hard. He waited another moment, but his vision didn't improve. This was as good as it was going to get.

Just as he began to step forward, it occurred to him that Harvey might not be alone. He'd had his girlfriend with him on the boat. What if she'd come home with him? What if she was lying in bed with Harvey, eyes open, watching? Waiting. Planning. Maybe Harvey kept a handgun in the nightstand drawer. The intruder knew what he'd do in the same situation. Move quickly and come up firing until the dark shape in the bedroom dropped to the floor. Hard to tell if there was a lump under the blanket at Harvey's side. Maybe. Maybe not.

Son of a bitch. This was crazy. Stupid. He'd just have to risk it.

But it was worth waiting a few minutes, which he did, until the air conditioner kicked on again. Good. That would mask any noise he might make.

He took one small step forward on the carpeted floor, and then another, and another. That's all it took. Now he was right beside the bed, with his thighs no more than eighteen inches from the nightstand.

He squinted. Best as he could tell, Harvey was alone. Harvey, who'd had one too many tequila shots and was now blissfully unaware of, well, just about everything.

The intruder bent forward slowly and reached toward the top of the nightstand. There was no clock of any kind, which was unfortunate, because a clock would've emitted some light and made it easier to see.

Slowly...slowly...grasping in the dark...palms open...

And there it was. Wait. No, that was a wallet. A random burglar would take it, so he stuck it in his pocket. He'd remove any cash later, then trash the rest of it.

He reached to the nightstand again and this time his hand landed squarely on Harvey's phone. It even had the charger cord attached. Harvey, in his inebriated state, had remembered to charge the ol' phone. Priorities, right?

The intruder disconnected the cord, gently placed it on the nightstand, and began to back away with the phone in his hand. As soon as he was outside, he would turn the phone off. That would disable the GPS tracking feature. Couldn't track it if it wasn't turned on.

Then, just to be sure, he would destroy it somehow.

Harvey was still snoring. Hadn't missed a beat.

The intruder turned and made his way for the bedroom door.

And right then, the phone came to life in his hands, blaring the unmistakable opening guitar riff of "Highway to Hell" by AC/DC.

2

I was lounging in bed on a September Sunday morning with a gorgeous blond woman when my biggest client called.

"Are you busy?" Heidi asked right off the bat.

"Not really," I said. "Just spreading joy and contentment around the world, one person at a time."

The blond woman elbowed me, then slipped out of bed, wearing nothing but panties, and made her way into the bathroom. I studied her closely, because the future isn't guaranteed, and if I was never in this enviable position again, I wanted to remember every detail. She had a small tattoo on her hip, above her right buttock. I'd known for several years that she had a tattoo, but I never knew what it was until recently.

"Could you spread a little of that goodwill my way?" Heidi asked. "I need a favor."

"I'll do my best. What's up?"

I could hear Heidi take a big breath.

"This is just me, now," she said. "Not acting as your client. And if you say no, I will totally understand and respect that."

I sat up in bed. The cold air in the room felt good on my bare torso. "Everything okay?"

"I don't know if you saw it on the news, but on Friday night, a twenty-two-year-old kid drowned in Lake Travis. He was out on a party barge, apparently jumped off the top, and never surfaced. They're still looking for him, but at this point, it might be a while before they find his body. Or maybe they won't find it at all."

"I did hear about that," I said. "Saw a headline but didn't

read the article."

"Unfortunately, he was my nephew."

"Oh, hell, Heidi, I'm sorry to hear that."

"Thank you. He's my brother's boy. His name is Jeremy Sawyer. Was. I didn't get the call until yesterday afternoon."

"That's really sad."

Heidi started to say something, but her voice choked up and she took a moment. I waited. I didn't know what to say. I'm not very good in situations like this.

Eventually Heidi said, "My brother and his wife are pretty torn up, as you can imagine."

"Absolutely," I said. "What a horrible thing to happen."

"Here's where the favor comes in," Heidi said. "Would you mind looking into it for me? Nothing elaborate. Just ask a few questions and see what you think. I'm not expecting a big investigation or anything."

I could hear the shower running in the bathroom.

"You know I'd do anything for you, Heidi—especially in these circumstances—but what exactly would I be looking into?"

"I don't know for sure. All I know is that something doesn't seem right."

"How so?"

"Everything the sheriff's office has told us is so vague. From what I understand, nobody even saw him jump off the boat, which seems odd. There were nearly fifty people out there. How could nobody see?"

It wasn't unusual for details to be sketchy in the hours or even days after this type of accident, but there was no need for me to point that out. Heidi already knew that. Instead, I asked if they'd assigned a detective yet.

"It's Ruelas," she said, laughing. "You knew it would be, didn't you?"

I'd be a real jerk if I complained about anything in these circumstances, so I said, "No problem. He's good."

"Yeah, he is."

"Tell me about Jeremy," I said.

"He was a smart kid, Roy. Not rash or impulsive. He doesn't even drink."

I didn't respond to that. I was guessing that Heidi—who was in her forties—might not know her nephew's party habits as well as she thought she did. One thing I remembered from the headline was that the drowning had taken place near Devil's Cove, a notorious party spot on Lake Travis. It wasn't unusual for hundreds of boats to gather in the cove—music blaring, alcohol flowing, nubile young ladies in bikinis gyrating on bows of boats like it was the set of some elaborate music video. The average age of the partygoers was probably twenty-two or twenty-three. In other words, there was a lot of potential for things to go wrong, even if everyone obeyed the laws and ignored the urge to do something stupid or risky.

"Who was he out there with?" I asked.

"Just a group of his friends, and I think one or two people from school. Plus some other people he didn't know. Jeremy and his group didn't have the boat to themselves."

"Where did he go to school?"

"Texas State. Oh, I forgot to mention—he was an amazing swimmer. He's on the swim team."

"Yeah?" I said.

"I sound like I'm grasping, don't I?" Heidi asked. "Like I don't want to accept what happened, so I'm looking for some other explanation."

"It's only natural," I said. "But that doesn't necessarily mean you're wrong."

"Doesn't mean I'm right, either," she said.

"True," I said.

"He literally never did anything crazy or irresponsible in his life," Heidi said. "This was a solid kid."

The shower was still running, and despite the grave nature of my conversation with Heidi, I couldn't help picturing myself in there with the blond woman. Warm water. Steam rising. Lots of lather.

Focus, damn it.

"Tell you what," I said. "Let me make a couple of calls and get back to you later today, okay?"

"You don't mind?"

"Absolutely not. Happy to help."

"If it looks like it was just an accident, well, so be it. I'll accept that."

This, right here—talking on the phone—constituted the majority of my relationship with Heidi. We had rarely met face to face. But that hadn't stopped us from getting to know each other well. Heidi was keenly intelligent, practical, and down to earth. If her instinct was telling her something wasn't right about her nephew's death, that was enough for me.

"I'll let you know if I find anything out," I said.

"Thank you, Roy. My brother and I would be happy to pay you for—"

"Heidi, come on. None of that."

"You sure?"

"Of course."

"You don't know how much I appreciate this."

"No problem. We'll talk soon. And, again, I'm sorry about your nephew."

A minute later, as I stepped into the shower, the blond woman—who also happens to be my business partner—said, "I swear, every time I see myself in the mirror, it catches me off guard. You still like it?"

Mia Madison ran a hand through her hair, which she hadn't gotten wet yet. She'd had the color changed less than a week earlier, and I was still getting used to it myself. The rest of her? Well, it was just as spectacular as it had ever been.

"Love it," I said. "But don't tell Mia."

I leaned in close and gave her a kiss. To hell with morning

breath.

"How is Heidi?" she asked.

"Not very good, unfortunately," I said.

"What's up?"

I explained the situation, and Mia asked some questions, and then she said, "We're not super busy right now. I can handle the Babcock case on my own."

"You don't mind?"

"Of course not. It's Heidi."

I nodded, but I was getting distracted, and my eyes were drifting downward. I know this sounds crazy, but I'd always found it difficult to maintain a conversation for very long while standing naked with Mia in the shower.

She said something else, to which I could only reply, "Huh?"

"Maybe we should resume this conversation after we dry off," she said.

"I think that's a great idea."

If I had accepted Heidi's offer to pay me for my services, I would've been in violation of the Private Security Act in the Texas Occupations Code for acting as an unlicensed private investigator. Mia and I are not private investigators, licensed or otherwise.

We are legal videographers.

I'm sorry, what?

That's one of the replies I typically get when I mention what I do for a living. To be fair, Mia and I aren't your typical legal videographers. Most of them concentrate on filming depositions or court proceedings, which is more complicated and demanding than it seems. And they work with stenographers to produce accurate transcripts.

Mia and I, on the other hand, specialize in capturing video

evidence when a claimant is suspected of committing insurance fraud. Ever seen footage of a guy playing soccer or windsurfing when he allegedly has a cervical fracture or a slipped disc? That's the kind of video Mia and I provide—if we're lucky, and if the subject is actually faking.

Our average day on the job involves a lot of surveillance, boredom out the wazoo, and then perhaps a few minutes of the subject toting a forty-pound bag of dog food to his car. Basically we follow people around and document their deceit and dishonesty. Truth is, it's nice work if you can get it. And we get it, because we are both extremely skilled at it.

Originally, it was just me—a one-man operation—and I would occasionally ask Mia for assistance. She was a bartender at the time, usually free in the daylight hours, and she didn't mind earning an extra hundred bucks here and there. And, of course, I appreciated the way she could help bring a case to a rapid end.

Imagine a guy walking out of Home Depot and he sees a tall redheaded knockout in a short skirt and heels attempting to wrestle a heavy object—say, a new propane grill in a bulky box—into the back of an SUV. What's he going to do? No question. He's going to trip over his own feet in the rush to offer a hand. Then he's going to pick that box up, despite his allegedly torn rotator cuff or ruptured knee ligament, and do the job by himself, happy to demonstrate that he is all man, from top to bottom. I've seen guys do that with a wife or girlfriend lingering nearby, glaring. And, of course, I'm always hidden in my van nearby, video camera running, usually grinning from ear to ear.

Working with Mia in this fashion gave rise to a great idea. Why not work together all the time? And not as boss and employee, but as partners? I ran it by Mia and she liked the idea, although it took some time for her to commit. She eventually did, with some nudging by me, and we'd both been thrilled ever since.

I hadn't told her at the time that I suspected I was in love with her. Wasn't long until I *knew* I was in love with her, deeply and thoroughly. Still took me a long time to tell her. What a wimp.

3

Mia left to run some errands and I stayed at her house in Tarrytown to do some research. I sat on the couch with my laptop and read every available online article about Jeremy's death, scanned the party barge website, and watched several YouTube videos about party barges on Lake Travis—but I didn't learn much more than Heidi had told me.

The party barge operated out of a marina just west of the main basin of the lake, off of Hudson Bend Road, and not far from Devil's Cove. You could rent the barge for a private party, or buy a ticket for one of its regularly scheduled cruises on the weekend. That's what Jeremy and his friends had done, meaning they hadn't known everyone on the boat, just as Heidi had mentioned. That might be relevant, or it might not.

The barge was twenty feet wide, fifty feet long, and had a tubular slide jutting out from the rear. This particular barge was named the Island Hopper and had a Caribbean theme, which, as far as I could tell, meant they played reggae music, or reggae-influenced music, during the cruise, and that was about the extent of it. As far as food and booze, you had to bring your own or hire a caterer.

Then I grabbed my phone. First call I made was to the detective, Ruelas. Disagreeable guy. Arrogant. Had an ego. I was prepared to leave a voicemail because he rarely answered when I called, but on this occasion he did.

"I was wondering when you'd call and start bothering me," he said.

I started to ask why, but then I realized he'd know that Heidi was the victim's aunt, and that Heidi was also my client, and he'd put two and two together.

"I bet you were quivering with anticipation," I said.

Did I mention that Ruelas and I don't get along particularly well? It's mostly because he's an ass, but he's able to hide that side of his personality from some people, like Heidi and Mia, when he chooses.

"I was hoping Mia would call instead," he said.

I'd always suspected that he had a crush on Mia, but that wasn't an outrageous assumption, because most guys did. Harvey Fierstein would've had a crush on Mia.

"She wanted to make the call," I said, "but she decided to place her hand on a hot stove instead. Said it would be more enjoyable."

"Well, we already know she has a masochistic side," Ruelas replied, "seeing as how she hangs around you so much."

It always irritated me when Ruelas managed to come up with a decent rejoinder to one of my scathing and witty remarks. I was tempted to shut him up by gloating about my relationship with Mia—*I've got her and you don't*—but she deserved better than that. Also, our relationship—the seeing-each-other part of it—was new, and I didn't want to jinx it.

So I said, "What can you tell me about Jeremy Sawyer?"

"Why should I tell you anything?" he asked.

"Because I'm charismatic and good looking," I said.

"And delusional. Dive team was at it all day yesterday and they're back out there today. No luck, but sometimes that part of the lake doesn't give up its dead. That's deep water, and one of the flood gates is open at the dam, so the currents are pretty strong."

"What exactly happened on the boat?" I asked.

Ruelas made a scoffing noise. "Had forty-six passengers aboard, and every last one was pretty much shitfaced. And they—"

"Including Jeremy?" I asked.

"His buddies said he was hitting it just as hard as everyone else, and from what I gather, he wasn't much of a drinker, so he was plowed."

This was running counter to the picture of Jeremy that Heidi had painted for me.

"Heidi says he supposedly jumped off the upper deck of the boat," I said.

"He did that a bunch of times," Ruelas said. "They were all doing it, which is pretty routine on one of those barges. And they kept doing it after dark, which ain't the smartest idea. All it takes is one log floating just under the surface. You hit that—bam—it knocks the air out of you, or if you dive in headfirst, you bust your head on it. I know a guy who dove in, then came up fast and slammed his head into the bottom of the boat. Lucky he didn't drown, but his neck is all fucked up and always will be."

"So is that how Jeremy drowned? Jumping off the upper deck?"

"It's a good guess, but we might never know for sure, even if we find the body."

An onlooker might wonder why Ruelas would freely share all of this information with me, considering our mutual disdain for each other. The reason was simple: reciprocation. In the course of our investigations, Mia and I often discovered valuable evidence of fraud and other crimes that we shared with the police. We had provided Ruelas and other cops in the area with some great leads in the past. Ruelas was an arrogant SOB, but like many police detectives I knew, he was driven by practicality and the ability to get results. He knew that if he helped me now, I might help him close a case later. And it worked both ways. Of course, he wouldn't share privileged information with me, but most of this stuff I could pick up by interviewing some of the partygoers. Ruelas was saving me some time and possibly mitigating the need for me to investigate Jeremy's drowning any further.

"Just seems weird that he went missing without anybody seeing anything," I said.

"You ever been on one of those boats?" Ruelas asked.

"Nope."

"Well, it can be hard to keep track of everybody. You've got some people on the bottom level, some on the top, everybody talking, drinking, eating. Somebody jumps into the water every few minutes, then climbs back onto the boat. Nobody is keeping track of anybody else in particular. They should do a buddy system out there, but they don't. There were only two completely sober people on the boat—the captain and the deckhand—and they can't watch everybody, right? Plus, everybody signs a waiver acknowledging that there isn't a lifeguard on board. Anyway, not long after sundown, suddenly one of his friends, Randy, notices he's gone."

"How long had Jeremy been gone?"

"Talking to Randy, it's pretty obvious it could have been a few minutes or half an hour. He thought it was just a few minutes, but he couldn't be sure."

"Was the boat drifting or anchored?" I asked.

I could picture a scenario where Jeremy jumped in, the boat moved, and then Randy noticed he was gone. If that were the case, they would've been looking for Jeremy in the wrong location.

"We don't know for sure," Ruelas said. "The boat was moving when Randy noticed Jeremy missing, but it had been anchored earlier. They stopped the boat where it was and four guys jumped in to look, but what're you gonna do fumbling around in the dark like that, especially when you're drunk? We're lucky we didn't lose a couple more. The captain had some spotlights, but they couldn't find him."

I hated to admit it to myself, but it sounded like Heidi's instinct had been wrong. Her nephew had been the victim of a typical drowning. Alcohol and poor judgment had combined to end in tragedy.

"I guess you've interviewed everybody that was on board?" I said.

Ruelas snorted. "No, genius, I'm using a Magic 8 Ball."

I deserved that. Ruelas was a thorough detective. Thoroughly unlikeable, too, but good at his job.

He said, "The deputies interviewed them Friday night, and when I got the case yesterday morning, I talked to everybody a second time, either in person or by phone, including Randy. Most of 'em didn't see anything. All they knew was suddenly everybody was looking for Jeremy. It took 'em a few minutes to even make sure he wasn't on the boat. They were thinking he was in the john, because the door was locked, but it turned out to be a guy in there getting a blow job."

Ruelas had few filters, at least when speaking to other men.

"Man, I hope they didn't hit any waves," I said.

"You and me both."

"So as far as you can tell, it was purely an accident?" I asked.

He hesitated for just a moment, then said, "Yeah, pretty much."

"Pretty much?"

"There was this one guy named Harvey Selberg on the boat. Totally fried, to the point that even after the initial freak-out, with everybody screaming for Jeremy and searching the boat, and then a couple of deputies showing up, Harvey still didn't know what was going on when the deputy talked to him. He was like, 'Somebody's missing? What happened?'"

"That's really drunk," I said.

"So the deputies eventually let everybody go home. Most of 'em had sobered up enough to drive, but Harvey was still pretty hammered, so his girlfriend drove him home. Anyway, Harvey crashes hard, and then he wakes up at about four-thirty with a burglar in his bedroom."

I hadn't known where this little side story about Harvey had been going, but I hadn't expected that. "What happened?"

"Moron should've kept quiet and let the burglar leave, but no, he gets up, yelling, and goes after him. Got his ass kicked bad, and now he's in Brack. Gonna be there a couple days.

Fractured orbital socket and a concussion. They just moved him out of the ER and into ICU."

"Brack" was Brackenridge Hospital, the oldest public hospital in Texas.

"Where was his girlfriend?" I asked.

"Lucky for her, she dumped him at home, then went to her own place because she was pissed about him getting drunk."

"That's a pretty eventful night for Harvey," I said. "He's out on a party barge where a person drowns, or appears to have drowned, and then he gets beat up by an intruder in his house."

Ruelas only grunted in response.

"You're as skeptical as I am," I said. "That's why you told me about it. It's bothering you, because you figure it can't be a coincidence."

Ruelas still said nothing.

"Right?" I said.

"If there's a connection, hell if I know what it is. You think you're a smart guy, so I'm sure you'll figure it out."

"Did the burglar get anything?" I asked.

"Wallet and phone."

"Did you try—"

"Of course we did," Ruelas said. "Nothing."

He knew what I had been planning to ask. *Did you try tracking the phone?*

I said, "I assume you're going to—"

"Yep," he said.

I was going to ask if they were going to monitor the cell phone for future usage, just in case. This was more effort than the sheriff's office would normally put in for a stolen cell phone, but when you factored in the resulting assault—and the possibility that the theft might have something to do with the disappearance of Jeremy—it was worth the extra effort.

"Any chance Jeremy swam to shore?" I asked. "Maybe it was a practical joke that got out of hand, and now he's too embarrassed or scared to come forward. He thinks he's going to get charged with something."

"We put the word out with his friends and family that if that's what happened, it's not a problem. We just need to know so we can quit wasting time on it. Not that I wouldn't give the little dickhead a hard time."

I had run out of questions.

"I don't know Jeremy's parents," I said, "but Heidi is a really great lady. So, when you find the body—if you find the body—"

"Yeah, what?"

"Just don't be, uh, your usual charming self," I said. I wanted him to take special care with the notification.

"You really are an idiot," he said. "You think I'd just walk in there and say, 'Sorry, ma'am. By the time we found him, the turtles were already snacking on his toes.'"

"Of course not," I said. "I don't think you'd say 'ma'am.'"

"You got any more questions or can I get back to doing real work?" he said. Before I could answer, he added, "Yeah, I thought so. Now just remember you aren't an actual detective and we won't have any trouble." Then he hung up.

I sat for a moment and wondered how I should proceed.

If I'd been doing this favor for someone I didn't like and respect as much as Heidi, I probably would've stopped there. I hadn't learned anything that made me think this was anything other than an accidental drowning. It happens about ten times a day in the United States. Nearly four thousand a year. Many of those people are experienced swimmers. And they aren't drunk. And they still drown. So why should I assume anything different had happened to Jeremy?

But this *was* for Heidi, so I decided I was going to speak with at least one person on that boat and hear a firsthand account of the evening. And I figured it might be better if that person had been sober when Jeremy went missing.

4

Instead of making a phone call and probably getting brushed off, I took a chance and drove out to the marina where the party barge was docked. This particular marina had five piers running like long fingers into Lake Travis, and there must have been at least forty or fifty motorboats of various sizes and models docked in each pier, for a total of nearly two hundred boats.

Still, from where I stood in the crowded parking lot above the marina, the Island Hopper was easy to spot, because it dwarfed every other boat in the marina. It floated in a special slip—twice as long and three times as wide as the other slips—at the end of the center pier.

I walked down some concrete steps to the pier area and saw that the place was bustling, mostly with families preparing their boats for excursions. Dads and moms did most of the work while the kids fidgeted or ran back and forth on the piers, making a nuisance of themselves. There was one group of college kids just departing in a large ski boat, rap music blasting.

As I walked along the pier and neared the barge, I saw a guy in his mid-twenties on the upper deck. Looked like he was mopping.

When I reached the near side of the boat—I had no idea if it was port or starboard—I called up. "Hey, there."

The guy was bigger than I first thought. Maybe six-three and about two-twenty. He stopped mopping and looked down at me. "You're a little early. Can't board until two o'clock."

So the boat was going out today. Well, why not? It had

been only forty hours since one of their customers had disappeared into the murky depths of Lake Travis, but they had a business to run, right? No reason to be all maudlin about it.

"I'm not a customer," I said. "But I am wearing a Speedo underneath my clothes, just in case."

He looked at me with absolutely no expression on his face. "What?"

"My name is Roy Ballard," I said. "Were you on the boat Friday night?"

"You a cop?"

"No, I work with the insurance company," I said.

That was plenty vague. Which insurance company? The one that covered the Island Hopper? Well, no. It was the one Heidi worked for, which otherwise had absolutely nothing to do with the death of Jeremy Sawyer. It wasn't my fault if this guy misconstrued what I meant, was it?

"You should talk to my boss," he said.

"The captain?"

"Yeah, him or the owner."

"Was he on the boat Friday night?" I asked. "The owner?"

The big guy grinned a little. "No. Not likely. I don't think he's ever set foot on it."

"Then I'd prefer to talk to you, if you don't mind," I said. "You were on the boat Friday night, right?"

"Unfortunately, yeah."

The boat itself didn't match well with the name Island Hopper. Tan carpet, beige seats, white fiberglass hull. Shouldn't it be all blues and greens?

"What's your name?" I asked.

"They call me Meatball."

Appropriate. Meatball had a thick torso and humped shoulders. His head was large and round. I was guessing you could punch him real hard and only hurt your hand.

"Interesting," I said. "What's your actual name?"

"Who are you again?"

"Roy Ballard."

"And you're like, what, investigating the drowning?"

Technically, that was true. So I said, "I'm looking into it, yes. Jeremy's aunt is my client."

"I thought you worked for the insurance company," Meatball said. He was leaning on the mop handle, and it looked awfully small in his hands. He was wearing khaki cargo shorts and a teal-colored shirt with an Island Hopper logo on the left breast.

"I'm a freelance legal videographer," I said. "Jeremy's aunt is my client. She works for the insurance company and she asked me to check into it."

All true, although a lawyer or pedant might argue that by saying "the insurance company," I was intending to be deceptive, since Heidi's insurance company had nothing to do with the party barge. I'm a scamp that way.

"Dude," Meatball said, "I feel like you're jerking me around. I don't like being jerked around."

"Who among us does?" I said. "And that's why I always promise a one hundred percent jerk-free experience. Just a couple of questions, that's all."

"The cops already asked me questions," he said.

My neck was starting to tighten from looking up at him.

"Can I come up there for a minute?" I said.

"Nope. Nobody is allowed on the boat except during cruises."

"Can you come down here?"

"Nope. Got work to do, so you'd better start asking if you're gonna ask."

"Did you interact with Jeremy much the other night?"

"Interact, like, how?"

"Talk to him," I said. "Did you and Jeremy have any conversations?"

"A little bit. I talk to everybody on board at some point."

"Did he seem drunk to you?"

"Dude, everybody seemed drunk. That's what happens on

these boats. People get drunk. They screw around. Sometimes bad things happen."

"Would you say he was just drunk or totally wasted?"

"No idea. I probably didn't talk to him for more than thirty seconds."

"What did y'all talk about?"

Meatball shook his head, clearly exasperated with my questions.

"Seriously?" he said. "How the hell am I supposed to remember that? I talk to a lot of passengers. Usually it's like, 'Hey, how much does this boat weigh? How fast can it go? This is a weird toilet. How do you flush it?' Bullshit like that."

I could feel the planks vibrating under my feet as a couple of kids ran toward us along the pier, but they stopped at a ski boat several slips closer to shore.

"Where were you when Jeremy jumped off the boat?" I asked.

"I don't know exactly when he jumped off, so I've got no idea where I was. Besides, I'm usually too busy doing stuff to keep track of everybody."

"Like what? What are your duties on the boat?"

"What does that have to do with anything?"

"Just curiosity, really."

He let out a sigh. "I run the passengers through the safety orientation before we leave the dock. I distribute life jackets if anyone wants one. I pass out the water toys when we anchor."

"Water toys?"

"Yeah, like floating noodles and that stuff. When we anchor for a while, people like to jump in and swim around. They usually like to float with a noodle. We also have some water blasters, which are basically big squirt guns. I do all the head counts—before we leave the dock, when we anchor, when we lift the anchor, and when we get back to the dock. I turn the gas grill on and off if anybody wants to use it. Some people bring meat to grill. If anyone hurls, I have to clean it up. I get ten bucks extra for that."

"Sweet deal," I said.

"You think I like cleaning up puke?"

"Well, probably not as a hobby," I said. "What do you think happened to Jeremy?"

"I think the dude drowned," Meatball said. "Sucks, but it happens. It's our first one, luckily."

"How long have you been working on this boat?"

"Four years."

"Did you know anybody on the boat that night?" I asked.

"Nope."

"No repeat passengers or anything?"

"Who knows? Not like I remember them all."

I saw a short, stocky guy at the far end of the pier, coming in our direction. He was also wearing a teal-colored shirt.

I said, "If Jeremy didn't drown—if something else happened instead—what do you think that would've been?"

"Man, I got no idea. Why would you want me to make a guess like that? What's the point?"

"Using your imagination can be fun," I said.

"Are you making fun of me?" Meatball asked.

"Not at all," I said.

Meatball thought about it and said, "Seems like he was flirting with a lot of the women. Maybe somebody got pissed off."

I said, "Who was he—"

"Dude, I got to get back to work," Meatball said, because he noticed the other guy in the teal-colored shirt, who was now twenty yards away. Meatball turned and walked to the other side of the boat, where I could no longer see him.

As the other man approached, I saw that he was about forty years old, with a red face, a round belly, and four or five days' worth of beard. He was wearing one of those corny captain's hats with an embroidered anchor patch above the shortened bill. He looked at me with some suspicion.

"Help you with something?" he asked.

"You the captain?" I asked.

"I am. Who're you?"

"Roy Ballard. I was hoping to ask you some questions about Friday night."

"You a reporter?"

"Even better. I'm a legal videographer. Jeremy Sawyer's aunt asked me to—"

"Nope," the captain said. "No questions," and he reached toward me, as if to escort me along the pier, toward the shore.

I stayed where I was.

"Just trying to figure out what happened to Jeremy," I said.

"He obviously drowned," the captain said, and now he grabbed me by the right biceps, again trying to get me moving away from the boat. He had a firm grip. I didn't budge.

"You know something?" I said. "I don't like it when short, tubby guys try to manhandle me. Not without any prior intimacy."

His face got even redder.

"You're trespassing," he said.

"There are no signs," I said.

"Yeah, but I'm informing you personally, which is better than any sign."

"You own this marina?" I asked.

He looked tongue-tied, which meant the answer was no.

"That's a nice hat, by the way," I said. "Did you borrow it from Thurston Howell?"

He gripped my arm tighter. "You need to leave right now."

He tried to move me, but I stayed where I was.

Meatball had come back to this side of the boat and was watching us. He looked uncomfortable with the situation.

I said, "You don't own this dock, and you don't own the marina, so you don't have any legal standing to ask me to leave. Now you need to remove your hand, because I promise you don't want me to do it for you."

5

"What did he do?" Mia asked.

"He waited about three seconds—just to prove he's tough, you know—and then he removed it," I said.

I was giving her an update by phone, while I sat in the air-conditioned comfort of my Dodge Caravan, still in the parking lot above the marina.

"Did he say anything else?" she asked.

"We set up a date for tonight. He has dreamy eyes. Other than that, no. Sure makes me wonder, though. Seemed like an overreaction on his part."

"He could be worried about a lawsuit," Mia said. "Or bad press. Or maybe he just feels guilty that one of his passengers drowned. So he's touchy."

Even from this distance, I could see Meatball and the captain on the upper deck, having an animated conversation. For all I knew, the captain was bitching about Meatball's mopping techniques—but I doubted that was the topic.

"But if you were me," I said, "you wouldn't drop it just yet, would you?"

"Oh, hell, no," Mia said.

I had a quick lunch at Rosie's Tamale House on Highway 71—the #4 plate—and then I met a young lady named Jayci Lewis at a coffee shop on William Cannon Drive in South Austin. It was busy, but not so busy that we couldn't get a corner table where we could chat with some privacy.

I guessed that Jayci was in her early twenties. Reddish-brown hair to her shoulders. Blue eyes. Looking cute in khaki shorts, sandals, and a turquoise tank top. She also looked great in a bikini. I knew that because I had seen photos on her Facebook page. Lots of them. They were unavoidable. Plus other photos of her in various low-cut tops or clingy dresses. And the privacy settings were such that anybody—even a skeevy older dude like me who wasn't friends with her—could see them. I think that was the point. She was a Kardashian wannabe. The more likes, the better.

My research earlier at Mia's place had revealed that Jayci had been on the Island Hopper on Friday night. It wasn't hard to find past passengers, because if you posted a photo on social media while you were on the boat, along with the hashtag #islandhopper, they gave you a ten dollar bill when you disembarked at the end of the cruise. Clever marketing.

I had messaged Jayci, explaining that I was looking into Jeremy's death, and asking if we could meet up and talk. I didn't think she would even answer, but she did. I found her reply after my phone call with Mia. Turned out she was in Jeremy's loose group of friends who had signed up for the cruise together. You got a better price if you bought ten tickets at once—more smart marketing.

"How long had you known Jeremy?" I asked Jayci.

"Since high school," she said. "I moved here my sophomore year from Nebraska."

"So you were pretty good friends?"

"We were sort of in the same circle," Jayci said. "We never hooked up, if that's what you're asking."

"Uh, I wasn't going to—"

"You know how you have some friends that you only see if you're hanging with the other friend you both know? He was one of those. Like, we wouldn't do stuff together, just the two of us, but in a group, yeah. I usually saw him when there were a lot of us doing something together. Maybe once or twice a year."

"Who was your mutual friend?" I asked.

"My what?"

"The friend you and Jeremy both knew."

"Caroline. Have you talked to her?"

"Not yet."

"They were together for a while, but they broke up. They were still cool, though, you know? It wasn't like an ugly situation or anything. They both just knew it was better to move on."

"Caroline and Jeremy?"

"Yeah. So are you like a cop or something?"

"No, I'm a legal videographer."

She nodded as if she knew exactly what that was, even though I was sure she didn't.

"I figured a cop wouldn't message me on Facebook," she said.

"Probably not."

"How old are you?" she asked, tilting her head to one side, assessing me.

"More than thirty," I said.

"But not more than forty, right?" she asked, and now she had a coy grin on her face.

I'm no idiot. I knew what was happening. She was flirting—but not because she liked me. She was the type of young lady who flirted because it earned her attention. It was the real-world equivalent of likes on Facebook. I could probably use that to my advantage.

"Of course not," I said. "I'm a long way from forty. Days and days."

"Really?"

"Okay, months. Years, even."

"You're funny," she said.

"But only in a humorous way," I said. "So Caroline was on the boat, too?"

"Actually, no. She was supposed to be, but she got sick and had to stay home."

"How big was your group?"

"Thirteen of us."

"And you didn't know anybody else on the boat?"

"Uh-uh. I mean, we all got to know each other as the night went on, because we were all talking and stuff. But at first, no."

"What did you think of the captain and the deckhand?"

She shrugged. "Fine, I guess. They gave us some safety instructions, but other than that, we didn't really, like, socialize with them."

"So all of the passengers were just drinking and having fun," I said.

"Pretty much," Jayci said.

"Everybody was pretty drunk?" I asked.

"Well, yeah," she said. "Some a little more than others. Or I guess a lot more. Some people were doing Jell-O shots."

"Including you?" I asked.

"Who, me?" she said playfully.

"Heaven forbid," I said.

"I try not to overdo it, because I make bad choices when I get drunk." She said it in a way that meant, *Oh, the stories I could tell! I'm so naughty!*

"Really?" I said. "You seem like such a demure young lady."

"I am!" she said with mock outrage. "But it's not my fault what happens when alcohol is involved. Everybody makes mistakes."

"True," I said.

"A couple of my mistakes were over thirty," she said, eyeing me closely.

Subtle.

"That's weird," I said, "because all of my mistakes were *under* thirty."

She laughed, but I could tell she didn't know how to take that.

"I bet," she finally said.

"So how about Jeremy?" I asked. "Was he drinking?"

She made a face then—not quite an eye roll, but close, combined with a little rueful shake of her head. "He was toasted, yeah, but I think most of it was because he doesn't drink very often. And we mixed up this big batch of punch that was pretty strong. Had, like, vodka and rum and some other stuff in it. The kind where it doesn't taste that strong, but it is, and before you know it…"

"Another mistake is on the horizon?" I said.

"Basically, yeah," she said. "That's how it happens. But, honestly, I wasn't too wasted. I remember everything. Seriously."

"How could you tell that Jeremy was drunk?" I asked.

"Well, he was just, like, being all goofy and everything. Cranking up the music real loud and dancing around all crazy. That's not how he normally is."

Jayci had surprised me earlier by ordering plain old black coffee, instead of some sort of caramel waffle cone blended crème Frappuccino topped with whipped cream and chocolate sprinkles. Good for her.

"How is he normally?" I asked.

"Kinda quiet. I mean, not like shy or anything, but he's not a loud guy. He's never the center of attention. He's the kind that suddenly makes a great joke or wise-ass remark out of nowhere."

"But Friday night he was different?"

I wanted to see if she would confirm what Meatball had said about Jeremy and the ladies on board.

"Totally," Jayci said. "Talking to everybody, including the other people who weren't in our group. He was all over the place—especially with the other girls."

"Oh, yeah? Hitting on 'em?"

"Well, yeah, but in a totally cute and harmless way. Everybody knew he was just drunk."

"Everybody did?"

"I think so," she said.

"So nobody got mad at him—like maybe some of the

other guys who didn't know him?"

She started to answer, then stopped. Her expression became more serious. She said, "Oh, crap. I forgot about that."

"About what?"

She took a moment, staring at some blank point in space, as if waiting for the memory to firm up in her mind. "At one point," she said, "when the boat hit a wave, Jeremy lost his balance and stumbled into this other guy at the railing. Big guy. So this dude totally shoved Jeremy and he almost fell down. He dropped his drink, I remember that. It was a totally uncool moment, but it was just a couple of seconds. I don't even know if anyone else saw it."

"So how did Jeremy respond?"

"He said he was sorry, and the other guy was just, like, 'Watch what you're doing!'"

"Was this other guy with a girl?" I asked.

"Yeah, a really hot one, too. Blond girl with the longest legs I've ever seen. And, like, great boobs."

"Any chance Jeremy flirted with her earlier?"

"Yep," she said, nodding with certainty. "He absolutely did. I remember that for sure."

"Could you hear what he said?"

"No, but she was laughing. She seemed to like it."

"And where was her boyfriend at the time?"

"I don't know. Not with the girl. Somewhere else on the boat. Probably getting a drink or going to the bathroom. Or maybe swimming."

"What time of day was this?"

"Still daylight. Probably late afternoon. That's as close as I can get."

"Any chance the boyfriend's name was Harvey?" I asked. A shot in the dark.

"No, I remember talking to Harvey, and it wasn't him."

"Do you remember the name of the blond's boyfriend—or the blond's name, for that matter?"

"I don't think I ever heard their names," Jayci said.

"If you looked at some pictures from the cruise," I said, "you think you could pick them out?"

"Oh, duh," she said, and she was already getting her phone out of her purse.

6

While this cute young lady was surprising me with helpful information, Mia was hoping to start working on the one active case we had at the moment. The Babcock case—and it was a doozy.

Some background to set the stage: A few years back, a woman made the news when she suddenly began to walk with highly erratic jerks and twitches, arms constricted and held close to her torso, like she was imitating a tyrannosaur. It was some sort of neurological malady, she claimed, and she'd found a doctor to back her up. Oh, and she—this woman from Mobile, Alabama—suddenly had a Scottish accent.

What caused all these problems? According to her, it was a routine flu shot. Vicious side effects, you see? If only she hadn't listened to the mainstream medical establishment. That's what she said later—and she added that the flu shot was nothing but a scam designed to generate money for Big Pharma. But now her eyes were open and she was no longer one of the sheeple.

Her story went viral pretty quickly, and then it disappeared just as fast. I have no idea what happened to her—or her lawsuits. Yes, she sued the manufacturer of the vaccine, because shouldn't they have warned her that she would end up walking like John Cleese and talking like a bad Sean Connery impersonator? She also sued the national drugstore chain where she got the shot, and she sued her doctor for recommending she get the shot. And, of course, it was the insurance companies for these three defendants that ultimately had to foot the legal bill.

You know what insurers worry about in this kind of situation? Copycats. If one woman with a suspicious burr can squeeze some money out of an international conglomerate, what's stopping others from doing the same?

And that leads us to Dennis Babcock, a twenty-three-year-old maintenance technician for an office building in downtown Austin. A little more than three months ago, Babcock scraped his arm on a rusty air conditioning duct and was advised to get a tetanus shot.

Two days after the shot—according to Babcock—he couldn't walk. When he tried, he took short, clumsy steps and would quickly lose his balance and fall forward. He claimed that his legs didn't feel any different than they had before, but somehow the wiring in his head refused to allow him to walk.

And then he discovered that he *could* walk—if he held his arms straight up above his head. With his arms raised, he could walk just as smoothly and efficiently as anyone else, for great distances, but as soon as he lowered his arms, the ability vanished.

Babcock got a lot of media attention, and much of it was the result of his sister and brother-in-law's efforts to spread the word about Dennis's physical impairment. His sister, Lorene, shot videos of her dear, sweet, afflicted brother trying to walk, and he couldn't, and she became so distraught each time, she couldn't help but break down and cry. It was heartbreaking, apparently, for thousands of Americans who voiced their support for Babcock in social media comments, many of them with the grammar and syntax of a seven-year-old. The most popular Dennis Babcock video wasn't a monster viral hit by YouTube standards, but it had gotten close to half a million views.

It was all bullshit, of course. Despite the fact that Babcock had found a doctor willing to diagnose him with some sort of idiopathic neurological disorder or deficit, it was all a crock. A scam. A hoax. But you know what happened in the month after Babcock's claim? Patients across the country began to refuse the tetanus vaccine. Not a lot of them, but enough to cause a concern, considering that tetanus kills about one in ten people who contract it.

So, to avoid any future litigation (because juries are sometimes comprised of the same people commenting on social media), and to prove that the tetanus vaccine was as safe as it had always been, the insurance company hired us to prove that Babcock was faking.

For the past five weeks, we had kept him under surveillance as frequently as we could, taking turns as necessary, and hoping to catch him walking normally with his arms down. No luck so far. The bigger problem was, in the past three weeks, he had become a recluse and hadn't left his house a single time.

Today, however, one hour after Mia and I spoke, the Honda that Babcock's sister Lorene routinely drove left their house. A few minutes after that, Babcock's truck also left the house. How did Mia know this? We had GPS devices attached discreetly to the underside of both vehicles.

Strictly speaking, not legal, but damn was it effective.

Mia climbed into her SUV and went to see what Dennis was up to on this fine Sunday afternoon.

I had learned some good stuff, but that didn't mean I knew how to proceed. I returned to my apartment and pondered the progress I'd made.

Thanks to Jayci, I now had several photos that included the leggy blond and her boyfriend. In all of the photos, Jayci had randomly captured the couple in the background—she hadn't set out to shoot them specifically—so the photos weren't all that great. In one of the photos, the blond was wearing a captain's hat. I figured she must've taken it off the captain's head, just goofing around, having fun. Women like her could get away with antics like that. Or maybe she'd brought her own hat. One of the photos showed the boyfriend from the back, and I noticed he had a shark tattoo on his left shoulder blade.

Jayci had also given me seven photos featuring Jeremy with various other people in his circle of friends on the boat, plus about two dozen other photos without Jeremy, the leggy blond, or her boyfriend.

None were particularly helpful. Just basic party pics. Young drunk people mugging for the camera or caught in the background. Nobody appeared angry or belligerent. Jeremy wasn't fondling anyone, inappropriately or otherwise. Most of the photos were taken during the daylight hours. That's because Jayci got increasingly drunk and taking pictures slipped her mind. That was my theory.

Maybe I should talk to Randy—the friend who had noticed that Jeremy was missing from the boat. Ruelas had said that Randy was blitzed on Friday night, but maybe I could get him to remember something new, like I'd done with Jayci.

It didn't sound particularly promising, considering that he had already been grilled by a deputy, and then by Ruelas. Might as well arbitrarily pick some other passenger on the boat. Or maybe the leggy blond. Or one of the other women on the boat Jeremy might've hit on.

I sat quietly and thought for ten minutes.

Then I scrapped all of those possible choices and went in a different direction entirely.

Like most hospitals, University Medical Center Brackenridge isn't exactly a fortress of security. If you want to see a patient in a general room, you can without any difficulties. If you call ahead to get the room number, you can usually go straight to the room without any physical interaction with any staff members.

Harvey Selberg, however, was in the ICU, so that presented a challenge. The Brack ICU, like most ICUs, had a door that could only be opened by hospital personnel. Fortunately, I've honed my skills over the years for situations like this. In other words, I'm practiced in the art of bullshittery. Didn't mean it always worked, but it would be worth a shot.

Two nurses—one male and one female—were present at the ICU desk when I approached.

The woman, standing at a computer, looked at me over the counter and said, "May I help you?"

The nurse behind her was seated and writing in a chart or something.

"I'm here to see Harvey Selberg," I said.

"Are you a family member?" she asked.

"I'm his cousin Roy," I said, which was true if you accept the theory of evolution, as I do. If you go far enough back in time—billions of generations—we all have a common ancestor. That makes us all brothers and sisters, doesn't it? Or cousins, one might say.

She looked at her computer and poked a couple of keys. "I'm afraid you're not on his visitor list."

"No surprise," I said. "I haven't seen him in several years. Probably fifteen, now that I think about it. But I have a feeling he'll be glad to see me, because I still owe him some money."

This I offered with a big grin. She did not grin back.

"Poker bet," I said. "I had aces and kings, but he had three twos. Boy, did I feel dumb."

Now I was just flat-out lying. It happens from time to time.

"Last time I checked," she said, "he was asleep, so there's not much—"

"Any chance you could check again?" I asked. "And if he's still asleep I don't mind waiting. I drove in from Luling."

Harvey's Facebook profile had revealed that he had family

in Luling.

The nurse pecked at her keyboard some more. I don't know what she was looking for, and maybe it had nothing to do with my request, but eventually she stopped typing, moved around the counter, and said, "Okay, hang on a second."

She hit a button on the wall and went through the double doors.

I waited.

From where I was standing, I couldn't see through the glass in the doors, so I couldn't even guess what was going on back there.

If Harvey was awake, the nurse would tell him that his cousin Roy was waiting to see him, and Harvey would respond...how? Confusion, obviously. But that didn't necessarily spell trouble for me.

Harvey had suffered a blow to the head. And if he was like most guys in their twenties, he wouldn't want the nurse to think he was still loopy—even if he had no frigging idea who was wanting to visit him. He wouldn't want to show any vulnerability or weakness. He wouldn't want to admit that he couldn't remember a cousin Roy. He might even start to wonder if he *did* have a cousin named Roy.

Conversely, if he firmly told the nurse he had no clue who I was, she'd think there was a possibility his memory had been compromised by the concussion. In that case, I wouldn't get in to see him, but at least she wouldn't call security.

I waited some more.

The other nurse—a guy in his thirties—was still writing away, paying me no mind. Who would've guessed that anyone would be writing something by hand in a hospital nowadays?

It was oddly quiet on this floor of the hospital. Very little activity going on. I saw no other visitors.

I felt my silenced phone vibrate in my pocket. I checked it and saw an incoming text from Mia.

FYI, just saw on the news that the dive team found Jeremy's body.

My heart sank, even though I hadn't even known Jeremy. Poor kid. I guess I'd been holding out some small bit of hope that he had swum to shore on Friday night and rambled into the darkness. Some stupid prank. Stranger things had happened. Much stranger.

I texted back: *That's a shame. I'll call Heidi later.*

Just as I slipped my phone back into my pocket, here came the nurse through the double doors. But instead of returning to the nurses station, she stayed where she was, holding one of the doors open.

"You can come on back," she said.

7

GPS trackers aren't just for cops, detectives, fleet managers, and ethically challenged legal videographers anymore. Smart engineers and product developers realized the potential for a much larger market, and now the general public uses them to track their pets, kids, vehicles, and spouses. I heard about one woman who put a unit on her husband's SUV—not because she suspected him of cheating, but because *she* was, and she wanted to have plenty of time to get her boyfriend out of the house before hubby got home.

The benefit for Mia and me is that trackers are cheaper, more accurate, and have longer battery life than they used to. We don't need to order our supplies from some obscure specialty shop, but instead we can buy some damn good trackers on Amazon at bargain prices. What used to cost five hundred bucks now costs seventy-five. Who cares if that unit was designed to attach to Rover's collar? It's just as easy to clip it to the underside of a fraudster's Nissan.

That's what Dennis Babcock owned—a Nissan Frontier. Brand new. Dual cab. Arctic blue. Nice ride. Mia, I learned later, caught up with Dennis Babcock's truck and followed him and his brother-in-law, Roscoe, to a Bill Miller Bar-B-Q on Ben White, where they went through the drive-through lane. Roscoe was driving, because Babcock's license had been suspended.

After that, the blue Frontier proceeded to the Academy store on Brodie Lane, where both Babcock and Roscoe got out and went inside. Babcock walked with his arms straight above his head, which earned some stares from passersby. Mia noticed one woman snapping a photo of Babcock, most likely because she recognized him from the news stories. She'd post it on Facebook or Instagram: *Hey, look, it's that guy that got screwed up from the tetanus shot! Hands up, mister! Gimme your wallet! Ha ha ha!*

The parking lot was fairly crowded, but Mia managed to find a decent spot for her Chevy Tahoe not far from Babcock's Frontier. Then she sat and waited. She didn't follow Dennis Babcock inside, and here's why: She can drive a plain-vanilla SUV that won't attract attention, but under no circumstances can Mia pass herself off as plain vanilla. No matter what she wears or how she presents herself, she's going to turn some heads. That's just a fact. Of course, sometimes we *want* her to turn heads—like when we're trying to sucker some dude into carrying a heavy object out to her vehicle. But in this case, she didn't want to get noticed by the subject.

So she waited, camera ready, AC running.

Twenty minutes passed. Could be a long wait. Maybe they were trying on every pair of shoes available. Or buying a hunting license. That would probably take a while. Probably more time than it would take to buy a hunting rifle.

Finally, after ten more minutes, here they came—Dennis Babcock with his arms over his head, Roscoe carrying a sack filled with whatever they'd bought. Mia realized that they were going to pass directly in front of her SUV, but that was okay. She lowered the camera before they could spot it through her tinted windows.

Mia didn't expect what happened next. How could she? Later, when she told me, I thought she was having a laugh— seeing if she could sucker me.

Dennis and Roscoe were passing in front of Mia's Chevy when Dennis made eye contact with Mia. It wasn't random. It wasn't chance. He found her eyes and he locked in, holding her gaze, with an expression of pleading desperation on his face.

Then he dropped something from his raised right hand.

Something small and white that fluttered gently downward, past Mia's hood and out of her line of sight.

One second later, the strange moment was over. Dennis and Roscoe climbed into the Nissan Frontier and drove away.

The instant they were gone, Mia exited her Chevy and came around to the front. She found the white object directly under her bumper. It was a small piece of paper, no larger than a matchbook cover to start with, and then folded twice.

Mia unfolded it and saw eleven small, scrawled words.

Please help, he's going to kill me. Don't call the police.

Harvey had no clue who I was, of course.

The door to his room closed behind me and I said, "I didn't bring a deck of cards this time."

He frowned, puzzled by my remark, so I figured the nurse hadn't relayed my highly entertaining poker anecdote. Or maybe it was a grimace, because a man in Harvey's condition had every right to grimace. One side of his face was badly swollen and bruised. His right eye was reduced to a slit. Otherwise, he was a healthy-looking guy. Thick all over, but not fat. Probably strong as hell. Hard to tell how tall. Probably six feet. He had black hair trimmed to half an inch and four or five days' worth of stubble for a beard.

"I don't have a cousin named Roy," he said. "Only thing I could figure is maybe you're the asshole that did this to me. So I said sure, let him in."

His speech was muffled, his teeth clenched, as if he couldn't comfortably open his mouth wide enough to enunciate, like a person who had just had a dental procedure. There were no bedside machines beeping or blinking. He did not have an IV attached to his arm. I assumed he was here merely for observation, which would not be unusual with a head injury.

"Wasn't me," I said. "And why would he come to your hospital room?"

"Hell if I know," Harvey said. "I thought it might be like returning to the scene of the crime. Wanting to see your victim, or something sick like that."

"I might be sick in the head," I said, "but it's a harmless kind of sick. I promise I wasn't in your house that night, and I know nothing about it. In fact, that's why I'm here—to learn more."

"Not a cop, though. Right?"

"Nope."

"Because a cop wouldn't have to lie to get in here," he said.

"Mind if I sit?" I asked. There was a padded chair beside the bed. I noticed a cluster of Dallas Cowboys helium balloons floating in the corner.

"Knock yourself out," Harvey said.

I swung the chair around so we could face each other.

"I'm friends with Jeremy's aunt," I said.

"Jeremy, the guy who drowned?"

"Right. His aunt is a client of mine." I explained what I did for a living, being straight up and honest. And then I said that Heidi had asked me to check into the situation.

"What for?" Harvey asked. "Last I heard it was just a drowning."

"And it might be," I said. "There's no harm in making sure, right?"

"I guess not, but won't the police do that?"

"Well, sure, and they can always use an unqualified civilian watching over their shoulder, don't you think?"

He started to grin, and then winced and cupped his jaw with his right hand.

"Sorry," I said.

He shook his head, like *Don't worry about it.*

"Mind if I ask some questions?"

"I've got nothing else going on."

"What was the evening like, in general?"

NOW YOU SEE HIM | 47

He lowered his hand and said, "Just a party, you know, for the first few hours. Then, like I said, I don't remember much about it."

"How many people did you know on the boat?"

"It was just me and my girlfriend. We kinda decided on a whim."

"What's your girlfriend's name?"

"Amelia."

I nodded. "I understand everybody was having a pretty good time with the adult beverages."

"Meaning everybody was getting hammered?" Harvey asked. "Absolutely."

"And that can screw your memory up pretty good, huh?"

"Hell, yeah," Harvey said. "I remember the first few hours, but after that, damn. Just bits and pieces. Guess I overdid it."

"Been there," I said, because I have, and because I didn't want him to feel self-conscious.

"But I didn't do anything stupid, according to Amelia."

"That's lucky," I said. "Tell me what you remember of the first few hours."

"Well, we all got on the boat, and we sat there at the dock for about thirty minutes, and then the crew member guy—"

"The deckhand?"

"Right. He ran us through a little safety drill—life jackets and all that crap—and then we took off. We took sort of a looping path up and around to Devil's Cove."

"And it was crowded, I bet."

"Mobbed. Boats everywhere. It's pretty wild. Ever been there?"

"Unfortunately, no. Too many of the women there have restraining orders against me."

He grinned again and then said, "Ow," returning his palm to his jaw.

"Is it broken?" I asked.

He shook his head. "Bruised, and I got a cracked tooth."

I waited a moment, then said, "Did you hang out with

Jeremy at all?"

"Nah, man. We sort of kept to ourselves. Amelia gets all uptight when I start talking to strangers. Says I'm obnoxious."

"But you knew which one was Jeremy, right?"

"Yeah, because he was wearing a bright-orange swimsuit. I remember that part. So when everybody was looking for him, somebody said, 'The guy in the orange suit.'"

"He wasn't memorable for any other reason?"

"Like what?"

Usually I preferred for people to tell me what happened, rather than the other way around, but in this case, I figured prompting him with real events might jog his memory.

"Did you see Jeremy flirting with any of the women?"

He said, "Well, yeah. But all the guys were flirting. The single ones, anyway. There were some smoke jobs out there."

"Yeah?" My tone said *Tell me more.*

"There was this one blond that could've been a friggin' model. Maybe she is, for all I know."

"Tall girl?" I asked.

"Right. Know who she is?"

"Someone else told me about her. I hear she was there with her boyfriend."

"Dude, I would give my left nut for a shot at a girl like that. Not that Amelia isn't great and everything, but this blond girl was, like, a friggin' goddess. Even the other girls on the boat were checking her out."

"You talk to her?"

I was starting to wonder if the boyfriend was the jealous type. Could that account for the intruder in Harvey's house?

"Not a chance," Harvey said. "Not with Amelia around. Or even if she wasn't, really."

"Did you catch her name? Or her boyfriend's?"

"No."

Dead end.

I sat with Harvey and asked questions for ten more minutes, but nothing useful came from it. Then, finally, he offered one ambiguous, but intriguing, comment.

I said, "So, after a couple hours, everything got a little fuzzy for you?"

"Pretty much, yeah. But there was one thing…I remember that something funny happened, and then something bad."

"Something funny and then something bad," I said.

"That's the only way I can describe it. You know when you're really shitfaced, sometimes you only remember, like, a mood or a feeling? You wake up and go, 'Wait a sec—something bad happened last night, but what was it?' And you can't remember until someone tells you. Or maybe even then you can't remember, but you still have the feeling. It's like this memory that won't quite come back."

"Did the something bad happen to you?" I asked.

"No, I think I was watching it happen."

"Does Amelia remember what it was?"

He shook his head. "She might not have been there when it happened, though."

"Where were you when the funny thing happened?"

"Probably on the upper deck, because I spent most of the cruise up there, except when I had to go downstairs to take a leak."

"Where on the upper deck?" I said.

Based on photos I'd seen of the Island Hopper, the upper deck was basically an open rectangular space—except that the staircase came through the floor near the rear of the boat, and near the front, a small bar occupied one corner.

"Probably near the bar," Harvey said, grinning. "My usual hangout."

"You remember if you took any photos?" I asked.

"I know I did early, and I bet I did later, but my phone's gone, so…"

"Do you store your photos on the cloud?"

"I never got around to setting that up. My phone was just a couple weeks old. This is like my fourth phone this year and it's getting ridiculous."

I was running out of questions about the barge party, so I changed topics.

"Tell me about waking up with an intruder in your house," I said.

"Freaked me out, dude. I hear AC/DC blasting—that's my alarm, 'cause I had to get up way early—but I go to grab my phone off the nightstand and it isn't there. I'm all groggy and hungover and shit, so it takes me a minute to figure out what's going on. Then I realize the phone is in another part of the house, and then I hear someone crashing around out there. I think the guy panicked and forgot how he came in, so he was banging against furniture. I should've just let him go, you know, but I went after him."

He cupped his jaw again. All this talking was probably giving him some pain.

"Want some ice water or something?" I asked.

"Nah, I'm good, thanks. I can take another pain pill pretty soon. Anyway, I start running down the hallway and bam! Somebody decks me hard."

"With their fist or an object?"

"Check this out," he said, and he lifted the hair off his forehead. I leaned in closer and saw a diamond-shaped pattern in the bruising above his eye.

"No idea what they used?" I asked.

"Nope."

"Think it was anything from inside your house?"

"I don't think so. I started to get up and they hit me again, this time across the side of my face. That time I stayed down."

"Did it knock you out?"

"Man, I don't know for sure, but I think so, because I suddenly realized the house was quiet and the dude was gone."

"Any idea how he got in?"

"I left a sliding-glass door unlocked. Bad habit."

"How long have you lived in that house?"

"Three years."

"You own or rent?"

"Well, rent, kinda. My parents own it."

"Got any roommates?" I asked.

He shook his head.

"Ever had any?"

"No."

"Anybody have any reason to be mad at you?"

A bungled burglary would be a good cover for someone who wanted to kick Harvey's ass. I've seen people concoct more elaborate schemes for payback.

"Not that I know of," Harvey said.

"No enemies?" I asked. "You're not sleeping with someone's wife or anything like that?"

"No, I'm generally against doing things that might get me killed."

"Wise choice," I said. "So let me ask you this: Does it seem odd that you'd get assaulted just a few hours after you were on a boat where someone drowned?"

Harvey had a blank expression. "Odd how?"

"I'll take that as a no," I said.

"Okay, but now I'm curious? You saying there might be some kind of connection?"

"Not really," I said. "I'm just shooting in the dark."

The disappointment he felt was obvious. He wanted to be part of a conspiracy.

"I'd give my left nut to find out who sucker-punched me," he said.

I could feel my phone vibrating in my pocket again. I ignored it for the moment and the vibration stopped.

"Dreaming about revenge?" I asked.

"Wouldn't you be?" he said.

I started to give him the trite reply about letting the cops handle it, knowing he probably wouldn't—and who could blame him?—but my phone began to vibrate again, which meant something urgent was happening.

"Excuse me a minute," I said to Harvey. "My pimp is calling."

8

"I have no idea what to think," I said, because Mia had just explained about the note from Dennis Babcock and asked me what I thought. I had left Harvey's room and found a small waiting room nearby with nobody in it. A TV mounted on the wall was tuned to a rerun of *That '70s Show*. "I have to ask— are you positive he dropped the note?"

"Absolutely. And the eye contact was unmistakable. He wanted to make sure I saw him drop it."

I took a seat in one of the padded chairs facing the doorway to the waiting room. There was a coffee maker nearby, but no coffee in the pot.

"For the first time in a long time," I said, "I'm at a loss for words."

"You've never let that stop you," Mia said.

I laughed.

Mia said, "You think he picked me at random?"

"Don't know," I said.

The truth is, no matter how skilled you are at surveillance, there is always the chance your subject will spot you. After all, we don't have an unlimited budget, so we have to use the same vehicles again and again. Eventually, even your average civilian will wonder why he keeps seeing a Dodge Caravan or Chevy Tahoe everywhere he goes.

"Has to be the brother-in-law, Roscoe," I said. "He's the 'he' in the note."

"Agreed," Mia said. "But the question is, is it legitimate? What if Dennis is just having a laugh at my expense?"

And she was right to consider that possibility. Fraudsters

didn't like being watched, and they could be unpredictable in their responses. Some simply came after us with threats or actual violence. Others tried to lose us. And a small percentage would come up with something really unexpected—even a practical joke.

"So do I call the cops?" Mia asked. "Even though the note specifically says not to?"

"Good question," I said.

"You're not helping much."

"I rarely do."

"We don't know what the situation is in that house," Mia said. "What if I call the cops and something bad happens to Dennis later as a result?"

"Don't want that," I said.

"But what if I *don't* call the cops and something happens to him?"

"Don't want that, either," I said.

"Your insight is breathtaking," Mia said.

"I think he's just jerking your chain," I said. "Wanting to throw you off."

"Yeah, and if I call the cops in that situation, I'd look like an idiot," she said.

"A beautiful idiot," I said. "But, yeah."

"Thanks."

"With a drop-dead gorgeous face," I said.

"You're sweet."

"And a body that would give a—"

"Focus, Roy," she said.

"Sorry."

A nurse trotted past in the hallway.

"I need to do some background on Roscoe," Mia said.

"I think so," I said. "Anything more on Jeremy?"

"Not that I've seen."

"Did they say where they found him?"

"About three hundred yards east of Devil's Cove," he said.

Another nurse rushed past. Somebody was having a bad

day in the ICU. I was glad they weren't going toward Harvey's room.

"They're sure it's him?" I asked.

She knew as well as I did what kind of condition the body would be in, and it wasn't pretty. We'd learned more than we wanted to know about that from a case involving a lovely young woman named Erin Gentry, who had been killed and hidden in a stock tank. I'd been the one who found her, and it had left an impression on me that would likely still wash me with sadness when I was eighty years old.

A body in water for nearly forty-eight hours in the Texas heat begins to bloat and decompose quickly, and then turtles and fish begin to nibble on the softer parts. Face. Genitals. And so on. Making a positive ID wasn't always easy without a DNA test.

"Nobody else is missing," she said. "Maybe they used dental records."

I nodded. "Want to do me a favor?" I asked.

"Call Ruelas?" she said.

"If you don't mind."

"Will do."

We both knew he was more likely to answer if she called.

"Any luck today?" she asked.

I brought her up to speed, and she said, "So where does that leave you?"

"No idea. I guess I could talk to some more people on the boat, but I'm not sure I see the point. I have no reason to believe it was anything but a drowning."

We were both silent for a moment, and then Mia said, "It was nice of you to look into it for Heidi."

"Of course it was," I said. "I'm a nice guy."

"Don't deflect," she said.

"But I'm good at it."

"You *are* a nice guy, Roy," she said. "The bestest guy. *My* guy."

I could feel my heart swelling and my face getting warm.

That I lived in a world where a woman like Mia could feel that way about me—well, it was more good fortune than any man deserved.

"Thank you," I said softly.

"You bet. See you at my place in a bit?"

I hadn't thought about where I'd stay that night, but now the question was a no-brainer. I'd swing by my apartment for a change of clothes, and then maybe grab some to-go dinner to take to her house in Tarrytown.

"Absolutely," I said.

After we hung up, I called Heidi and got voicemail.

"Hey, it's Roy," I said. "I heard the news today. I'm sure your brother and his wife have gotten an update from the sheriff's office, but Mia and I are going to talk to Ruelas and see what the situation is. If we learn anything valuable, I'll call you again. I hope that's later tonight, but it's almost six now, so it might be tomorrow. I'm really sorry about Jeremy, Heidi. Please give my condolences to everybody, okay?"

I sat quietly for a moment, just thinking, but nothing came of it.

I went back into Harvey's room and saw that he was asleep. I left a short note thanking him for his help. As an afterthought, I added my phone number, but I doubted I'd talk to him again. There was nothing to investigate.

Still, though, as I walked out to the van, I kept remembering one thing he said.

Something funny and then something bad.

What did that mean?

Ruelas didn't answer when Mia called, but he called her back shortly after. By the time I reached her house in Tarrytown with some Chinese food, he had told her what we both had expected.

The cops couldn't say how Jeremy had died or whether he had any injuries or wounds that hadn't occurred post-mortem. Ruelas also stressed that they had no reason to think a crime had been committed. The autopsy would take place in the next few days, and it would likely confirm that Jeremy had drowned. It would also reveal his blood alcohol content.

"Guess I should call Heidi again," I said after we'd finished eating. We were on the couch with the television volume turned low.

"You don't really want to, huh?"

"I feel like I let her down."

"But why?"

"Because I didn't really find anything out."

"That's because there isn't anything to find out," Mia said.

I didn't reply.

"You don't think he drowned?" Mia asked.

"I don't know. He could've drowned, but that doesn't mean something else didn't happen."

"Like what?"

"Like someone pushing him off the boat when he was too drunk to swim. Or punching him, and he fell overboard. He could've been unconscious when he went into the water."

"But you have no reason to think that's what happened," Mia said.

"No reason to think it didn't," I said.

"Well, in that case, we have no reason to think winged monkeys didn't pick him up, drop him in the water, and hold his head under."

"I looked into that," I said. "Nobody remembers any winged monkeys."

The one thing still bothering me was the burglar in Harvey's house just hours after Jeremy's death. Maybe it really was a coincidence. Coincidences *do* happen now and then, which is why there is a word for such an occurrence.

"Want me to call Heidi for you?" Mia said.

"Thanks, but I'll do it. First, tell me what you learned about Roscoe."

"Nope."

"Why not?"

"Call Heidi, and then we'll talk about Roscoe."

"You've got something good, don't you?"

"Maybe."

"Tell me."

"Nope."

"You little minx."

She just smiled.

So I called Heidi, and she answered this time. I told her what I had learned throughout the day, which wasn't very much. But she was understanding and appreciative, anyway. That's the way Heidi is. She and her other family members had already spoken to several different people from the sheriff's department, including Ruelas and a victim services counselor, and they had told them the same thing Ruelas had told Mia. *Looks like a drowning. Wait for the autopsy, but don't anticipate anything surprising.*

When I got off the phone, Mia came back from the kitchen with two bottles of beer and handed me one. Then she sat down again.

"His full name is Roscoe Trout. Twenty-eight years old. Originally from Bastrop. Divorced, with two kids. Works as a roofer when he can get—"

"Blah, blah, blah," I said. "Get to the good stuff."

She raised an eyebrow at me. "Always in a rush, aren't you?"

"Hey," I said. "Not *always.*"

She waited a long moment to test my patience. Then she said, "He's been busted three times for writing bad checks, once for petty theft, and three years ago…he was charged with insurance fraud."

"There we go," I said. "Details?"

Now she grinned.

"He set his car on fire and claimed it was an accident. The investigators detected accelerant splashed all over the inside of the car. He eventually confessed in exchange for a plea agreement. He is currently on probation."

"This is fantastic," I said.

"Still…" Mia said.

"Yeah, I know. We still don't know what's going on with Roscoe and Dennis. Whatever it is, maybe they're in on it together."

Repeat offenders like Roscoe would try just about anything to muddy the waters and keep their scam running. They might decide that if Mia and I were busy trying to figure out if Dennis was really in danger, we'd have less time to try to catch him walking with his arms down. And they were right. This was a distraction. It would take time to determine what was really happening. And they knew if we called the cops about it, we could end up as laughingstocks.

Then again, Dennis might not be faking. Maybe he really needed help. Or maybe the truth was somewhere in between.

Evidently, Mia was thinking the same thing, because she said, "Remember the pizza delivery guy with a bomb around his neck?"

I did. Bizarre story.

A balding, middle-aged pizza deliveryman in Erie, Pennsylvania, robbed a bank with an odd device attached around his neck. When the police found him minutes later, he claimed that the device was a bomb—which it was—and that he had been forced to rob the bank. He started to panic and say the bomb was going to explode at any minute. And it did. The pizza deliveryman died three minutes before the bomb squad arrived.

Later, however, prosecutors alleged that the pizza man had helped plan the doomed scheme. One of his alleged co-conspirators confirmed that the pizza man was indeed involved, except that he didn't know the bomb was going to be real. They'd double-crossed him. Supposedly. But it was a confusing, tangled case, and plenty of crime experts weren't sure it had ever been completely sorted out.

I didn't expect the Dennis Babcock case to be that complicated, but at a minimum, it was prudent to remember that things weren't always necessarily what they seemed.

"How can we figure out if Dennis's note is legitimate?" I asked.

"That's the question, isn't it?" Mia said, as she rose from the couch and went into the kitchen. I heard the snap of the dead-bolt lock on the back door.

"Maybe we should just walk right up to the front door and talk to him," I said.

"Maybe so," Mia said. She came out of the kitchen and went into the master bathroom off a small central hallway. This being a Tarrytown house that was nearly one hundred years old, it wasn't nearly as large as most modern homes.

"Want to do that tomorrow?" I asked. I figured I might as well help her with the case again, now that I was done investigating Jeremy Sawyer's death.

I heard the splash of water in the tub as Mia started to draw a bath.

"Mia?" I said. She hadn't answered my question.

A moment later, she appeared in the bathroom doorway. She was no longer clothed.

"Sweet Jesus," I said. My heart was already beginning to race.

"How about we forget Dennis Babcock for the night?" she asked.

"Who?"

"That's better," she said. "Gonna join me?" She turned and went back into the bathroom.

9

We had just fallen asleep when Mia's doorbell rang.

I looked through one of the small inset windows and saw two uniformed Travis County deputies on the porch. I recognized one of them—a guy named Leo Bricker, who wasn't my biggest fan. He was one of those cops who didn't appreciate guys like me poking around in investigations, although he would grudgingly accept any helpful information I might share with him. Come to think of it, he was a lot like Ruelas in that way, except that Bricker had zero sense of humor and no ability to roll with a joke. The other deputy was a young woman I'd never met.

I opened the door and said, "Whatever it is, I didn't do it."

"But you don't even know why we're here," Bricker said.

See what I mean? As humorless as a pile of rocks.

"That's true," I said. "I guess you could be handing out good-citizenship awards."

Bricker didn't even smirk. "Not likely. You should answer your phone every now and then. We wasted time driving over to your apartment before we came here."

"You called?" I said.

"About thirty minutes ago."

"I must've been in the middle of my beauty regimen. What's up?"

He said, "You know a man named Gilbert Holloway?"

"Herbert Hoover's vice president?"

"He captains a party barge on Lake Travis."

"Oh, that guy," I said, wondering where this was going. "I didn't know his name until now."

"Did you see him at the lake earlier today?" Bricker asked.

"I did, yeah. Why?"

"Wanna tell us what happened?"

It's never good when a law enforcement officer shows up and starts asking you questions, especially late at night.

"I talked to the deckhand for a few minutes about Jeremy Sawyer, and then Holloway showed up and ran me off. Said I was trespassing. Of course, he doesn't own the property, so..."

"And what else?" Bricker asked.

"We swapped chicken salad recipes," I said.

"Come on, Ballard. Quit screwing around."

I turned to the other deputy and stuck my hand out. "I'm Roy Ballard."

She shook my hand. "Shandra Lewis."

"I hope you're teaching Leo how to be a proper deputy," I said.

"He does all right," Lewis said.

"Ballard," Bricker said. "Give me your side of the story. That's why we're here."

"My side about what?"

Mia came up beside me wearing tan shorts and a blue T-shirt. "Hey, Leo," she said.

"Hi, Mia," he said.

"This is Shandra Lewis," I said.

Mia and Shandra shook hands.

"What's going on?" Mia asked.

"I was asking Roy about an incident at a marina on Lake Travis earlier today," Bricker said.

"It was an incident?" I said. "And here I thought it was merely an occurrence."

"You always gotta joke around like that?" Bricker asked.

I started to answer, but Mia grabbed me by the elbow.

"Annoying, isn't he?" she said. "But he has a heart of gold."

"Fool's gold, maybe," Bricker said, and then he grinned with surprise at his own joke.

"Hey, not bad, Leo," I said. "There's hope for you yet."

"What was the supposed incident?" Mia said.

"That's what I'm trying to get from Roy," Bricker said. "I want him to tell me what happened."

Everybody was looking at me now.

"Am I suspected of a crime?" I asked.

"We are conducting an investigation," Bricker said. "I'm giving you the opportunity to explain what happened, and I'd encourage you to take it."

I had no idea what Gilbert Holloway was claiming I'd done, but whatever it was, the normal course of an investigation would flow as follows: Deputy arrives on scene, in this case the marina, takes the alleged victim's information, and asks if he will come to the substation to meet with a detective and make a sworn statement. If the answer is yes, the detective receives the deputy's report a few days later and makes contact with the victim to get the statement. Several days after that, the detective writes a probable-cause affidavit to get an arrest warrant. The county attorney's office reviews the affidavit and might take several weeks to actually issue the warrant. All of this could take place without a deputy or detective ever contacting or interviewing the alleged perpetrator. But Bricker knew me, and he knew where he could find me, so he was giving me a chance to clear things up. Had to give him credit for that.

So I said, "Like I said, I was talking to the deckhand—he calls himself Meatball—when Gilbert Holloway showed up. He asked who I was and what I was doing there. When I explained, he said I was trespassing and grabbed me by the arm. I could file on him for that, by the way, but my biceps are made of titanium and no damage was done. I did, however, inform him he'd better remove his hand before I removed it myself."

I stopped talking.

Shandra Lewis said, "And what happened next?"

"He removed his hand and I left."

"Nothing else happened?"

"A couple of young ladies complimented my backside, but I'm used to that," I said.

Bricker had a poker face, but Shandra Lewis was grinning a little.

"Do I get to hear what Holloway is saying?" I asked.

"Okay," Bricker said. "He says he asked you to leave, but you refused. So he told you he was going to call the police, at which point you punched him in the face."

"Ah, man," I said, shaking my head. "Not true at all. He's making it up. Look at my hands."

I held them out for the deputies to inspect. Even a well-thrown punch was likely to result in some abrasions or bruising. A poorly thrown punch could easily break a bone or sprain a ligament.

Shandra Lewis glanced at them, but Bricker said, "Problem is, this guy Meatball is backing up Holloway's story. Why would he do that?"

I didn't sleep well, but I woke up next to Mia, so I didn't really have a right to be grouchy, did I?

It was 6:24 in the morning and light was just beginning to sneak around the edges of her bedroom curtains. She was still asleep, so I lay still and continued to ponder the two issues that had kept me awake most of the night.

What should we do about Dennis Babcock?

More important, what should we do about my own damn self? Despite giving my side of the story to the two deputies, I would eventually get arrested for the bullshit assault charge. When an alleged victim had an alleged witness to the alleged assault, it was more or less a given that the alleged perpetrator was screwed. Allegedly.

But why would Gilbert Holloway concoct the story? And why would Meatball play along with it? No matter how I looked at it, I could only arrive at the conclusion that they wanted to stop me from investigating the drowning of Jeremy Sawyer. It sounded so cliché—like something out of an episode of *The Rockford Files*—but what other explanation was there?

And if they were trying to stop me, the next question was…why?

Mia stirred, stretched, and yawned. Then she turned her head toward me and said, "You're still here? Thought you'd be in lock-up by now."

"No cell can hold me," I said.

"Good to know."

"And I'm glad you could sleep so peacefully while certain imprisonment looms over my head."

"It's a gift," she said.

I could hear a wren starting to chirp in one of the trees outside the bedroom window. We didn't speak for several minutes.

"Meatball is the weak link," I said.

"Yeah?"

"I think so. He was actually somewhat cooperative until Gilbert showed up. Then he didn't want to be seen talking to me. Maybe he's just dumb."

We hadn't discussed the problem much after the deputies had left. I had simply assured Mia that I had *not* punched Gilbert, but we were both too tired to discuss it beyond that.

"Unfortunately," Mia said, "Meatball is off limits."

He was a witness, which meant I, as the defendant, could get in trouble for contacting him. Even if I simply asked questions, I would be exposing myself to a charge of witness tampering. If Meatball was willing to lie about the alleged assault, he would have no problem saying I tried to coerce him into changing his story. He might even claim I threatened him.

"Roy?" Mia said, because I hadn't responded to her last comment. "He's off limits."

"Of course he is," I said.

"You have to leave him alone."

"I know I do."

She grabbed me by the chin and turned my head so she could look me in the eye. "I mean it," she said. "Let the sheriff's office sort it out. They'll pick Holloway's story apart, or Meatball's, and charge them with filing a false report."

"And perjury," I said.

"Right. So let the detective handle it."

"I wouldn't have it any other way," I said.

I drove out to the marina later that morning and checked the barge from the parking lot with my binoculars. Meatball—whose actual name was Adam Dudley, according to the deputies—was nowhere on the barge. Neither was Gilbert Holloway or anybody else. Too early. Or maybe they didn't have a cruise today. After all, it was Monday. Not a busy day on the lake, even during the pleasant early fall days.

Mia, meanwhile, had left her house not long after our conversation, because Dennis Babcock was on the move again, or at least his truck was. We had not reached a conclusion about that situation. I suggested the best she could do right now was follow Babcock and see if he dropped another note. Or, even better, if she could get a moment with him alone. Maybe he would tell her what was happening. We had wondered if we should contact Babcock's sister, but had decided against it. If Roscoe, the brother-in-law, really was threatening Dennis, his sister could very well be in on it. It can be difficult for anyone with ethics to imagine that sort of betrayal, but I was long past any such naiveté.

Now I had time on my hands, so I drove south to Fitzhugh Road, west of Austin, and turned on a caliche driveway between two cedar posts. I continued another fifty feet and parked. This was a nine-acre tract with one hundred feet of frontage on Barton Creek. Heavily wooded, gorgeous, and all mine.

I got out of the van and walked several hundred feet downhill to the creek. I stopped five feet from the water and simply stood still, enjoying the solitude.

I had purchased the property with the intent to build a house on it. And it was right here that I'd finally worked up the nerve to tell Mia that I loved her. It had been the most nerve-wracking moment of my life. I'd had no idea how she would respond. Would it freak her out? Alienate her? Ruin the friendship and partnership we both valued so highly? It was risky, but I'd reached the point where I couldn't bear the status quo anymore. I had to take the gamble. So I told her. And her reaction had been better than I'd ever hoped. She had grabbed me and kissed me and things had progressed from there, and we'd ended up wrapped around each other in the pristine waters of the creek.

Best day of my life. Truly, it was. Only one thing could have made it better, if I were going to quibble. She could have told me she loved me, too. She didn't, though, and she still hadn't, but I was being an idiot for fixating on that.

Right?

Give it time. No need to rush things. After all, just a few months earlier she had gotten out of a relationship with a guy named Garlen Gieger.

Garlen, it turned out, had been a drunken, lying scumbag, but he'd managed to hide it from Mia until she'd developed serious feelings for him. Ultimately, I had been instrumental in breaking the two of them up, which had angered him enough to chase me down in a fit of road rage that had covered more than thirty-five miles and crossed county lines. I'm happy to say it had ended poorly for Garlen—both the chase and his relationship with Mia.

On the other hand, if Garlen hadn't forced my hand, would I have told Mia how I felt? Maybe not. Maybe I owed

Garlen a debt of gratitude. What a weird twist that would be.

Okay, but what about this tract of land? I didn't regret buying it, but I had to wonder about the future. I wasn't being presumptuous, and I certainly hadn't broached the issue yet with Mia, but where would our relationship go? If I had my way, it would go on and on, for years and years, and—dare I think it?—might even lead to the M word.

If that happened—if I was that damn lucky—where would we live? Mia's home in Tarrytown had been in her family since the 1920s. No way would she part with it, and I wouldn't expect her to. On the other hand, I could sell this tract in a year or two and probably make a decent profit. Wouldn't be easy, though. The place already had special meaning to me, because of the aforementioned moment when I told Mia I loved her. So, for now, I was simply holding on to the property and waiting to see what would happen.

I could hear a deer snorting somewhere in the brush on the other side of the creek. The gurgling of the water was almost mesmerizing. White-winged doves cooed steadily in nearby live oaks. Occasionally a vehicle passed by on the road seventy yards away. Then I heard a noise behind me—a heavy thud, followed quickly by another, and another.

I spun around and saw a very large man charging right at me.

10

There wasn't time to step aside or try to run, so I braced myself as best I could. He hit me in the upper torso—like he was hitting a tackling dummy—and drove me backward. The force knocked me completely off my feet, airborne for a moment, and then I was plunging upside-down into the cool waters of Barton Creek, the stranger on top of me as I resisted the urge to gasp for breath.

He was trying to grab my throat when my back hit the creek bottom, which was about four feet deep with the water at its current level. The only good news was that his weight advantage was minimized here in the water. I managed to grab his shirtfront and twist him off of me, and now I was able to burst to the surface and get some air.

And then he was all over me again, trying to wrap me up with powerful arms. I snapped a hard left jab and got him directly in the nose. Blood began to flow.

I finally had a decent look at the guy—and I had no idea who he was. Average height, but stocky, with broad shoulders. Short blond hair. Clean shaven. Late twenties.

I noted all that in my head in half a second, and then he was coming after me again, surging forward in the water and trying to grab me, blood still dripping from his nose.

I backed away, saying, "This won't end well for you."

Mind games. Always show confidence. Talk trash.

He grunted and grasped for my shirt again, but I managed to lean back and make him miss.

Ever walked backward in four feet of flowing water with rocks on the bottom? Not easy.

"Why are you here?" I asked. "Doing Gilbert Holloway's dirty work?"

He wasn't going to respond. He had a look of pure animal aggression on his face—totally focused on harming me. I doubted my words even registered.

"You're leaving here in an ambulance," I said.

If he was concerned, he didn't show it.

He moved closer, and I let him. I had my left foot in front of me, right foot trailing behind. Classic boxer's stance. But the current made it difficult to keep my balance.

I shot another left jab at his face, knowing it wouldn't connect because he was still too far away. But he flinched, and that was a good sign. So I jabbed again. He pulled back, plainly wanting to avoid another shot to his nose. I threw yet another jab and he tried to grab my extended arm this time.

I started to make my way toward the bank, but he moved to cut me off. I wanted to be on land, because if he managed to get ahold of me again in the water, he might have the strength to wrap me up and hold me under. Even better if I could reach the van, because I had my nine-millimeter Glock tucked in a secret compartment under the rear passenger bench. A weapon would give me a clear advantage.

A weapon.

Oh, man. Now the solution was obvious.

I pumped another jab toward his nose, and when he flinched, I surged backward and dropped into the water. I kept my feet moving, pushing myself backward, while simultaneously feeling around on the creek bottom. Lots of rocks. Wonderful rocks. Most were too big or too small.

Then I found a good one. About the size of a baseball.

I came up out of the water and he was even closer than he'd been before. I had the rock in my right hand, just under the surface of the water, where he couldn't see it.

I jabbed with my left, and jabbed again, then raised my right and hurled the rock right at his upraised hands. The rock was slick with moss, so it slipped between his hands and caught him hard in the forehead, instantly opening a large gash.

"Fuck!" the guy screamed. "Shit!" He was cupping his forehead with his right hand. A serious amount of blood was leaking between his fingers.

"You might want to let a veterinarian look at that," I said.

"Ow!"

I went under for another rock, but when I came up, he was already wading toward the bank, giving up. He was no danger to me now. Retreating to tend his wounds.

I threw the rock anyway, hitting him squarely in the back as he stepped from the water. He let out an anguished moan and began to jog up the slope.

Just for grins, I threw one more rock at him when he was about twenty yards away.

Missed him, but it made him trot faster.

Good times.

A minute later, I heard a car door slamming.

Right about the time I heaved that third rock, Mia decided to deal with the Dennis Babcock situation head on. Not honestly, necessarily, but head on.

She parked in front of his house—not in her Chevy SUV, but in her classic Ford Mustang, which she can't use for surveillance, for obvious reasons—and walked up the sidewalk to the front door. Gave the doorbell a good ring.

A full minute passed.

She rang the bell again.

Remember, Dennis Babcock had made national headlines several times. He'd been the discussion of scores of heated online debates. This meant that Babcock had had dozens of uninvited visitors show up at his home since his name first went big. This included reporters and journalists. Conspiracy theorists and other nut cases. Neighborhood kids wanting a selfie. Homeopaths and naturopaths who were convinced they could cure him.

This also meant that even if Babcock's affliction were totally real and not a scam, nobody could blame him for not answering the door anymore. Who would want to deal with those kinds of headaches? The only real surprise was that none of the three residents had thought to put any no-trespassing signs on the property.

Mia rang the bell a third time, and then she followed that with a firm knock. She knew that Dennis Babcock was probably home, because his vehicle had returned to the house, and his sister's hadn't left. Roscoe didn't appear to own a vehicle, so that meant all three of them were likely inside the house, unless they had walked somewhere. Unlikely, because even though it was September, the daily high was still in the upper nineties.

Mia thought she heard some movement inside the house.

"Dennis?" she called out.

No answer.

"Hello?" Mia said. "I just need a minute of your time."

Nothing.

"I don't know how to get in touch with you," Mia said loudly, "but I have something important I want to share."

They weren't going to open up. So now Mia had to go for broke.

She said, "My brother got a tetanus shot last weekend. Now he can't walk unless he holds his hands behind his back. It's really sad."

Mia waited to see if that would do it. Still, though, no answer. What if they really weren't home?

"You understand what this means?" Mia continued. "We can team up and work together. Don't you think two plaintiffs would be more believable than one? Just ask your lawyer. Bet he agrees."

It was a brilliant angle, when you thought about it. If the

note Dennis Babcock had dropped yesterday was a prank or a red herring, there was no way anyone inside would open the door. Why would they? There was nothing to gain. They'd know why Mia was really there.

But if the note was legitimate and Dennis Babcock was being threatened—and if we were right to conclude that Roscoe was the person making the threat—how would Roscoe respond?

He might be intrigued, because Dennis's case would be bolstered if a second person appeared to be injured by the tetanus shot, even if that person's claim was every bit as fake as Dennis's.

Roscoe might also be wary, because teaming up with a stranger on the scam could be risky. If this strange woman's brother was a sloppy amateur, he could ruin everything.

Or, perhaps most likely, Roscoe might be suspicious and think Mia's offer was a trap. She was trying to sucker him and expose the fraud. Maybe she'd been hired by the pharmaceutical company, or she was a cop of some kind.

Mia, for her part, didn't really care about all of that. She only cared about two things: One, would someone open the door? And, two, who would it be? The answers to those two questions would shed a lot of light on the situation. Unless, of course, all of our educated guesses were way off base and nothing was as it seemed.

She knocked again.

"Dennis?" she said. "You in there? A lot of people think you're running a con job, but that will change if a second person steps forward. Plus, it doesn't hurt that my brother has a spotless record. He teaches seventh-grade history. You'll never find a more reputable—"

The deadbolt popped and the door began to swing open.

Instead of walking directly up the slope to the van, I took a winding route through the trees, moving slowly, just in case the guy from the creek was still hanging around, despite the door I had heard. Looked like he was long gone.

Who the hell had that guy been? Where had he come from? I could only conclude that he must have followed me here. I decided I would think of him as Creek Guy—creative, huh?—until I knew his real name.

Okay, so what could I conclude from the fact that Creek Guy had followed me? I had come here directly from the marina, hence he had probably spotted me there and followed me over. What had he been doing at the marina? Keeping an eye out for me? Or he just happened to see me? Did it matter? Regardless, the logical conclusion was that he was connected to Gilbert Holloway or Meatball or both.

Interesting.

I reached the van and sat for a few minutes in the driver's seat with the door open, weighing the pros and cons of my next move.

The biggest pro—assuming I was right about Creek Guy following me from the marina—was that I felt confident I could easily find a link between him and the men from the party barge. People like Meatball, Gilbert Holloway, and Creek Guy were out of their depth in this type of situation. They didn't know how to avoid mistakes. Hell, they'd already made mistakes. The blood that Creek Guy had dripped on the way up the slope would support my story. The marina might have security cameras, which would show Creek Guy's vehicle following me off the property.

And what about cons? The biggest one, and maybe the only one, was that I'd have to admit I'd been at the marina this morning. That wouldn't look good, vis-à-vis my making an attempt to influence a witness.

Under normal circumstances, I would figure out who Creek Guy was and respond accordingly. But I had an assault charge hanging over my head, and Creek Guy's lame attempt to harm me, or intimidate me, or make me quit looking into Jeremy's death, was my ticket out of that tight spot.

So I called the sheriff's office.

11

It was Roscoe. He was wearing cargo shorts and a stained green tank top with PARTY, SLEEP, REPEAT written on it in neon letters. He smelled of cigarettes and fried catfish.

"Dang," he said. "We've had a lot of folks knock on our door, but ain't none of 'em looked like you." He was openly letting his eyes roam all over Mia's body, and they came to rest on her breasts for a long moment.

"Uh," Mia said.

Then he looked over her shoulder, out to the street, where her red Mustang was parked. "Sweet ride. Got a 289 in it?"

"It's a 302."

"Even better. Please tell me it ain't no automatic."

"Four speed."

"Praise the Lord. I bet you get guys running off the road tryin' to catch up with you. How many miles on her?"

He had the accent of a man trying as hard as possible to sound like a redneck. Some of it might have been authentic.

"About a hundred and sixty thousand," Mia said. "Still runs great."

"AC, too?"

"Fortunately."

She'd talk about the car all day if it would get her a few minutes with Dennis Babcock. She was hoping Dennis or his sister might show up behind Roscoe, but Mia couldn't see very far into the darkened interior of the house. She could feel cool air flowing outward.

"I love that fastback look," Roscoe said. "Straight outta *Bullitt*. What year is it?"

He stepped onto the porch and closed the door behind him.

"Sixty-eight," Mia said.

"I prefer sixty-nine, if you know what I mean." He grinned at her with yellow, crooked teeth.

"You should write comedy for a living," Mia said.

He pointed at her, like she'd nailed it. "You know, people have told me that before. I wonder how a guy gets started in that bidness."

"With your level of talent, you should just drive out to Hollywood and knock on some doors."

He squinted at her. "Now you're jerking my chain."

"Just a little," Mia said. "Hey, is Dennis around?"

"Who're you?"

"My name is Mia Madison."

He waited, but Mia offered nothing else.

"So what's your deal, Mia?" Roscoe asked. "Selling Tupperware?"

"I was hoping to speak to Dennis."

"About what?"

"Did you hear what I was saying earlier?" Mia asked.

"About going to Hollywood?"

When I first embarked on my career as a legal videographer, I made the mistake of thinking most insurance scammers would stack up as cunning and worthwhile quarry. I was pleased to learn in short order that most of them are about as smart as a wheel of cheese. The only reason some of them ever get away with their scams is dumb luck and limited manpower—and willpower—at the insurance agencies they rip off. Sometimes it's easier and less expensive to pay the scammers off. Sad state of affairs.

"No, I mean before that," Mia said. "Before you opened the door."

"Yup," Roscoe said. "I heard it. And you must think I'm a friggin' idiot."

"Not at all. Why do you say that?"

"Who ya work for?"

"A flower shop," Mia said.

"Bullshit."

"Pardon?"

"You don't work for no flower shop."

"I really do."

"What's it called?"

"R&M Flowers," she said.

"Never heard of 'em."

"Which flower shops have you heard of?" Mia asked.

He opened his mouth, but nothing came out.

"See?" Mia said. "Besides, we don't do any advertising. We're a small shop."

"So small it don't exist," Roscoe said, and he followed it with a knowing snort.

Mia shrugged and said, "Okay, hang on a minute."

She walked out to the Mustang, feeling Roscoe's eyes on her backside the entire time, and returned with a business card. She could have kept one of the cards on her, but it appeared more convincing to get it from the car—like she wasn't expecting to have to prove who she was, but when pushed, she certainly could.

She handed the card to Roscoe and he looked at it closely. Then he looked at her again and said, "Name some flowers for me. Ones I ain't never heard of."

Mia pretended to suddenly understand Roscoe's reluctance. "Oh, you think I'm a reporter or something? Is that what this is about?"

"More like a TV lady, looking the way you do," he said. "Trying to arrange an interview or something." He stuck the card into his pocket.

Mia smiled, and I knew from experience that the smile alone would be enough to make Roscoe believe just about anything she was about to say. He'd *want* to believe. "Okay, flowers you've never heard of. Let's see. Bluebonnet. Daisy. Yellow rose."

He was frowning, totally puzzled.

"Kidding," Mia said. "There's the Dutch amaryllis, which is one of my favorites. Calatheas are nice. Frangiponi. Heliconias. Cryptopodium…"

"Yeah, okay," Roscoe said.

Of course, she had practiced for just such a question. We both had, because we used this cover, and others, on a regular basis. We even had metallic signs we could stick on the side of the van during a surveillance job, and we had a separate cell phone to service that number. If you called it and we didn't answer, you'd get a bubbly voicemail for R&M Flowers. *We're busy with a customer at the moment, but please leave a message and we'll call you right back!*

"So," Mia said, "can I talk to Dennis?"

"Nope."

"Why not?"

"He don't wanna talk to nobody. I handle all of it for him, so he don't have to deal with it. He's sick of all the bullshit—people calling him a freak or a liar. People are just mean, you know?"

"I understand, but I would totally be cool."

"Cain't do it," he said.

Mia waited, because she sensed Roscoe had more to say.

He pulled a pack of Marlboro reds from his cargo shorts and shook one loose. He lit up and said, "Your brother got the tetanus shot?"

"He did, yeah."

"What for?"

"Got bit by a ferret."

"A what?"

"A ferret."

Roscoe was obviously entertained by that possibility. "One of them weaselly sons a bitches?"

"Exactly."

"Damn. That's friggin' crazy. Why was he messing around with a ferret?"

"Fun and games, mostly," Mia said. "Drinking beer and things got out of hand. You know how it goes. Suddenly the ferret was out of the cage and that was all she wrote. Never poke a ferret. That's the bottom line."

He looked at her as if he didn't know whether she was pulling his leg or not.

"Sheesh," he said. "A friggin' ferret."

"I know, right?" she said. "Here's the important thing: my brother got the shot a few days *before* Dennis made the national news. Anybody who got the shot *after*—and then claims to have a similar neurological problem—well, people are going to wonder if they're just trying to jump on the bandwagon. Know what I mean?"

"Got video of him walking?" he asked.

"I do, yeah, but his lawyer said I shouldn't show it to anybody yet."

Roscoe took a long drag on his cigarette and blew the smoke out his nose. "Y'all got a lawyer? What's he saying?"

"*She*," Mia said. "She's saying we got a good case, but that we should team up with Dennis. She said she couldn't contact Dennis directly because that would be a breach of ethics. That made me laugh—a lawyer worrying about ethics."

Mia had no idea if it was true that her imaginary brother's imaginary lawyer couldn't contact Dennis, but it sounded convincing.

Roscoe flicked some ashes but didn't reply.

"My lawyer could talk to your lawyer and work out the details," Mia said.

"We ain't got a lawyer," Roscoe said.

"You *still* don't have a lawyer?" she said with disbelief. "I thought for sure you'd have one by now."

"Thought about it," Roscoe said. "Don't see why we need one."

What an idiot. Then again, a guy like Roscoe would think he could single-handedly negotiate an amazingly complicated legal settlement. Fine by us.

"Fair enough," Mia said.

Roscoe took another drag of his cigarette, then flipped the butt into the yard.

"Way I look at it," Roscoe said, "Dennis got sick first, so he deserves a bigger slice of the pie. Know what I mean?"

This was his way of saying, *We both know it's a scam, but your brother is a copycat, so he doesn't get half. Agreed?*

"I'd have to talk to his lawyer about that," Mia said. "But I'd really like to talk to Dennis first."

"Why?"

"No offense," Mia said, "but I have no way of knowing if you really do speak for him, and—"

"I do," Roscoe said.

"—it only makes sense to hear it from him. Wouldn't you do the same thing if you were me?"

"If I were you," Roscoe said, "I'd look at myself in the mirror all day. Among other things."

Mia wasn't above flirting to gain an advantage, but this guy was just a total creep, and she suspected she wasn't going to get any more out of him today. So she did what she had to do.

She said, "Okay, well, you should think about it. Here, let me give you my cell number."

He returned her business card. She wrote the number on it and handed it back.

He looked at it and grinned. "I bet you can get pictures on your phone, huh?"

"You bet," she said. "What kind of pictures would you be sending me, Roscoe?"

"Oh, this and that," he said, grinning.

"Roscoe?"

"Yeah?"

"You seem like a decent guy," Mia said, stretching the truth to its breaking point, "but if you send me pictures of your dick, I'll come back over here and kick your ass." That last part wasn't stretching the truth at all.

"Jeez," Roscoe said. "It was just a damn joke."

"Don't forget that the cops might get a warrant to search your cell phone some day," Mia said.

"*My* phone?" Roscoe asked. Obviously that possibility had not occurred to him.

"Absolutely. And whatever they find will make the news. You don't want to come across as some sort of letch or weirdo, right? You want to look trustworthy. Normal. In case it ever gets to trial. You want a jury to see dick pics you sent? See, this is why you need a good attorney, who can warn you about stuff like this. Maybe my brother's lawyer could represent Dennis, too. A team effort." She could tell that Roscoe was overwhelmed by everything she was throwing at him, and still somewhat suspicious. "Think about it. Call me."

"We'll see," Roscoe said.

Mia nodded, then walked out to her car. Before she pulled away, she looked toward the porch and saw Roscoe still there, watching her.

To his right, in one of the windows, there stood Dennis. He was holding a sign that said: NO COPS!

12

All social media is helpful, but Facebook is the undisputed king if you want to snoop into a person's life. Or if you simply want to identify someone. Like, say, after some dude randomly assaults you on your own property in a fairly remote location.

It was nine o'clock that evening when I decided to hunt for Creek Guy online. I was on the far right end of Mia's couch. She was stretched out, occupying the remainder—the soles of her feet pressed against my left thigh, her head on a pillow at the other end, already dozing.

The TV was tuned to a rerun of *COPS*. A trucker had parked in a lot for the night and gotten robbed by a woman he'd invited into his cab. Not unusual, except the trucker was dressed in a black teddy and high heels. His legs were pretty good, actually, and I had to hand it to him for not appearing embarrassed at all. He just wanted his wallet back.

I started by searching for Gilbert Holloway and found a handful of people by that name, but none were in the Austin area. So I searched for Adam Dudley, known affectionately by friends and family as "Meatball." Lots of results. Scrolled downward. And downward still.

There he was, the burly bastard.

I checked his timeline and didn't see much. Either he rarely posted, or he had his privacy settings tightened up. His friends list was hidden.

By default, every Facebook user's current profile and cover photos are viewable by the general public, and so are previous profile and cover photos, unless you remember to change the setting for those. That's what Meatball had done. I could see just one profile and cover photo, and there were no comments underneath them. Made me think he had deleted them.

Anyone wanting privacy and security—like Meatball, apparently—would be better advised to deactivate the account until it was safe to go online again. Deactivation didn't delete the account, it simply made the account dormant—and thus invisible to everybody on Facebook, including friends. I knew some people who were such sticklers for privacy, they deactivated their accounts every night and reactivated in the morning.

I was logged in as Linda Patterson, a fake profile I'd created a few years earlier. She was attractive and friendly, or that's how she appeared in the stock photos I'd gotten from a site somewhere in eastern Europe. She lived in Austin, but she didn't say where she went to school, where she worked, or whether she was married. Linda frequently sent friend requests to people just like Meatball. And she would do that in a minute. But first...

I wrote a status update for her that everybody would be able to see, including Meatball, even if he didn't accept the friend request: *Such a tragedy what happened on the lake this weekend. So close to home. Prayers for the family.* I added a crying-face emoji. Nice touch, right?

This would make Meatball wonder if Linda Patterson had some connection to the barge party. Did she know Jeremy Sawyer? Had she been on the cruise? Why did she want to be friends? I sent the friend request.

I jumped over to the profile for Jayci Lewis, the young woman I'd interviewed at the coffee shop. She had already given me all the photos she had taken on the party barge, but maybe someone else had posted photos and tagged her in them. Sadly, there was only one new photo—a selfie of Jayci in a tight dress when she'd gone out to dinner last night. I studied it diligently for several minutes but didn't see any clues.

Now on *COPS*, some slow-witted guy without an ID was

saying his last name was spelled D-L-F-U-M. He couldn't name the year he was born. No surprise that he ended up in handcuffs.

Speaking of cops, the young deputy who had responded to my call earlier had done exactly what I'd wanted: he'd taken a report and collected some blood samples off the ground. I'd told him I'd been accused of assault by Gilbert Holloway, and that I suspected Holloway was trying to prevent me from investigating the death of Jeremy Sawyer, and that I further suspected Creek Guy had been sent by Holloway to send me a message. I kept it as brief as possible, and the deputy took it down, but ultimately I would have to tell it all to the detective who would get assigned to the case. Yes, just as a detective would be assigned to investigate Holloway's claim that I'd assaulted him, a detective would be assigned to this case, too. Not the same detective, obviously. If I could identify Creek Guy and connect him to Holloway, that would go a long way in clearing me. More important, it might help me figure out what happened on the party barge.

Mia stirred. She lifted her head a few inches and looked at me, still half asleep. "What're you doing?"

"Surfing porn," I said.

"Finding anything good?"

"Well, if you like whipped cream, you'd love the video I just watched."

"Mmkay," she said, and lowered her head. Out again in seconds. Investigating Dennis Babcock had tuckered the poor girl out.

We'd had a discussion regarding whether she should alert the cops, but we both still agreed that we shouldn't. We figured there were three possible scenarios: Number one, Dennis and Roscoe were playing mind games, because they were just that bored, holed up in their home, and because they were pinheads, getting their jollies by wasting Mia's time. Number two, Dennis really was in some type of danger, but until we knew what it was, we might cause him harm by alerting the police. Look at the pizza delivery guy with a bomb around his neck. Or, number three, something was happening that we didn't understand—yet—and that's why Mia should keep after it.

I went to Google and tried an advanced search for "adam dudley," and I limited it to results from Facebook. This would allow me to see some comments Adam Dudley had made on profiles or pages that were viewable by the public, and I'd be able to see if he had been tagged in comments other people had made on those pages. The drawback was that there were dozens of Adam Dudleys on Facebook, so I'd have to sort through a lot of junk to find anything useful.

It's my job to thoroughly understand the workings of Facebook, and this was one area in which I was admittedly confused. You'd think there would be thousands of comments on public pages by people named Adam Dudley, but for reasons I didn't understand, the search results were always much smaller than anticipated. In this case, there were 985 hits.

I quickly learned that there was a voice actor named Adam Dudley. And an author named Adam Dudley who wrote business books for entrepreneurs. And an Adam Dudley who worked for some sort of hunting-related organization. Plus lots of other Adam Dudleys with a wide range of interests and activities. But I wasn't seeing any comments from Adam "Meatball" Dudley.

Until I got to the eighth page of hits.

He had commented on a page for a beer joint near Lake Travis called the Bock Dock. I had been in there a few times myself. Always an interesting collection of people—from bikers and frat boys to rednecks and millennials. Meatball had been there three weeks earlier for something called Miss Mermaid night, which was basically a bikini contest that had nothing to do with mermaids, but it tied in to the nautical theme set by the name of the place. Come on down! Half-price drinks for ladies in bikinis, and trophies for the three who get the most votes for the title of Miss Mermaid. The top vote-getter gets a cash prize of $250.

Whoever managed the Bock Dock page had posted an album of photos from that night—eighty-three in all, with the majority featuring women posing for the camera. A long list of comments followed—mostly from men offering their opinions on the event. A few were clever. Many were crass. Adam Dudley had said, *Some fine lookin lady's!*

I began to click through the album photos one by one, and there were additional comments for the women in each individual shot. In some cases, the remarks went from crass to obscene. Frankly, I was beginning to feel embarrassed for my gender. In other words, it was just another day online.

Photo after photo showed a solo woman, or sometimes a couple, or an occasional group shot. Every now and then, a man or two would be in one of the shots—not as the subject, but as a nearby ogler or catcaller. I didn't see Meatball in any of them.

But I did see someone I recognized—a leggy blond with perfect boobs, to paraphrase Jayci's description of her. And Harvey had said this woman could be a friggin' model.

Yep. Same girl from the barge party.

She was wearing a tasteful red two-piece swimsuit and a kimono-style wrap. Standing beside her was a pretty brunette wearing a minuscule black bikini, and her chest was crossed by a white sash declaring her Miss Mermaid. The smile on her face indicated that she was quite proud and excited.

But back to the leggy blond. Interesting to see her and Meatball in the same beer joint at the same time. Could be a coincidence. After all, there was a small population of young, hard-core partiers whose weekends revolved around the lake. It wasn't necessarily surprising that a woman on a party barge on Devil's Cove would appear at a bikini contest at a nearby bar, or that a deckhand on the boat would also attend that contest.

The photo of the leggy blond and the sash-winning

brunette included a caption: *Introducing this month's Miss Mermaid, Amber Graeber!*

I began reading the comments.

Based on the writing skills, some of the men hadn't finished grade school, and some of them were intoxicated or stoned. Some of the comments didn't even make sense. Punctuation was a thing of the past.

Then I found a comment from Meatball: *Starlyn always looks great too!*

He had tagged her, and I followed the link to her profile. Starlyn Kurtis. It was locked down tight. I couldn't view any of her photos or posts.

Starlyn always looks great too!

Obviously Meatball knew Starlyn Kurtis fairly well. So why had he told me he hadn't known any of the customers on the barge the night Jeremy Sawyer died? Why had he lied?

13

"I just don't understand how it could work," Mia said quietly, so nobody could overhear. "At some point, Dennis would have a chance to get away, don't you think? I mean, for instance, instead of dropping that note for me, why not just make a break for it? There were people all around. It's not like Roscoe could pull a gun on him or anything, right there in the Academy parking lot. There would be witnesses. Dennis could run into a store and beg for help. For that matter, all he has to do is walk with his hands down and the jig is up."

"Hands down, jig up," I said. "Clever."

"But if Dennis and Roscoe are pulling a prank, why would Roscoe have that long conversation with me?"

"To make the prank seem that much more realistic?" I said.

"Maybe," she said. Then, after several more seconds, she added, "But I think it's scenario number three."

We had gone over all of this last night, but she was feeling the need to discuss it further, and I didn't blame her at all. Sometimes, when you came at it a second time, you saw things you didn't the first time around.

"Which one is that again?" I asked.

"Something is happening, but we don't know what it is yet," she said.

"That's pretty vague," I said. "And not very helpful at all."

"Right. You came up with that one," she said.

"Sounds about right," I said.

We were having breakfast on Tuesday morning at Magnolia Café on Lake Austin Boulevard, about two miles from Mia's house. It was almost nine o'clock and the place was packed. We were drinking coffee and waiting for our food to arrive. Two tables away, a college-aged guy with a pretty woman his age was sneaking glances at Mia every chance he got. She had her hair in a ponytail this morning. I liked that look. I was starting to get used to the blond.

Speaking of blonds, I was still pondering the relationship between Kurtis and Meatball. What did it mean, if anything? Meatball had said he didn't know anybody on the party barge, but that was untrue. What was he hiding?

"—don't you think?" Mia said.

"I'm sorry, what?"

My mind had been wandering for a moment, but she didn't chide me for it, because it happened to her sometimes, too. Earlier that morning, I had told her what I'd found on the Bock Dock's web page, so she knew I had a lot to mull over.

"If it's scenario two, Dennis's wife has to be in on it, too, don't you think? Because we know there are times when she leaves the house by herself. She could go straight to a police department."

A waiter brought our breakfasts—huevos rancheros for me, poached eggs on an English muffin for Mia—and we went quiet for a few minutes, just eating and enjoying.

"Maybe I should just tell APD what's going on," Mia said.

"Yeah, but the note—"

"I know," she said.

"I'd have to vote no on that," I said.

"If you got a vote," she said. "It's my case now. Don't worry your pretty little head about it."

"Yesterday you wanted my opinion," I said.

"What can I say? I'm fickle. Besides, you have your own case to work on."

"You're gorgeous when you act tough," I said. "Or when you don't."

She gave me the kind of smile that could make an otherwise normal man consider writing poetry. I could even come up with a decent title: *I told her I loved her, but she never told me back, so should I say it again or wait for her to say it?* And now you know why I don't write poetry.

We continued eating, both of us unsure where to go next on our respective cases. I caught the college kid checking out Mia again, so I gave him a wink. He grinned and shook his head at me. I knew what he meant.

Mia's phone was on the table and it vibrated. She picked it up, read for a moment, then leaned closer and said, "Ruelas got the autopsy results. Jeremy Sawyer drowned, no question about it now. No sign of any trauma."

Mia and I split up in the parking lot and I wandered aimlessly for a few minutes. Then I pulled into Zilker Park and found a shady spot near the canoe rental. Good memories.

Mia and I had rented a canoe in the summer—or, rather, I'd surprised her by bringing her here and renting a canoe. Spur of the moment type of thing. She'd been dating Garlen at the time, and he'd later confronted me about the canoe ride, because he'd thought it was some sort of romantic overture on my part. He'd been drunk, obnoxious, and absolutely right. Not that I would've even admitted it to myself at the time.

I kept the AC running in the van because it was already heating up outside. September in Texas isn't much more comfortable than August.

Yeah, that canoe ride.

What kind of jerk would make a move on his partner while she appeared to be in a happy relationship with a handsome, wealthy guy? Funny thing is, I didn't feel bad about it in the least, and Garlen had eventually revealed himself to be an abusive stalker type.

After the car chase, if I'd had my way, Garlen would've spent several years in prison, and I made it plain to the county prosecutor that I wanted that to happen. But Garlen hired a high-dollar lawyer who negotiated a plea deal that centered around Garlen joining a treatment program and staying sober for three years. Sucks, but I understood the reality and practicality of the situation.

Back to things at hand.

I could probably track down Starlyn Kurtis and ask her some questions, but my gut told me I shouldn't do anything else until I'd managed to identify Creek Guy. Figuring out his identity might just bust the entire thing open, whatever this entire "thing" was.

I knew now that Jeremy Sawyer had in fact drowned, but that didn't necessarily mean it was an accident. Somebody might have tossed or pushed him over, and in his drunken state, he had floundered in the water and finally succumbed. But how did Meatball and Gilbert Holloway and Creek Guy fit in?

I had to step back and consider how I might behave if I were the captain of the barge, or even a deckhand, and some poor, drunk kid had fallen, jumped, or gotten pushed off into the darkness and drowned. How would I react? How would most reasonable people react?

Sadness.

Disappointment.

Regret.

Yeah, maybe a sense of responsibility or guilt, even if those feelings weren't merited. One captain and one deckhand couldn't possibly ensure the safety of fifty passengers, especially if those passengers were drinking. But the bottom line was that adults should be expected to behave like adults and not endanger themselves or others, right?

On the other hand, what if there was a reason for Meatball and Gilbert Holloway to feel guilty?

The interior of the Bock Dock was one large room, with a bar running down the left-hand side and tables, booths, and two pool tables taking up the remainder of the space. When I walked in, there were exactly two customers—a middle-aged man and woman seated in a booth in a far corner. They had mugs in front of them and a half-empty pitcher of beer. It was 11:15 on a Tuesday morning, but maybe they were on vacation or something. There were no windows, so the place was fairly dim. The AC was working well.

I grabbed a stool at the bar and nodded at the bartender, a tall, thin guy in his early thirties. I recognized him from at least one previous visit.

"What can I get you?" he asked, tossing a coaster in front of me.

What the hell. It would be noon soon enough. I could see the beers on tap behind him. "Fireman's Four," I said.

"Nice," he said. "My favorite local."

He filled a chilled pilsner glass and set it on the coaster. I took a drink and it was just as refreshing in the morning as it was at night. Go figure.

The bartender started washing some glasses. Guess they were left over from the previous night, because there wouldn't have been many dirty glasses from the present crowd. A TV above the bar was tuned to a foreign soccer game, but the sound was off.

"I've always been curious about something," I said.

"What's that?"

"You've got sort of a nautical theme going on here," I said. "A pelican on the sign outside. Big nets hanging from the ceiling. Sea shells. An octopus painted above the urinal in the bathroom…"

"Right."

"But that's ocean stuff," I said, "and you're on a lake."

"Ha," he said. "I never thought about that. Doesn't make a lot of sense, does it?"

Friendly guy. Open to conversation. Perfect. Helped that

the place was dead.

"And the Miss Mermaid contest," I said. "Do mermaids live in lakes?"

"I guess the owner didn't think about it much," he said.

"Who *is* the owner?" I said. "I've been in here several times, but I don't think I've ever met him. Or her, as the case may be."

"Lawrence Crider."

The name sounded familiar, but I shook my head, indicating I didn't know him.

"He's the original owner?" I asked.

"Yep. He's been in this area for a long time."

I extended a hand over the bar. "My name's Roy."

He wiped his right hand with a towel, then clasped mine. "Zane."

I took another drink of my beer and he went back to washing glasses.

"I've never been to one of those Miss Mermaid contests," I said, "but I know one of the winners."

"Yeah?"

"Amber Graeber."

"Sure, Amber. She's a cool girl."

"And she's friends with Starlyn Kurtis, I think."

"Right. So how do you know Starlyn?"

"Met her at a friend's party. I don't know her well."

"But she's the kind you remember," Zane said, grinning.

"That's a good way to put it," I said.

There was a wink-wink tone to our conversation. We didn't know each other well enough to say, "Damn, she's got a smoking body, doesn't she?" And, of course, I was much too refined to make such a comment.

So I said, "I met her boyfriend, too, but I can't remember his name."

"Anson Byrd."

"That's right. You know them pretty well?"

His shrug said they were just acquaintances. "They come

in now and then," he said. "I think she's going off to get her master's degree somewhere this fall."

"Oh, that's cool. In what field?"

"Don't know, but don't let her looks fool you. She graduated with honors from UT. She's been interning for a state rep. Or maybe it's a senator. I can't remember."

"Interesting," I said. "She never mentioned that to me. Beauty, brains, and modesty, all in one."

"Hard to beat that," Zane said.

"Bet she could win Miss Mermaid in a landslide," I said.

"Yeah, if she ever entered, but she doesn't."

"How come?"

"Probably wouldn't sit real well with the congressman."

"Good point. Is Starlyn planning to run for office herself someday?"

"Wouldn't surprise me."

"Otherwise, why intern for a congressman?" I said.

"Exactly."

At this point, I figured if I asked any more questions about Starlyn, Zane might get suspicious. So I veered in a different direction.

"Hey, I bet you know Meatball, too," I said.

"Oh, sure," Zane said. "Everybody knows Meatball. He gets around."

"He sure does," I said. "He come in here a lot?"

"Here, there, and everywhere," Zane said. "I think he goes out every night of the week, when he isn't working."

I nodded knowingly and took another drink.

"Shame about what happened on the party barge," I said.

"Yeah, no kidding," Zane said. He was done washing glasses. "Hey, hang on a second." He came around the bar and went over to check on the couple in the far corner. He came back with their empty pitcher, refilled it, then took it back.

When he returned behind the bar, I gave it a minute, then said, "I guess Meatball was working that night, huh?"

"Which night?" Zane asked.

"Friday night," I said. "When the guy drowned."

"Yeah, I guess so, since he's the only deckhand Gilbert's got right now."

"That's gotta be pretty freaky," I said. "Being out there and suddenly someone's missing."

I heard the familiar and unmistakable sound of pool balls cascading downward in a coin-operated table. I glanced backward and saw that the couple from the corner had decided to play.

Apparently Zane didn't have much more to say about the barge, so I had to keep the conversation going—without sounding like I was more than a guy stopping in for a beer.

"I almost drowned once," I said. "Tubing on the Comal. Got sucked under on some rapids and almost didn't make it out. I wasn't expecting it, so I didn't have a chance to take a breath before I went under. I'll say one thing—it made me realize how quickly it can happen, even when you're a good swimmer."

"Yikes," Zane said.

"I've never been on one of those party barges, though," I said.

"It's fun," Zane said. "As long as things stay mellow. Problem is, there's usually at least one asshole on board, and you're stuck with him for the duration. Sometimes it's a group of dudes seeing who can be the loudest and most obnoxious. Want another beer?"

"Sure."

He poured a fresh one and sat it in front of me.

"Thanks. I guess it's a good thing most of those boats have two levels. So you can move away from the obnoxious guys."

"Yeah, but if you're a good-looking lady, they follow you."

"Speaking of which," I said, "I heard Starlyn was on that cruise, too. On Friday night."

"I hadn't heard that, but it doesn't surprise me. She goes out on that boat a lot, considering she gets free rides. Obviously."

I tried not to appear too interested. "She does?"

"Well, yeah, if it's not sold out."

"Why? They like to have pretty ladies on board?"

I figured it was another marketing tactic: give free rides to beautiful women and pretty soon men would want to ride that boat. Similar to having a bikini contest at a bar. It brings in the men, who spend money.

"Well, yeah, that doesn't hurt business," Zane said. "But also because her stepdad owns the boat."

Now, finally, I was getting somewhere.

14

At 11:32, Mia got a call from Roscoe Trout on her cell phone. "Ah, fuck it," he said right off the bat. "Guess we should throw in together and see how it goes."

"Who is this?" Mia said, just because she couldn't resist needling him a little.

"Roscoe Trout," he said, indignant as hell.

"Yeah, okay," Mia said. "First thing we should do is set up a meeting between Dennis and my brother's lawyer, so we can—"

"Whoa," Roscoe said. "Hold on."

"What?"

"No meeting. Not with Dennis. The lawyer can meet with me."

"But she'll have to talk to Dennis eventually. There is absolutely no way around that. And I don't understand why Dennis is so reluctant to meet with anyone. What's the deal?"

Mia had decided it was time to push Roscoe harder. If he and Dennis were stringing her along—i.e., scenario one—there would be no harm in pushing. If it was scenario two or three, she stood to gain an advantage by trying to force a meeting with Dennis. As for actually producing her imaginary brother and his imaginary lawyer, Mia could and would handle that when the time came. It was not an insurmountable obstacle by any means.

"Roscoe?" she said, because he hadn't replied.

She could hear him let out a long sigh.

"What's the problem?" Mia asked.

"Dennis is the problem," Roscoe said. "He's...different."

"In what way?"

"He's always been a little out there. There's no telling what he might say or do."

"Okay, well, could you give me an example?"

"Not really. He just has a weird sense of humor, that's all. He likes to say stupid stuff."

A weird sense of humor? Was that why Dennis had dropped the note for Mia?

"Again, can you give me an example?" Mia asked.

"Man, I don't know. Not really. He's just flaky, but not all the time. He can be a smart-ass and a goofball. Reason I bring this up is that your lawyer might not like the way Dennis acts. In fact, we met with a lawyer when all of this started, but he wasn't interested in the case. I think Dennis turned him off."

Mia had no idea what to make of this. Was Dennis Babcock's alleged neurological affliction nothing more than a joke that had gotten out of hand? Not a scam, just a joke, but Dennis got carried away with it? Or maybe Roscoe and his wife had believed it, so Dennis kept the act up.

So Mia had to ask the obvious question—without screwing up the potential partnership she was suggesting by merging Dennis's case with her imaginary brother's case.

"Roscoe, did the lawyer think Dennis was faking it?"

There was a big difference between asking that question and asking whether Dennis was in fact faking it.

"Got no idea," Roscoe said. "All he said was he couldn't take the case."

"Okay, well, can't you just tell Dennis to quit screwing around?"

Roscoe snorted. "That just makes it worse."

"We'll deal with it," Mia said. "The important thing is to arrange a meeting and move forward with the lawsuit. We need to put pressure on the manufacturer of the tetanus shot."

She could hear Roscoe sucking on a cigarette, but he didn't say anything.

"Won't be long before the media won't care about Dennis

anymore," Mia said. "They'll move on to the next thing. That means your case will lose momentum. So will my brother's. We'll miss the window of opportunity."

"How do you know so much about all this shit?" Roscoe asked.

"Our lawyer," Mia said. "And doing research on my own. I want to get some serious cash for Roy. Enough to go around, if you know what I mean."

"Who the hell's Roy?"

"My brother."

Another long pause. Then Roscoe said, "I'm gonna have to think about this some more."

"If you study these kinds of cases," Mia said, "you'll see that we'll be stronger together, and that means we'll get the biggest settlement possible."

"Settlement?"

"Well, yeah, unless you want to wait five or ten years to go to court. Roy's lawyer can explain all these things."

Roscoe gave her a noncommittal grunt.

By this point, Mia was confident that Roscoe was not pulling some sort of prank in conjunction with Dennis. A scam, yes, but not a prank. If Dennis's note was a joke, Roscoe wasn't in on it. In which case he would be the key in helping Mia expose the scam for what it was. Without knowing, of course.

"Tell me what you're thinking, Roscoe," Mia said. "We need to get on the same page."

"I'll get back to you," he said, and he hung up.

So close. Mia felt she was on the verge of breaking this one open. If she had to orchestrate a meeting between Roscoe, Roy, and Roy's attorney, she'd make it happen.

Five minutes later, the cell phone for R&M Flowers rang. Mia had been monitoring that line ever since she'd given the business card to Roscoe yesterday.

Caller ID listed the caller as unknown, but she answered anyway.

"R&M Flowers," she said. "What can we arrange for you?"

Nobody spoke for three seconds, and then the call disconnected.

I was still at the Bock Dock, nursing my second beer. Zane had gone into a small room behind the bar. Replacing a keg, probably. Checking the inventory of bottled and canned beer. That sort of thing. When Mia had been a bartender, I had watched her work often enough to know what the job entailed.

Here's what I knew so far:

Jeremy Sawyer had gotten drunk and flirted with some women on the party barge. Both behaviors were out of character for him.

One of the women was Starlyn Kurtis, the stepdaughter of the boat's owner, who was named Eric Moss. Starlyn's boyfriend, Anson Byrd, was also on the boat.

At some point, Jeremy had gone overboard and drowned, and nobody realized he was gone until it was too late.

Meatball had denied that he'd known anyone on the cruise that night, but he obviously knew Starlyn and probably Anson. Meatball was wary when questioned, and the captain, Gilbert Holloway, was downright hostile.

Then, right after I'd left the marina, Creek Guy had shown up at my acreage and assaulted me. He may have been simply trying to discourage me from looking further into Jeremy's death, or he might have been trying to outright kill me.

The conclusion I drew from all this was that Meatball didn't want to discuss Starlyn because she was somehow involved with the death of Jeremy Sawyer. Or maybe Anson Byrd was. But how? What had happened? And how had it happened without any witnesses? Surely, even in a group of drunk partiers, there would have been one or two witnesses who were also sober enough to tell the deputies what had taken place.

And what about the burglary and resulting assault at Harvey's house? Was that related? Was it possible that Harvey held the key to the mystery? Was that why his phone had been stolen? Or could it have been something in his wallet? Or maybe something else had been stolen, but Harvey hadn't realized it yet.

The couple was still playing pool behind me. I'd watched them for a few minutes, and boy, were they bad.

I'd asked Zane quite a few follow-up questions, of course, when he'd mentioned that Starlyn's stepdad owned the party barge.

First one was, "Excuse me?"

Then I'd kept digging and learned that the stepdad—Eric Moss—had grown up in this area. Star athlete back in the day for Lake Travis High School. Football, baseball, track. Sort of a golden boy. Was a baseball walk-on at UT and made the team. Played one year in a limited role before injuring his shoulder. So he began to focus on his studies instead. Graduated with honors, just like his stepdaughter. Opened a boat rental company that was wildly successful from the start. Not party barges at that point, but ski boats. Now he had fleets of boats on lakes all over Texas.

Finally I reached a point where I had milked all of the information from Zane that I was going to get. Time to take off, but first, I hit the men's room. When I came out, a new customer was at the bar, three stools down from mine.

I took two more steps, then froze, totally taken aback.

Mystified.

Befuddled and bemused, even.

Unless I was mistaken, there, sitting twenty feet away, casually drinking a bottle of Budweiser, was Creek Guy.

Very often, in my line of work, you have to react to a particular situation in a matter of seconds. This was one of those times.

I was staring at Creek Guy's profile, knowing he might turn my way at any moment, and I had to make a decision. Zane and the guy were making small talk, so neither of them was focused on me, but that could change at any time.

Should I confront him? Or attempt to sneak out behind him, and then follow him later when he left? At a minimum, I wanted to identify him. Assuming it really was Creek Guy. I was about ninety percent sure it was.

Sometimes you just have to wing it.

I walked back to the bar and sat in my stool sideways, facing him. Oh, yeah, it was definitely him. He was wearing a baseball cap, but I could see that the upper portion of his forehead was bandaged.

Zane was talking to him, saying something about some skis he had bought recently, when Creek Guy slowly turned to see who had come out of the bathroom.

I was waiting. Grinning big.

His gaze settled on me, and his eyes got real big.

"Fuck," he said, but it was no more than a whisper—just something that escaped spontaneously.

"We meet again," I said. "I know it's trite, but I've always wanted to say that in a situation like this. It's just so perfect."

Then Creek Guy did something entirely predictable. He tried to pretend I hadn't just surprised the hell out of him, and that everything was fine, because he didn't know me at all—right? He ignored what I'd said and turned back toward Zane, trying to act cool.

But Zane had seen what had just happened, and he was confused by it.

"Y'all know each other?" he asked.

Just as Creek Guy began shaking his head, I said, "You bet. This guy tried to drown me yesterday, but I beaned him in the head with a rock. It was actually kind of fun."

Zane said, "Uh…"

"Then I nailed him with another rock square in the back as he ran away."

Creek Guy attempted to appear as puzzled as possible, saying, "Dude, I got no idea what you're talking about."

"You didn't take a drama class in high school, did you?"

"Now I'm really lost."

"You're overacting."

"What the fuck're you—"

"Okay, then tell us. How'd you hurt your head?"

"None of your damn business."

Zane said, "Guys, I don't know what this is about, but you need to take it down a notch."

"What's your name?" I asked Creek Guy.

"Fuck off," he said.

I looked at Zane, hoping he'd tell me, but he said, "I'm staying out of this. Y'all just be cool."

"No problem at all," I said. I turned back to Creek Guy and kept my voice low and relaxed. "Here's the thing," I said. "You left a trail of blood at my place. I called the sheriff's office to file a report, and a deputy collected some of that blood. You're looking at a charge of attempted murder."

"Shit, that's not even—"

"You tried to drown me," I said.

"Bullshit."

"Guys," Zane said.

"It's all in the report," I said. "Everything I told them will match up. They'll see the injury on your head and probably a big bruise on your back, right? They'll do a DNA test and that blood will come back to you. You'd better get yourself a damn good attorney. Even then, well, you're looking at major problems, especially if you have a record already, and I bet you do."

Creek Guy said nothing. Took a drink of beer and tried to look unconcerned. Had both elbows up on the bar, eyes on the silent TV.

"You might do okay in prison," I said. "For awhile. But the gangs—they'll wear you down. Make you do stuff you won't find pleasant."

Zane said, "Dude, seriously, you should probably leave."

I looked at Zane again. "I don't want to cause trouble for you, okay? But this guy here is a suspect in an attempted murder. You want to give me his name?"

"Not particularly," Zane said.

"Fair enough," I said. "But if you do know his name and don't give it to me, you could also be opening yourself up to some charges. I'm willing to ignore all that, but I'll leave when I'm ready to leave. Understood?"

Zane held up his hands. *We're good. No issues here. Take your time.*

I returned my attention to Creek Guy. "When I go outside, I'll see a new vehicle in the parking lot. Yours. I'll take a picture of the plate and it will be easy for the cops to find you. At that point, you will have no more options. You hear me?"

I waited a moment, but Creek Guy kept quiet, staring straight ahead, trying to ignore me. He hadn't had any experience with this sort of thing. He didn't know what to do.

I grabbed a cocktail napkin from a nearby stack.

"Here's the only way you're gonna avoid screwing up the rest of your life," I said. I took out a pen and jotted my cell number on the napkin. I said, "And now I'm about to deliver another cliché. You ready? Here it comes. I need to know who sent you."

Creek Guy didn't respond—as I knew he wouldn't—so I placed the napkin beside his glass of beer.

"I need a name, and I won't tell anybody where I got it." I looked at Zane, who hadn't budged. "You won't tell anyone either, will you?"

"Hell, no," he said. "I don't even know what y'all are talking about."

Back to Creek Guy. "You're in way over your head," I said. "You've got twenty-four hours to call me with a name. After that, you really are fucked. That's a promise. But if you do call with a good name, I might forget what you did yesterday."

He still wasn't looking at me, but the sour expression on his face said I'd shaken him up plenty.

I left a twenty on the bar for Zane and walked out. There I saw a newish Chevy Avalanche parked right beside my van. I snapped a photo of the license plate and took off.

15

Of course, I didn't need the cops to run the plate for me. I had access to a website that allowed me to obtain that kind of information myself, for a reasonable monthly fee.

An hour later, back at my apartment, when I got around to running the plate, the name of the registered owner almost made my laugh. Almost.

Dirk Crider.

Good Lord, this couldn't get any more convoluted. Everything was linked.

Lawrence Crider owned the Bock Dock. I was betting Lawrence was Dirk's daddy. Could be an older brother. Or maybe a cousin.

I ran Dirk through my usual screening process and came up with less than I expected. One arrest for possession of marijuana under two ounces, and the mug shot confirmed without a doubt that Creek Guy was Dirk Crider. That's all I found. If he was on Facebook or any other social media, I couldn't find him. Probably used a nickname.

I wanted to know the exact family connection between Dirk and Lawrence Crider. Not that it mattered, necessarily, but it wouldn't hurt to find out. I found Lawrence Crider on Facebook, but I couldn't see his friends list or many of his posts. I found other Criders who lived in the Austin area, but I couldn't tell if they were relatives or not.

So I did the next-best thing and logged in to a popular ancestry website. Very often I could find complete family trees for anyone I was investigating, and that could be incredibly helpful, assuming the trees were accurate. I didn't know if the information would turn out to be helpful this time, but in less than ten minutes, I learned that Lawrence Crider was indeed Dirk's uncle.

I could hear Rita, the resident in the apartment directly across the breezeway, closing her door as she entered or exited her apartment. She was great, as neighbors went. A cashier at Whole Foods Market. Quiet. Didn't have a lot of people coming and going.

I'd been meaning to move out of this damn apartment for several years, which is why I'd bought the acreage on Barton Creek. But then Mia and I had gotten together, and that muddied the picture. Or it did for me, at least. I would move in with her tomorrow, if she asked. Or I'd build a dream house for the both of us. Maybe I needed to tap the brakes a little. I'd never been the type to rush things before. Why do it now?

Contemplating the situation with Mia was making me restless.

At a minimum, maybe I should move to a different apartment. Something nicer and bigger, in a complex with people closer to my age. Get a lease that was a year long, max. Six months would be even better.

Now I spent some time researching Anson Byrd, but there wasn't much to find out. If he had a Facebook account, I couldn't find it. He had a Twitter account, but he didn't tweet much, and none of his tweets were helpful. I learned that he played lacrosse in high school, and he had boxed for a few years at the Golden Gloves level, which was kind of unusual for a white kid who had grown up in western Travis County. He had never been arrested, or if he had, it had been expunged from his record. He didn't own any real property in Travis County. He wasn't registered to vote. Dead end after that.

I was sitting on the couch with my laptop. I placed it on the coffee table and stretched out.

At the moment, I wasn't sure what to do next. I'd hit a roadblock. But I'd hit them before many times, and I'd learned that often you simply had to set the problem aside for awhile, then come at it from another angle later.

So I took a nap. Two solid hours. Woke up at nearly four o'clock.

It was still warm outside, so I went to the pool for an hour. I had it all to myself. Not unusual on a weekday.

While I was there, I called Mia and got an update on her situation with Dennis Babcock. She sounded tired and a little stressed, so I told her to have a good evening and I'd touch base in the morning. Some alone time wouldn't hurt anybody.

I returned to my apartment and had a quiet evening. Went to bed at ten. Read a Tim Bryant novel for a while, then set my Kindle aside and lay quietly in the dark, thinking.

I'm not exactly sure what I would do if I were ever in Dirk Crider's position, mostly because I've never been in that position. Squeal on somebody or face criminal prosecution. Tough choice. I guess, for me, it would depend on who I would need to squeal on. Was it a relative? A friend? Ouch. But an acquaintance or someone I didn't know at all? Much easier decision.

But I knew one thing for sure.

Once I decided that I would squeal, I would make the call in the middle of the night, just to inconvenience the person who had forced me into that position. Just to wake him up and enjoy that small measure of satisfaction.

And that's exactly what Dirk Crider did.

The ringing woke me at 2:47.

Maybe he'd been drinking, or doing drugs. It was hard to know for sure, because I didn't know the guy. He sounded agitated, by any measure.

"This fucking sucks," he said.

"I'm sure it does," I said. "But you're doing the right thing."

"So if I tell you, we're good—me and you?"

"As long as it's the truth," I said, easing myself out of bed.

"No charges for what happened at the creek?"

"As long as you tell me the truth, and you weren't involved in anything else. And you answer all my questions—now, and later if I have any."

By now I had grabbed a little digital recorder and was holding it up by my ear to capture our conversation. Just in case. It was legal in Texas for one party to record a call without the other knowing—not that it would have stopped me if it hadn't been legal.

"And you won't tell nobody I told you?"

"That's the deal."

A fellow has to stretch the truth on occasion.

"Okay," Dirk said. He took a deep breath. "It was Gilbert."

"Gilbert Holloway?"

"Right."

"How do you know him?"

"I used to work for him."

"On the boat?"

"Right. I was a deckhand."

"On the Island Hopper?"

"Right."

"When was this?"

"Coupla years ago."

"And you quit?"

"He fired me. But Eric made him do it."

"Why was that?"

"I screwed up on a cruise and didn't have enough life jackets on board. Totally my bad. The friggin' game warden wrote us a ticket, and Eric said we could've lost our insurance because of that. So Gilbert had to fire me."

"You're talking about Eric Moss?"

"Right."

"How well do you know him?"

"I met him a couple of times, that's all."

"How long did you work on the boat?"

"Four years, but just during the summer."

"I assume you heard about Jeremy Sawyer."

"Who?"

"The guy who drowned last Friday."

"Oh, man. Is that what this is all about? I didn't remember his name."

What a jerk.

"Did you talk to Gilbert or Meatball about it?" I asked.

"A little, yeah. To Gilbert, not Meatball. I haven't seen him in a while."

"And what did he say?"

"I just told you I didn't talk to him."

"I'm talking about Gilbert."

"Oh. He said it was just an accident and nobody did nothing wrong. The guy jumped off when nobody was looking and he drowned. End of story. But Gilbert was pretty stressed about it. He's a sensitive guy."

That made me grin, but I didn't laugh.

"Okay, so tell me about the reason you came after me."

"Well, Gilbert called and said he needed a favor, and he wanted to get together and talk about it. I asked what kind of favor, but he didn't want to say on the phone. He said I could earn five hundred bucks if I'd help him out with something. So I met him at the marina yesterday afternoon."

I knew what was coming.

Dirk said, "We were talking in his truck, and he was saying there was a guy that was giving him some trouble, and he was wondering if I'd, you know, kick this guy's ass. I asked him what the problem was, and he just said it wasn't anything too important, but this guy deserved an ass kicking, and if I didn't want to do it, that's fine, but he'd find someone else who wanted to earn the money. I figured, like, Gilbert probably had a pretty good reason to be asking, so I said yeah, I'd do it."

I couldn't help being disgusted with the guy.

"That's all it took?" I said. "You didn't even ask any more questions?"

"Hey, man, I was gonna, but before I even had the chance, Gilbert says, 'Holy shit, there he is now.' And he points to your van. We could see you scoping the place out with your binoculars."

Yep. That's what I had suspected. Terribly sloppy work on my part. The kind of thing that could blow a case or get me seriously injured. Stupid. Couldn't do anything about it now except learn from it.

"And then what?" I asked.

"Gilbert was rushing me, saying I'd better make up my mind right now, because this would be a great chance to follow you and take care of it."

"So that's what you did," I said.

"Yeah."

I couldn't resist asking, "How'd that work out for you?"

"Dude," he said, "that rock hurt. I still have a headache."

"Did you go to a doctor?"

"Yeah. Got seven stitches."

What do you do with a guy like this? Lecture him and hope he learns from it? I wasn't in the mood.

"Are you the one who broke into Harvey's house?"

"Who?"

"Harvey Selberg."

"I got no idea who that is."

"Then I'll put it this way. Have you broken into *anyone's* house lately?"

"Hell, no. I don't do that kind of thing."

"He wound up in the ER."

"Wasn't me, I swear. I don't know him."

"You know Starlyn Kurtis?" I asked.

"Sure. What about her?"

"I want her phone number."

"Ah, man. What for?"

"None of your damn business, really, but I'll tell you anyway. She was on the boat that night, so I might want to ask her some questions."

"That's all?"

"Yep. I'm not even sure if I'll call her or not. And I won't tell her where I got the number."

He reluctantly gave it to me.

"I might have more questions later," I said. "Don't dodge me if I call."

"Yeah, okay," he said with all the enthusiasm of a kid kicking the dirt.

16

I managed to sleep late and woke up the next morning at eight o'clock in a much better mood.

Gilbert Holloway had an assault case pending against me, but now I had an ace card to play against him. He'd sent someone after me—not just for retribution, but to stop me from investigating the death of Jeremy Sawyer.

But the question remained: Why?

The other question: What was I going to do about it?

I had the recording of my conversation with Dirk Crider, and despite what I'd told him, I'd use it as leverage to force Holloway to drop his assault case, if need be. But that wouldn't get me any closer to figuring out why there was a cover-up in regard to Jeremy's death.

I texted Mia, but she didn't reply right away, so I showered and shaved.

When I was done, she had sent a reply. *Good morning. Slow start today.*

I didn't know if she was referring to me or her.

She'd added a little heart emoji. Was that the same as saying she loved me? Of course not.

I said: *What's your plan today?*

Again, she didn't reply right away, so I went outside and climbed into my little gray Toyota. That was my back-up vehicle when the van had been seen too many times by a subject. I stopped at Maria's Taco Xpress for a couple of breakfast tacos with egg, bacon, and cheese, and then I decided to grab a few extra and make a stop at Mia's. If she'd already eaten, that was fine. She could save them for tomorrow.

I made my way up to Tarrytown, and as I approached Mia's house, I saw a shiny new BMW with dealer plates parked in her driveway.

Something weird happened. I started to pull over to the curb, but I changed my mind—don't know why—and kept going instead. Drove past her house. The curtains were all closed.

I went to the end of the block and pulled over for a moment. Why was I having an odd feeling about this? Partly because Mia generally texted me back fairly quickly, especially if she was at home, as opposed to out running errands or tailing a subject.

And who would be at Mia's place at 9:12 on a Wednesday morning in a spiffy new BMW? An answer sprang to mind, but I didn't want to believe it.

I double-checked my phone. Mia still hadn't answered my last text.

I turned around and drove slowly back to her place. This time I pulled to the curb. I knew from being inside her house that, with the curtains drawn, nobody inside could see me. I got out and walked to the BMW. Put my hand on the hood and immediately felt an overwhelming sense of relief.

The hood was warm.

The car hadn't been parked there long. Not overnight.

I checked the dealer plate, but the handwriting was so poor, I couldn't make out the name of the new owner.

I got back into my Toyota and drove to the other end of the block. I knew I should do one of two things: either go back to Mia's and knock on the door, or go on about my day without a further thought. She had a visitor. So what? Could be a neighbor. A friend.

I made it as far as Lake Austin Boulevard, and then I turned around.

Drove back to Mia's block and parked at the curb, thirty yards down from her place. I was in the shade of an enormous Spanish oak, but if Mia should happen to come outside and glance this way, she'd recognize my Toyota immediately. I couldn't see her front door, but I could see the BMW in the driveway.

What was I doing?

Just checking, this one time. Just making sure. After this, never again. That was reasonable, wasn't it?

The bag of tacos was in my passenger seat, but I had no appetite now.

Fifteen minutes passed.

Still no text from Mia.

A couple of cars drove by, but in general, this was a quiet street. The walkers and joggers had probably already finished their morning routine, when it was ten degrees cooler.

Fifteen more minutes passed.

I realized that I could be sitting here for hours. Was I ready to do that, considering that I was feeling more pathetic with each passing minute?

The answer, apparently, was yes.

Ten more minutes passed.

I reached for the key, and right then I saw a man walking toward the BMW.

There was no mistaking who it was.

Garlen Gieger, Mia's former boyfriend.

I drove.

Probably a danger to everyone else on the road.

Pulled over in a grocery store parking lot.

Sat quietly for a few minutes and tried not to let my emotions get the best of me. It wasn't easy.

I don't know if I'd ever felt more betrayed.

She had texted me back just moments after Garlen had left her place, but I hadn't answered yet. Too angry. Without question, I would say some things I'd regret.

But here's something I knew deep down inside. She wasn't seeing him again. There would be some other explanation—and I wouldn't like it—but she wasn't seeing him again. I would bet my life on it. Literally.

Not that Garlen wasn't trying to make that happen.

I pondered my options.

One was to confront Garlen and possibly beat the living hell out of him. Oh, so tempting. Stupid, though. Especially since I was currently suspected of assaulting Gilbert Holloway. Didn't want to establish a pattern.

The second option was to call the cops, which is what Mia and I were supposed to do if Garlen reared his ugly head, because we both had active protective orders against him. There was supposed to be zero contact between Mia and Garlen. Not even a text, an email, or a phone call. Not a smoke signal or a carrier pigeon. The cops could enforce the protective order even if Mia hadn't reported the violation herself. I'd been flustered watching Garlen walk out to his car, but I'd had the presence of mind to snap a couple of quick photos. Great evidence, if needed. Garlen would go to jail, his plea deal scrapped. But why hadn't Mia reported it?

Ten minutes ticked by and eventually I began to calm down a little.

The mature course of action—if I insisted on doing something—would be to tell Mia I'd seen Garlen walking out of her place, and ask her in a measured, trusting tone of voice why he'd been there. That would be reasonable. After all, the guy had nearly killed me. I deserved to know why he'd been at her house. There would be a logical explanation. Still, I couldn't imagine what she might tell me that would make me any less upset. I had helped her out of that abusive relationship, and I felt that I deserved to know what was going on. Right?

I exited the grocery store parking lot and drove eastward.

When I stopped at the light at the intersection of Lake Austin Boulevard and Loop 1, a scruffy-looking guy was standing in the median with a sign saying MY HOUSE IS AN OVERPASS. I lowered the window and gave him the bag of breakfast tacos.

I was almost back at my apartment—with no clear agenda for the remainder of the day—when my phone rang with a number I didn't recognize. I took a chance and answered it.

"Hey, it's Harvey," a voice said.

In my semi-agitated state, it took me a moment to process the name. Then I had it. Harvey. The guy I'd interviewed in the hospital.

Something funny and then something bad.

"Oh, hey," I said. "You sound good."

"I'm learning to talk without moving my mouth as much," he said.

"Good to know," I said. "You still in the ICU?"

"Nah, man, I came home a little while ago. You wanna know how much my bill was?"

This was exactly the kind of distraction I needed at the moment.

"I'm afraid to guess," I said.

"Seventy-four thousand dollars," Harvey pronounced with as much disgust as he could muster between clenched teeth.

"Yowser," I said. "Are you, uh, insured?"

"Yeah, but I've got a deductible of five grand. Think I've got five grand sitting around? Like hell. They'll have to settle for a hundred bucks a month for a long time."

I was in traffic on Lamar, but I pulled over into the BookPeople parking lot. I was hoping Harvey had something good for me, but I wasn't counting on it.

"Well, I'm glad you're doing better," I said.

"Kind of weird to be home," he said. "The scene of the crime. Don't tell anybody, but I'm buying a gun."

"Don't blame you," I said, "but be careful with it, okay?"

"Yeah, sure."

"Are you prepared to shoot someone if you have to?" I asked.

Harvey, to his credit, appeared to have already considered that question. "Not for stealing my wallet, no," he said. "But if someone tries to take my head off again, yeah. Fuck that shit. I'll do what I gotta do."

I waited. He'd tell me in his own time.

"What should I get?" he asked.

"You mean what kind of gun?"

"Yeah. Something cheap, though."

"For use at home, and that's it?"

"Yeah."

"Done much shooting?"

"Not much. A twenty-two when I was a kid."

"Are you prepared to practice a lot, so you're a good shot?"

"Yeah, I guess."

Which meant no.

"You should probably get a shotgun," I said.

"Yeah?"

"Or maybe a security system instead," I said.

"How much do shotguns cost?"

"Couple hundred bucks for a basic one," I said.

"Hmm. Hey, I was just wondering—you made any progress on your case?"

He was still hoping to find out who had decked him. Understandable.

"Not much," I said. "Still working on it."

"Will you keep me posted?" he asked.

"You bet," I said, and it could very well be true, depending on what I learned.

"I appreciate it," he said, just as I heard a call-waiting tone. I checked it and saw another number I didn't recognize.

"Hey, I have another call coming in," I said.

"No problem. I'll catch you later."

I answered the other line and heard a female voice say, "Is this the infamous Roy Ballard?"

"It is. Who's this?"

"Jayci, silly. Have you forgotten me already?"

Her tone was a mock pout intended to be flirtatious—but I would guess that she sounded flirty when calling for a pizza delivery. That was her way.

"What's going on, Jayci?" I said.

"Well," she said, "I think I might have something for you."

"Oh, yeah? Like what?"

"I'm not giving it up that easily," she said. "Why don't we meet for happy hour?"

17

"I was trying to take some pictures earlier today at lunch," she said, "and I got one of those warnings that my phone was running out of storage space. Ever get one of those?"

"Sure," I said. "Usually when I'm shooting selfies of my pecs."

We were on the front patio of Star Bar on West Sixth Street. I hadn't been there in several years, but I'd been relieved to see several people about my age. It was still a popular place with the type of customer who is always looking past his or her date to scope out the action at the next table over.

"Okay, so, you know you usually have to delete some stuff, right?" Jayci said.

"Right," I said.

She was wearing a red V-neck halter top that was showing off a lot of cleavage. Occasionally, through no fault of my own, I could catch a glimpse of her bra, which was also red. She wasn't in the same league as Mia, of course, but she was pretty cute.

She said, "What I do sometimes—I'm like so totally scattered—is I forget to empty the trash folder in my photos app. Like, for weeks. So I end up with all of these old pictures and videos in there. Sometimes *hundreds* of them. And so, today at lunch, I started to do that—to ditch all that junk—and then I realized I had some pictures in there from the party barge last weekend."

"I like where this is going," I said.

"You can thank me later," she said, and she took a sip of

her drink—something called a Jalisco Sally. It was almost gone. I was drinking Jameson on the rocks. Slowly.

I waited patiently for Jayci to say more. She was obviously enjoying the process of stringing it out. She liked having an audience—even just me—hanging on her every word.

She finally set her glass down and said, "Okay, so most of the pictures are a lot like the ones I already showed you, but there's one in particular…" She reached into her purse and pulled out her phone.

Please let this blow the case open, I was thinking. I was ready to be done with it and move on. I was suffering from a combination of impatience and a bad mood.

While Jayci scrolled through her photos, I took a discreet look at my phone, because I had felt it vibrate earlier with a text.

Coming over tonight? Mia had asked seven minutes earlier.

We had sent a few texts back and forth earlier in the afternoon. She had made no further progress on the Dennis Babcock case, because he hadn't gone anywhere that day, and Roscoe hadn't called Mia back about meeting with her fictional brother's attorney. She hadn't said a word about Garlen. I hadn't asked. Yet. I decided I wasn't going to answer this text right away. Make her wait. Passive aggression—ain't it lovely?

"Here it is," Jayci said.

She passed her phone across the table to me. I studied the photo on the screen, which had been taken sometime after sundown on the night of the cruise.

"That's me and my friend Cady," Jayci said.

And indeed it was—both of them in bikinis. Cady was a little taller, but equally cute and nubile.

"My eyes were glowing from the flash," Jayci said. "I guess that's why I deleted it. I don't remember."

I made a show of raising my gaze to a point higher on the photo. "Oh, right. Your eyes. I see them now."

"You're bad!" Jayci said, and she took another drink.

It was a selfie—the camera in Jayci's right hand—and as with a lot of selfies, Jayci had held the camera up high, slightly above her head, to provide a more flattering angle of their faces. As a result, you could see the area behind them well—and that was the most intriguing portion of the photo. Three people were visible behind Jayci and Cady.

In the upper-left portion of the photo, Jeremy Sawyer was in the process of going backward over the hip-high railing, flipping into the darkness. You couldn't actually see the railing itself, or Jeremy's lower body, for that matter, because Cady's pretty head was in the way. But it was obvious from the tension in Jeremy's arms and the angle of his back that he was hoisting himself up and over. He was also making a funny face. Hard to describe, exactly, but it was the type of expression a guy makes on a basketball court or soccer field when he does something sudden and unexpected—a look of mock surprise that says, *You weren't ready for that, were you? I totally suckered you.* That was the only way I could explain it.

Approaching Jeremy, in the upper-center portion of the photo, was Starlyn Kurtis's boyfriend, Anson Byrd—or rather, his shoulders and the back of his head. Obviously, I couldn't see his face, but I spotted the shark tattoo on his left shoulder blade that I'd seen earlier in another photo. Byrd had the kind of muscular, athletic physique that would intimidate a smaller guy like Jeremy Sawyer—enough to make him jump from the moving boat and make a joke out of it as he went.

To the right of Byrd, in the upper-right quadrant of the photo, was Starlyn Kurtis. She was facing forward, but her head was turned to her right, watching Jeremy go over the railing. It appeared she was behind the small bar that occupied one corner of the upper deck.

I realized that I had been studying the photo so intensely that I missed something Jayci had just said.

"Sorry?" I said.

"So that's it, right?" Jayci said. "That is the last time

anyone saw him? Don't you think?"

"It could very well be," I said. "Probably."

"Is it helpful?"

"It might be. Can you email it to me?"

"Sure, but it'll cost you." Her tone suggested she wasn't talking about money.

I would be able to check the metadata to see what time the photo was taken. The cops could too, and because they probably had every photo taken by every person on board that night, they could determine if any other photo with Jeremy in it had been shot after this one. If this photo did turn out to capture Jeremy Sawyer's last moment aboard, well…so what? Frankly, I wasn't sure it would help much.

"Dude," Jayci said.

"What?"

"I thought you'd be more excited by this."

"I'm sorry," I said. "No, this is really great. Thanks for sharing it with me." I tried to sound as enthusiastic as possible.

"I guess I need to send it to the cops, too, huh?" Jayci asked.

"Yeah, you do."

"You want me to wait?"

"No, go ahead and send it."

I looked at the photo again. If there was an answer in there somewhere, I didn't see it.

Something funny and then something bad. That's what Harvey had said.

What was funny? Jeremy flipping over the rail? The way he did it? Did he say something silly as he did it?

I was getting frustrated with this investigation, and when that happened, it wouldn't be long before I'd want to do one of two things: either do something rash to spur the investigation along, or give up completely.

I passed the phone back to Jayci just as our waitress swung past our table.

"Another one?" she asked, pointing at Jayci's drink.

"Yes, please."

The waitress looked at me.

"I'm good."

After she left, Jayci quickly emailed the photo to me, then leaned down to put her phone in her purse, providing the best view yet down her halter top. I felt like a creep for looking, even though I was confident the display was intentional. Didn't really make me any less of a creep, though, did it?

Jayci said, "You know, I'm still not sure exactly what it is you do for a living."

"I haven't figured that out myself," I said.

"But you're not a private detective, I know that."

"No, I'm not."

"You catch people who try to cheat insurance companies."

"That pretty much sums it up."

The waitress whizzed past our table and dropped off Jayci's drink.

"Is it fun?" Jayci asked.

"It can be."

"Tell me about a fun case," she said.

So I did, sharing the story of a slip-and-fall artist who tried to fake a slip in a grocery store and accidentally tipped a pyramid of beer cases, which all crashed down on him, knocking him unconscious.

By the time I was done—no more than five minutes—she had already sucked down her second drink. The loopy grin told me she was feeling a strong buzz.

"You're, uh, not driving anytime soon, are you?"

"Nope," she said. She pointed to the north. "I live about three blocks in that direction."

"Oh, yeah? In a condo, or..."

"A house," she said. "It used to be my dad's office—he's an attorney—but he retired last year, so I moved in to it."

Any house in the area she indicated had to be valued at a million dollars or more.

"That's handy," I said.

"Yep." She arched an eyebrow playfully at me. "Wanna walk me home and see how handy it is?"

I've read some interesting articles about self-destructive behavior.

Why do people abuse alcohol? Do drugs? Overeat? Why do we sabotage relationships that make us happy?

I noticed that the experts often seemed to reach varying conclusions as to the root causes of self-destructive behavior, but they generally agreed that it was a coping device. For instance, a person might be afraid of screwing up a stable, thriving relationship, and the ongoing anxiety from that fear is so great, he intentionally engages in conduct that will cause a crisis and possibly end the relationship, thereby relieving the stress.

Or something like that. Didn't make a lot of sense to me.

But the point is, a person prone to self-destructive behavior would've jumped all over Jayci's kind offer.

I'm happy to report that I did not. Didn't consider it for a second. Oh, I might've *daydreamed* about it later, and been flattered by the attention at the time, but I did not consider it.

I *did* walk her home—but just to her front porch, to see her safely inside—and then, as I was returning to the Toyota, I sent Mia a text.

Gonna stay home tonight. Case going nowhere. Sucks.

18

The reason I hadn't yet contacted Starlyn Kurtis—or her boyfriend, Anson Byrd, for that matter—was simple. I hadn't wanted her to know I was investigating Jeremy's death. I didn't even want her to know I existed. Sometimes you wanted to know everything you could possibly know about a person and the situation they were involved in before you made a move. Sometimes that could yield an advantage. Most of the time, however, it led nowhere. I was realistic enough to understand that.

That's why my impatience finally got the best of me the next morning and I called Starlyn Kurtis. Got voicemail, which was not a surprise. A woman like Starlyn Kurtis wouldn't answer a call from a number she didn't recognize.

"Hey, Starlyn," I said, "my name is Roy Ballard and I'm—well, it's kind of complicated, but I'm looking into Jeremy Sawyer's death. I have a couple of quick questions for you, if you don't mind. Could you call me back? I would really appreciate it. Won't take long. Thanks!"

I hung up, expecting to receive a return call from her about the same time we colonized Mars.

Then I sent a text to Heidi: *Nothing new to report, but still working on it.*

Then I texted Mia.

"So…where to?" she asked.

It was an hour later, and I was standing in her living room as she did all the little things she normally did when she was getting ready. Currently she was in the bathroom, applying the final touches to her makeup.

We were planning to grab a late breakfast and spend an hour or two brainstorming on both cases. Fresh perspectives and all that. In fact, I'd been entertaining the idea that we should swap cases for a few days and see if that got us anywhere. Better than giving up.

"Kerbey Lane?" I said.

"Works for me," she said.

But first, I needed to get the Garlen issue out of the way.

"Hey, I need to ask you about something," I said.

"Yeah?"

She came out of the bathroom.

I said, "Yesterday morning, I brought a bag of breakfast tacos over to your place. I saw a BMW parked in your driveway…"

Her expression changed, but it wasn't one of guilt or shame. More like the look of someone who just realized her morning wasn't going to be as pleasant as she had hoped.

"And then I saw Garlen walk out," I said.

I was conveniently omitting the part where I parked down the street and staked out her place for more than half an hour. And the part where I'd checked the BMW's hood to see if it had been there overnight.

"I was planning to have this conversation with you soon," she said. "But I didn't know it would be right now."

"No time like the present," I said.

"Yeah, okay," she said. She grabbed me by the hand and we sat down on the couch, facing each other. "I need you to be patient and understanding. Can you do that?"

"I don't have a history of that kind of behavior," I said.

"You can start now," she said cheerfully. "It will be fun!"

"I'll be the judge of that," I said.

"Well, the bottom line is, Garlen joined AA."

"The auto club?" I said. "Guess I can't blame him, with a nice car like that."

She smiled, but she was just placating me. I could tell she was nervous.

"He hasn't had a drink since the accident," she said.

"Not to be petty," I said, "but it wasn't an accident, it was a wreck. He wrecked because he was trying to run me off the road. Fortunately he really sucked at it."

"Fair enough," Mia said. "But he hasn't had a drink since then. And he's been doing the AA steps. I don't really know what they all are, but one of them involves apologizing to people."

"Making amends is what they call it," I said. I'd heard that phrase plenty of times on TV shows.

"Right. Anyway, he wanted to apologize to me. So I let him."

"Even though it violated the protective order?"

"It was a one-time thing."

I took a breath.

"Doesn't it seem ironic that a guy wanting to make amends would start by violating an active protective order? Now he owes you an amend for that, doesn't he?"

Mia didn't reply.

"How did he contact you?" I asked.

"His sponsor—who probably doesn't know about the protective order—sent me an email. It went from there. Roy, listen. Garlen is trying to turn his life around. Surely you can respect that."

She was alluding to some troubles I'd had of my own not so many years earlier. I'd gotten a second chance from some key people in my life, and shouldn't Garlen be granted that same opportunity? Sounded reasonable, but Garlen had had plenty of chances, in my opinion. Too many.

"Can't he turn his life around without pestering you?" I said, grinning.

She knew it was a rhetorical question.

Here's the thing. Deep down, I knew she wasn't opening the door to a renewed relationship with Garlen. She was willing to let him make amends solely because she had the most forgiving heart of anyone I knew. There was nothing more to it than that, and I should've admired her for it—but I simply couldn't tamp down the anger I was feeling. The jealousy. Even when I knew it was all ridiculous.

Then she made the situation worse.

She said, "The thing is, he'd like to make amends to you, too."

"Not a chance," I said immediately, pulling my hand from hers.

"Roy."

"Do you remember everything he did? Do you remember that he basically stalked you, and you had to threaten him with physical violence if he didn't stop?"

"I remember."

"And that he could've easily killed me on that little jaunt west of town?"

"You don't have to be sarcastic."

"I'll damn well be sarcastic if I want to be."

She held both hands up, palms facing me. "We can talk about this later," she said.

"My answer isn't going to be any different," I said.

"Maybe not, but I'm hoping you'll be less angry then."

"I have a right to be angry, and so do you."

"I was," she said, "but I've gotten past it. There's no use in holding on to it forever."

"You deal with it your way, I'll deal with it mine. My opinion is that a guy like Garlen says whatever it takes to fool people a second time. Or a third, or a fourth. Anything, he'll say it."

"You don't know that."

"I may have had my issues," I said, "but it's not even close to what he pulled."

"I know that," Mia said, "and I was never implying it was. I'm just talking about second chances. If he screws up again, fine, then I'll know for sure what kind of person he is. But he hasn't had his second chance yet."

That wasn't true.

At one point, he had come over to my apartment, fairly drunk, and grilled me about the canoe ride Mia and I had taken together. He was plainly worried—correctly, I'll admit—that I was interested in Mia. When he left, he'd had a minor fender bender, and he told Mia it had happened on his way home from work. He'd supposedly swerved to miss a deer and ended up hitting a small tree instead. He omitted the part about being drunk and coming to see me. So I'd told her. She deserved to know. She then revealed that she had caught him in some lies before, or what she called "bending the truth."

But it hadn't stopped there. My telling Mia the truth prompted her to break up with him, which in turn caused him to come after me in a rage outside my apartment. He threw some clumsy punches, which I ducked, and I bloodied his nose.

After that, he continued to call and text Mia, begging her to let him back into her life. Then he began to drive past her house, keeping tabs on her, until she finally had to threaten to press charges.

The last straw came when he tailed me in traffic one day. He actually bumped my Toyota with his Audi, then followed me on a long and winding chase west of town. Later, he hit me even harder from behind, and then harder still. I knew that he had a concealed-carry permit, so I was taking it very seriously. I tried to call 911 but had no cell signal.

So I used my superior driving skills and knowledge of the road to evade him. He tried to keep up—but he lost control and rolled his car several times. Wound up in the hospital, lucky he hadn't died. Now his case was slowly working its way through the system. I realized he would probably take a plea bargain and serve very little time, or none at all. Rehab would be mandatory, so his joining AA could be seen as nothing more than a feeble attempt to impress a judge.

Mia knew all this, and she could see the cynical expression on my face now.

She said, "What I mean is, he hasn't had a second chance *after* making the decision to stop drinking."

I raised an eyebrow at her. *Do you realize how that sounds?*

"That is a legitimate distinction," she said.

"I don't know why we're even discussing this," I said, "because I don't want to see him—don't want to hear his apologies—and I don't intend to change my mind."

"I'm sorry to hear that."

"And I wish you wouldn't have seen him, either."

"I'm a big girl, Roy. I can take care of myself."

Then I said something so amazingly stupid, it could have gotten me into the Hall of Fame for dumb comments. I said, "Apparently not."

The temperature in the room dropped by ten degrees. Maybe I was more inclined toward self-destructive behavior than I'd thought.

"Did you really just say that?" Mia asked.

"Yeah, but in my defense, I'm a patronizing ass sometimes."

"You need to leave."

"I apologize. That was a ridiculous thing to say, and you know I didn't mean it."

"Roy, seriously, just go. I'm not in the mood for this right now."

"I'm sorry, Mia."

She didn't reply.

"I'll call you later," I said.

Still nothing.

So I left.

As I was walking to the curb, I heard a voice.

"Hey, there, Roy."

I turned and saw Regina, Mia's neighbor, watering some hanging plants on her front porch.

"How you doing, Regina?"

"Not bad. Everything okay?"

Her tone of voice—a slight hint of concern—suggested that she had seen Garlen yesterday morning. Regina knew the situation. She and Mia had developed a friendship after Regina had extinguished the flames when a lowlife scumbag had tried to set Mia's house on fire.

I walked closer.

"I hope so," I said. I also hoped that Mia wasn't watching us through the window.

"You know about the, uh, visitor she had yesterday morning?" Regina asked.

"Yep."

"I wasn't sure what to make of that. I almost called you."

I wanted to say, *I wish you had*, but that would've made her feel bad.

"We just had a talk," I said. "It didn't go well."

"Please tell me she isn't getting back together with him," Regina said.

"No, not that. He wanted to make amends."

"Oh. Well. Was he allowed to do that? To make contact?"

"Nope."

"So what happens now?"

"Nothing. She didn't report him for the violation."

Regina was searching my face, looking for answers, but I had none.

"That sucks," she said.

"Yeah, it does," I said.

19

Ever wanted to get in your car and drive to another state?

Or park at the airport and grab the next available flight to an attractive destination?

That's where my mind was at the moment.

Get the hell out of town and take a break.

Everything was going to hell.

Instead, I put the Toyota into gear and drove east, then south on Exposition.

Had to distract myself.

Gilbert Holloway was the key. Of course, I'd suspected that for a while now. But I'd made almost no progress in finding out what he was trying to cover up or what had really happened on that party barge.

I stopped at a traffic light and checked my phone real quick. I was hoping to see a text from Mia. Something along the lines of: *I'm sorry. You're right. Come back and let's go to breakfast.*

Nope. Nothing.

I continued straight ahead when the light changed, just driving.

And a new idea occurred to me. What if something else had happened on the Island Hopper—something unrelated to Jeremy Sawyer's death—that was freaking Holloway out? But what? I couldn't even imagine. I spent ten minutes trying to come up with any sort of scenario that would cause Holloway to send a tough-guy wannabe after me, but I got nowhere.

Hard to think straight. I was in a truly foul mood.

I thought of a question I should've asked Mia. *Did Garlen*

ask if you were seeing anyone? If he had, that would've given some insight into his true intentions. And how would she have answered? None of your business? A simple yes? Or would she have told him she was seeing me and was happy as can be?

I was vacillating between anger and indignation. Didn't I have the right to be concerned for Mia, and to be upset that she'd agreed to see a man who had caused us both so much trouble?

Maybe so, but it was the "Apparently not" that got me.

She was using that—my one little rude comment—to turn the tables and be mad at me, instead of having a conversation to address the problem at hand, which was Garlen. Now that she'd allowed him to make contact without reporting him, he could use that to justify contact in the future, and he could very well avoid prosecution that way. If she ever did file a report, he would say that she'd set a precedent by allowing him to come over to her house. She knew all that, too, which is what made it even more frustrating.

A driver behind me honked his horn. I'd been sitting at another red light, which had since turned green. I squealed my tires, then took a random left on Woodmont Avenue. I pulled to the curb in front of a gray two-story home.

Still no text from Mia, so I sent her one: *It was just concern, that's all.*

Waited a full two minutes. No reply.

Some older guy with white hair and glasses was watching me from the porch of the home.

I got on my phone and Googled Eric Moss, the owner of the Island Hopper. It didn't take me long to uncover the name of the corporation he'd created to support his party barge business, and after that, I was able to find a phone number fairly quickly. Not his personal number, of course, but a number that would be answered by someone who could contact him.

No more screwing around.

I was just about to dial, but now the white-haired man was

coming down the steps of the porch toward my car. He came to the passenger window, so I lowered it.

"Can I help you with something?" he asked.

"No, thanks," I said. He was plainly expecting me to say more, but I didn't.

"Is there a reason you're parked at my curb?" he asked.

"Because it's my curb, too," I said.

"How so?" He had a condescending manner about him that, at that particular moment, pushed my buttons—not unlike my encounter with Gilbert Holloway.

"I can explain it to you," I said, "but I should warn you that I am in a bad mood and I don't have time for any shenanigans or tomfoolery."

"Go right ahead."

It was a dare—like nothing I said could possibly justify the gall I had for parking right there at that particular moment.

"It's a public street," I said. "I pay taxes for it, same as you. And parking is allowed here."

"But this street is too narrow for—"

"I'll be here for about five more minutes," I said, talking over his protest. "Maybe ten. If you want to turn this into a conflict, bring it on. Otherwise, why don't you turn your cranky old ass around and get back on your porch?"

He glared at me—then retreated.

I raised the window and dialed the number. A young-sounding guy answered on the second ring. "Moss Enterprises."

I was either going to blow the case open or crash and burn entirely.

"Who is this?" I asked.

"Ernie."

Okay, Ernie," I said. "My name is Roy Ballard. I need you to listen very closely to what I am about to say. While you're at it, grab a pen."

About that same time, the line for the fictitious flower shop rang. The screen listed the caller as UNKNOWN.

"R&M Flowers," Mia said. "What can we arrange for you?"

"Can we talk on this line?"

"I'm sorry, who is this?"

"Roscoe. Jeez. Who did you expect?"

"I get dozens of calls every day," Mia said.

"Yeah, well, it's me."

"What's going on? Coming to your senses?"

"What's that supposed to mean?"

He sounded nervous. Wound too tight.

"I was just wondering if you and Dennis were ready to move forward and meet with my brother's attorney," Mia said.

"Okay, yeah," he said. "Let's go ahead and do it."

"And Dennis will be there, right?"

"Yeah, fine. But there's gonna be some ground rules."

"Like what?"

"First of all, we meet here, at the house, not at some fancy office."

"Okay. I'm sure she'll be fine with that."

"No cameras. No recorders. Nothing like that."

"No problem," Mia said.

"Also, Dennis probably won't talk much. He likes lawyers even less than me. Unless he's in one of his weird moods. Then there's no telling what he might babble about."

"Well, I understand, but he'll need to answer some basic questions," Mia said.

She could hear Roscoe sucking on a cigarette. So gross.

"What kind of questions?"

"You know—height, weight, shoe size. The usual."

Roscoe grunted and said, "We gonna fool around all day?"

"I can't say for sure what she'll ask, but the questions will be about his case. She'll probably want to know how he feels, whether he thinks he's getting any better—things like that."

"He's liable to say just about anything," Roscoe said.

Roscoe seemed to be preparing her for a strange encounter with Dennis. Why? It gave her an idea. Some bait, in the form of an excuse.

"Has he always been that way?" she asked.

"Pretty much, yeah."

The answer she expected.

She said, "Are you sure the tetanus shot isn't also affecting his mental capabilities? I mean, it if can affect him physically, why not mentally?"

A long pause followed. Roscoe was weighing the pros and cons of his answer. Then, sounding much more upbeat, he said, "Now that you mention it, yeah, I think the shot is making him a little wacky. That's pretty smart of you to think of something like that."

"Thanks."

"Like really smart," Roscoe said. "It's perfect."

Mia could tell that Roscoe was thinking she had just solved a major problem for him. Any bizarre behavior on Dennis's part could be blamed on the shot. Why hadn't he thought of that?

Mia said, "Okay, well, I'll check—"

"Those fuckers screwed up his brain, too!" Roscoe said, sounding downright giddy. "They owe him even more money for that!"

"Slow down," Mia said. "One step at a time. Let me talk to Roy and Adrienne and get something set up. The sooner the better."

"Who the hell's Roy?"

"My brother. I already told you."

"Who the hell's Adrienne?"

"His lawyer."

She waited to see if Roscoe had any other questions, but all he said was, "Poor sumbitch done got his brain fried. That just ain't right."

20

Less than two hours after talking to Ernie, who probably officed out of some cubicle downtown, I was sitting across from Eric Moss, who officed out of his home on a magnificent bluff overlooking Lake Travis. To my left was a wall of floor-to-ceiling windows that must've provided an amazing view of sunsets over the water. I was on the visitor side of Moss's desk, seated in a leather chair that truly cradled my butt like warm butter. If I'd been in a better mood, I might've appreciated it more.

Moss was about fifty years old and maybe six-two. He'd been a star athlete back in the day, but now he was about twenty pounds overweight, with thinning hair and bags under his eyes. Still, he carried himself with the confidence of a man who had scored plenty of victories in life and knew how to get what he wanted. The kind of guy who wouldn't feel the need to involve his lawyers in this conversation, because he was pretty damn sure he knew more than they did anyway, right? Ernie might have been intimidated by my forceful pitch earlier, but Moss plainly wasn't.

"Your name again?" Moss said as he took a seat behind the desk.

Which was a load of crap. He knew my name. It was a power game.

"Roy Ballard," I said. "But most people refer to me as Roy Ballard." I placed a business card on the desk, but he didn't make a move to take it or even look at it.

"And you told Ernie you wanted to talk about a crime that

Gilbert Holloway allegedly committed. Do I have that right?" He was shaking his head, as if this was all very confusing and couldn't possibly be true.

A small, fluffy dog—maybe a Maltese—had barked at me when I'd arrived, and now it was sniffing my shoes.

"Well, there's no 'allegedly' about it," I said. "But we'll get to that. The point is, I'm going to give you a chance to work with me before I get him busted. Maybe we can avoid that."

"Boy, you cut right to it, huh?"

"I don't want to waste your time, or mine."

"I appreciate that, but work with you how? I have no idea what you're even talking about."

"That's not surprising, since I haven't told you yet. But as soon as I tell you, then you'll know. See how that works?"

He stared at me for a long moment. "I don't care for your tone," he said.

"Frankly, I'm not a big fan of it myself, so we're in the same boat. Speaking of boats, let's talk about Gilbert."

"I have about five minutes," Moss said.

Another power play, but I didn't care to dawdle anyway. So, as succinctly as possible, I told Moss exactly who I was, what I did for a living, and why I was looking into the death of Jeremy Sawyer.

Then I described my first visit to the marina, where I first encountered Meatball, and then Gilbert Holloway.

"Oh, you're *that* guy," Moss said, mildly amused, or pretending to be. "From what I understand, you're the one who committed a crime, not Gilbert, and I bet the sheriff's office would frown on you being here."

"They frown on me being anywhere," I said. "What they don't know is that Gilbert sent a goon after me. Kid named Dirk Crider. You know him?"

I was being facetious, but Moss actually said, "Nope. Never heard of him."

The dog finally gave up on my shoes and pranced out of the room.

"That's odd, considering that he used to work for you," I said.

"A lot of people have worked for me," Moss said. "I literally cannot remember them all."

"He was a deckhand on the Island Hopper until a few years ago."

"Okay, yeah, I remember now. The kid got us written up once."

"Right. His uncle is Lawrence Crider. Owns the Bock Dock?"

"I know Larry," Moss said.

"I know you do," I said. "I found several photos of you and Larry together at various business functions." My way of revealing that I'd done my homework and I knew more than he knew I knew.

"To be blunt, so what?" Moss said.

"You know Larry, but you had trouble recalling that his nephew Dirk worked for you?"

"If you have a point, please make it," he said.

"Dirk Crider attacked me on a piece of property I own. He tried to drown me in Barton Creek."

Moss let out a short laugh of disbelief. "Are you high? That's the most ridiculous thing I've ever heard."

"Why would you have an opinion on it if you can't even remember Dirk? How would you know what he might or might not do?"

"Because you're implying that Gilbert is behind it. Because it's like something out of a dime-store novel. Laughable, really."

"I guess it's natural to protect the captain of your boat. Is he your partner in the business?"

"Why should I answer your questions?"

If you've ever seen the show *COPS*, you know that most people will talk when they should remain silent. Many of them are concerned that they will appear guilty if they refuse to answer questions. Even someone like Eric Moss could succumb to that tendency, if you handled him correctly.

I said, "So he *is* your partner?"

"No, he's an employee. Why would I make him a partner? But he is buying the Island Hopper from me. Not that it's any of your business."

"So he has a lot to protect," I said. "His future."

Moss gave a sharp laugh. "Good Lord. You are obviously desperate to counter the charges Gilbert has against you, so you're trying this lame bullshit."

My phone was in my hand, with the recording of Dirk queued up and ready to go. I held my phone up and hit the Play button.

We were talking in his truck, and he was saying there was a guy that was giving him some trouble, and he was wondering if I'd, you know, kick this guy's ass. I asked him what the problem was, and he just said it wasn't anything too important, but this guy deserved an ass kicking, and if I didn't want to do it, that's fine, but he'd find someone else who wanted to earn the money. I figured, like, Gilbert probably had a pretty good reason to be asking, so I said yeah, I'd do it.

I hit the pause button.

I couldn't read the expression on Moss's face now.

I said, "I wouldn't call that lame bullshit. Would you? In case you were wondering, that was Dirk."

Moss didn't say anything.

"Dirk Crider, your former employee," I said. "The one you can't remember."

"I have nothing more to say," Moss said. "Call the cops and see where that gets you."

Now it was my turn to give him a long stare.

"Are we done here?" he asked.

"Apparently Gilbert doesn't like me asking questions about the night Jeremy Sawyer died. I figure that's why he sent Dirk after me. He probably sent someone over to Harvey Selberg's house, too. Maybe Dirk, or someone else."

"You are delusional."

"Did you not hear the audio I just played?"

"That could be anybody. Some actor you paid."

"But Dirk will confirm that it's him."

"I don't think he will."

"Voice analysis will prove it."

Then the tenor of our conversation changed.

Moss said, "I have a hunch he'll say he was just jerking your chain. Making stuff up to string you along."

He smirked at me and the implication was clear. Moss would coerce Dirk to recant his story. Now I knew that Moss was involved in the cover-up.

"Why would he do that?" I asked.

"He has a lively sense of humor."

"Weird. On the one hand, you say you don't even remember him. On the other, you seem to be familiar with his comic sensibilities. Can you understand why that would make me question your veracity?"

"Question whatever you want. Your five minutes are up. Besides, I bet a good attorney could stop that recording from being played in court."

"Couldn't stop it from making the rounds online, though," I said.

"I would sue you into oblivion," he said. "I would totally destroy you."

I waited a beat, then said, "You forgot the evil laugh that's supposed to come after that."

"Are you a mental defective?" he asked.

"Probably. Your stepdaughter was on the boat that night," I said.

He pointed a finger at me. "You leave Starlyn out of it."

"I didn't know she was in it," I said.

"She's not."

"What is it?"

"There is no it."

"Then how can she be out of it?"

"I don't know what you're talking about."

"I tried calling her," I said, "but she hasn't called me back."

"And if you call her again," Moss said, "I will have you charged with harassment. Starlyn is a great girl. She has a bright future and doesn't need some half-ass detective trying to drag her name through the mud."

Very defensive. Maybe I was getting warmer. Which meant I should keep poking.

"I'm not a detective," I said.

"Then stop acting like one."

"I saw that she interns for Barry Blanche," I said.

I'd dug up everything I could about her, of course, and I'd learned that she worked in the office for the state representative in District 47. Blanche was your basic garden-variety Texas conservative, always placing an emphasis on smaller government. He had a reputation, however, as a reasonable, intelligent man who understood the value and necessity of bipartisanship. Rare nowadays.

"What about it?" Moss asked.

"I just thought it was interesting," I said. "If Starlyn has political aspirations herself, she doesn't need to be caught up in some scandal."

Moss leaned forward. "Follow me closely on this. There is no scandal. Nobody did anything wrong. Why are you trying to make something out of nothing?"

"I just want to ask her some questions, in case she saw something on the barge."

"Like what?"

"I don't know. That's the point of asking questions."

"If she saw something, she would've told the cops about it."

"Maybe she saw something and doesn't even realize it's important. Happens all the time."

"And don't you think the cops would've figured that out by now? Or do you think you're some kind of superhero who has to fly in and save the day?"

"Just a concerned citizen doing my civic duty," I said.

"Now you're just wasting my time," and he began to push

his chair back.

"What about Anson?"

"What about him?"

"Several people told me Jeremy Sawyer was flirting with Starlyn that night, and it makes me wonder how—"

"Forget it," Moss said. "Anson isn't a hothead. Besides, come on, just look at him. Good-looking guy. Built like a Cowboys linebacker. You think he's worried about someone flirting with his girlfriend? He *steals* girls from the Jeremy Sawyers of the world, not the other way around."

"That's something to be proud of, huh? Something for the résumé."

"You are really beginning to annoy me," Moss said. "I didn't even have to talk to you, but I did, and all I get in response is a lot of accusations and smart-ass comments."

"Fair enough," I said. "In that case, I'll just ask you one more question, and I would appreciate it if you'd give me an honest answer."

"That's what I've been doing all along," he said.

I waited.

"What's your damn question?" he said. "Last one, and then we're done."

I gave the question all the gravity it deserved.

"What happened out on that boat, Eric?"

He shrugged impatiently, like *Really? Haven't we covered this already?*

"Some poor guy jumped off and drowned. That's it. There's nothing else to it. Nobody was responsible for his death except himself."

I was disenchanted and my motivation had bottomed out. What now?

I checked my phone, but Mia hadn't texted. Instead I saw

that Regina, Mia's neighbor, had called a few minutes earlier.

I sat in my car with the AC running and called her back.

"Look," she said, "you know I'm not a busybody or a tattletale."

"Of course not."

"And I believe in letting adults make their own decisions and live with the consequences. Within reason."

"I'm with you on that," I said. "Within reason."

"But I need to tell you something. I'm not positive, but I'm about ninety percent sure I saw that same BMW drive by about fifteen minutes ago."

"The BMW that was at Mia's yesterday?" I asked.

I noticed that both of us were avoiding mentioning his name. No real reason for that.

"Right," Regina said.

"Did it pull over or what?"

"Just drove by slowly."

"And you haven't seen it since?"

"Nope."

"Could you see the driver?"

"The windows were too dark."

"Did it have dealer plates?"

"Damn. I didn't even notice."

"Don't worry about it."

The Toyota was starting to cool off, but I was still sweating.

"What should I do if I see it again?" Regina asked.

"Let me ask you something. Do you happen to have any rocket-propelled grenades?"

She laughed. "I wish. I'd take that son of a bitch out in a heartbeat."

"I bet you would."

"But I'd probably better just call you instead," she said.

"I would appreciate it," I said. "And maybe take a few pictures of him and his car. From a distance. Don't confront him."

We both remained quiet for a moment.

"I don't want to piss her off," Regina said, "but at some point, we can't worry about that anymore, right?"

That insight hit me like a stone in the middle of the chest. Shouldn't I do whatever was best for Mia, even if she became furious with me for it?

I nodded, looking out at the quiet street.

"Might not've even been the same car," Regina said. "But I think it was."

21

I resisted my earlier impulse—an overwhelming urge to do whatever I thought was right for Mia—for the longest time. It wasn't my business. Mia and I were partners, and we were dating, but that didn't give me the right to butt into her affairs.

I resisted.

But I couldn't help wondering: If I *were* going to do something, what could I do?

The most tempting option was still on the table, as far as I was concerned. Find Garlen and give him a beating he would never forget. Break his legs. Better yet, destroy his knee ligaments. Put him on crutches for the long term. Make him aware that he had crossed the line too many times. Let him know he would receive a beating every time he contacted Mia. The only drawback? I'd go to prison. I couldn't give him beatings from prison.

Next idea.

Go ahead and call the cops and tell them Garlen had violated the protective order. Mia would say I'd derailed Garlen's sincere efforts to make amends and start a better life, but so what?

Maybe the solution was somewhere in the middle. Contact Garlen—preferably by phone, so I'd be less inclined to do something rash—and gently inform him that he was walking on thin ice. Reason with him. Allude with subtlety to potential repercussions. All of which would be a waste of time. Men who abuse and stalk women don't think like normal people. Same goes for women who abuse or stalk men. Or anybody who abuses or stalks anybody else.

There was a tiny part of me that was hoping—for Mia's sake, as well as Garlen's and mine—that he would stay true to his word and not contact her again. I decided to assume that would be true, while also putting a safety measure in place.

He had a new job now, because his previous employer had let him go after the arrest. I found the name of the place on LinkedIn. Ten seconds later, I had an address in Westlake Hills. I drove over there, hoping he would be in the office. Fortunately, it was a multi-tenant three-story office building with lots of vehicles parked in front, on both sides, and in back. That way I wouldn't be so conspicuous cruising the parking lot slowly.

I spotted the BMW in the back, tucked between a Mercedes and a GMC truck. I drove past and found a spot fifty feet away. Parked and sat and watched. Studied the building itself. Not many people coming and going at this hour. Plenty of windows looking this way, but that was a chance I'd have to take. I could see a pair of security cameras mounted to the rear of the building, above the entrance, pointed toward the lot. I would be recorded, but I wasn't concerned about that, even though I was about to commit a crime.

I stepped from the Toyota wearing a baseball cap, sunglasses, and—believe it or not—a fake mustache. You could buy a pack of six for ten bucks on Amazon. They were comically large, but I trimmed them down to normal size. From a distance, it looked fine. Up close, I looked like a 1980s porn star.

I was carrying a GPS tracker—one of the best I owned—in a plastic grocery sack. Each new generation of trackers improved on accuracy and battery life. The promotional materials for this particular model claimed it could operate for one hundred days on a single charge. I didn't know if that was true, but even if it were half that, I'd be in good shape. Had a good, strong magnet to hold it in place.

I strode purposefully across the lot and stopped between the BMW and the GMC truck. Dropped to the ground and quickly shimmied underneath the front end. It was a tight fit, but I was able to tuck the tracker into a discreet spot where it wouldn't be visible to anyone looking at the engine compartment from above, with the hood raised.

I slid out from underneath the car and casually strolled away. Got back into the Toyota and drove off, hoping nobody had seen me from the windows of the office building.

Mia had called while I was creeping around under her ex-boyfriend's car, so I called her back.

"Hey," she said.

"I was wondering when you'd come crawling back," I said.

I figured, why not counter the tension with some humor? It was a gamble—and it didn't pay off. I didn't hear the slightest hint of a giggle. Which told me something about her mood, and where we still stood.

"Too soon?" I said. "It was just a joke. Sorry."

Mia said, "I might be making some progress with Dennis Babcock. Figured you'd want to know."

"I do, yeah. What's the story?"

"Got a meeting set up with Roscoe, Dennis, me, my fake brother, and his fake lawyer."

"Should I fake being excited?" I asked.

Another lead balloon. She obviously wasn't in the mood for world-class wit and banter.

"Now I just need to finish setting it up. You remember Diana Tait?"

"You bet."

Diana Tait was a forty-year-old local actress with high

cheek bones, long brown hair, and the uncanny ability to play just about any role—from Desdemona in a stage production of *Othello* to a folksy southern mayor in a popular prime-time dramedy currently airing on cable TV. Twelve years ago, she'd landed a nice gig as the national spokeswoman in ads for a popular brand of processed cheese product that you shot out of a can. (*Tastes like real cheese!*) We had used her once before for a staged sting and she had proven herself to be a great improviser.

"I think she'll make a fantastic lawyer," Mia said. "Don't you?"

"Absolutely. Need any help from me?"

"That depends. How's your case going?"

Even though we were ignoring the fight we'd had earlier, I was grateful we were talking about anything. So I gave her a one-minute update on what I'd been doing since that morning, omitting my visit to Garlen's place of work, obviously.

"I think you're making progress," she said.

"Then why do I feel so lost?"

"Name a case where we didn't feel lost at some point," she said. "Besides, you've got ample evidence that some kind of cover-up is taking place. Just keep twisting the screws on the major players and somebody will give in eventually, or make a mistake."

"Oh, damn, that's what I forgot," I said. "Twisting the screws. I've been driving the nails and, uh, stapling the staples."

"Stapling the staples?"

"I'm not sure what else you do to them."

"You know I'm right," she said.

"Probably so," I said.

"So what is your plan right now?" she asked.

"Ha," I said. "Plan. Good one."

"Would you prefer to take a break instead?"

"By playing the role of your brother?" I asked.

"Exactly."

"When?"

"Hoping tomorrow afternoon, if Roscoe agrees."

"When will you know for sure?"

"I left a voicemail. Waiting to hear back. Roscoe is one skittish dude. Wouldn't surprise me if he backs out entirely."

"Well, just let me know," I said.

I was hoping it would occur to Mia that we should get together and create a backstory, so we could put on a convincing show. Roscoe obviously assumed I was faking a neurological disorder, same as Dennis, and that we just wanted in on the scam, but he wouldn't know I wasn't actually Mia's brother. If he began to suspect that wasn't true, he'd become suspicious.

And what about Dennis and his note to Mia? We still didn't know what that was about, but maybe the meeting would help us clear it up. Because there was still the chance that Roscoe and Lorene were somehow forcing Dennis to participate in their scam—perhaps under threat of physical harm—I intended to be carrying a weapon. Maybe not my Glock, since it wasn't easy to conceal that, even if I wore a jacket. But I had a small .38 I could strap to my ankle. Wear some baggy khakis and I'd be good to go.

We had these details and more to discuss, and I was hoping Mia would ask me to come over to her place. Unfortunately, all she said was, "I'll text you later," and she hung up.

And she did, at 9:47 that night.

Finally heard from Roscoe. 2:00 tmw at his house. That okay?

I'd been sitting around most of the evening, watching TV and moping.

I gave her a thumbs up, then said: *Need to talk strategy?*

She said: *Will call in the morning.*

I said: *Okay. Miss you.*

She didn't reply.

I lay in bed later, wide awake. I could feel the vibration of music from my neighbor's apartment. Not loud, just lots of bass.

My phone was on the nightstand. If Garlen's BMW came within three hundred yards of Mia's house, I would hear an alert. I sincerely hoped my phone would remain silent throughout the night, and in the days to come. I didn't want any drama. I just wanted Garlen to disappear and not come back. Maybe fall off a building or move to a different country. Was that too much to ask?

22

The home smelled of cigarettes, neglected litter boxes, and unwashed dishes. The walls were scuffed and dirty, the ceiling was covered with that old blown foam "popcorn" popular back in the 80s, and the carpet was eight different shades of brown, none of them from the factory.

Roscoe and Lorene were seated on a plaid couch, Diana—aka Adrienne, the attorney—had taken an upholstered chair at a right angle to the couch, and Mia and I were in two of the three dinette chairs Roscoe had pulled in from the kitchen to accommodate us. We formed an oval of sorts. That left one remaining chair—which was quite obviously for Dennis—but Dennis wasn't present.

"So the shot fucked you up, too, huh?" Roscoe said, looking at me. I had walked from the car and into the house with my hands behind my back.

Diana had been well versed by Mia on how to respond to various scenarios. "Let's hold off on any discussion until your brother joins us."

"Well," Roscoe said, "I ain't so sure he's gonna. Hard to predict. We might oughta hash this out between the five of us."

Diana was shaking her head. "The purpose of this meeting is for Dennis and me to talk, so I can determine if he would make a suitable client, and for him to decide if he wants me to represent him. Or am I mistaken?"

Roscoe shrugged. "Ain't much I can do about it."

"Okay, in that case..." Diana stood up, preparing to leave. Mia and I followed suit.

"Jeez," Roscoe said. "Take it easy. Just hang on a second." Then he yelled, "Dennis!"

Five seconds passed.

"Dennis!"

Then came a reply— "What?" —from a hallway that led to the rear of the house.

"Come out here for a second," Roscoe yelled.

We all waited silently. About ten seconds later, I could hear someone coming. Then Dennis walked into the room, his arms straight above his head. "Don't shoot," he said, and he gave everyone in the room a broad grin. He had probably used that joke dozens of times by now.

"Everybody, this is Dennis," Roscoe said, with all of the enthusiasm of someone describing a recent bout of stomach flu.

"Hello, Dennis," Diana said. "My name is Adrienne Guthrie."

But Dennis's gaze lingered on Mia, and he gave her a small nod of acknowledgment. Obviously, he recognized her from the parking lot at Academy, and from her front-porch conversation with Roscoe four days earlier. We'd been wondering, of course, what might happen at this moment. If Dennis had written that note for Mia because he knew she was trying to document the fraud he was committing, would he drop the pretense now and ask us to leave? If the note was authentic—indicating that Roscoe and possibly Lorene were forcing Dennis to play a role in this scheme—would he use this opportunity to get help?

"Hi, Dennis," Mia said. "I'm Mia Madison, and this is my brother Roy." She gestured in my direction.

But Dennis's eyes remained on Mia. "I have a dentist appointment later," he said. By now he had lowered his arms.

"'Member when I told you about that lawyer?" Roscoe asked. "Well, here she is. Sit down for a second and talk to her."

"I got a lotta stuff to do today," Dennis said.

"Dennis, damn it," Lorene said wearily.

"Just sit for a second," Roscoe said.

Dennis raised his arms again to step over to the empty chair, and after he sat, he lowered them again. "Can't be sitting around talking all day," he said. He looked at Diana, then at me, and then at Mia again. His focus was on Mia.

"You need to talk to this lady," Roscoe said. "She's—"

"I'm here to talk to you about the problem with your arms," Diana said. "May I ask you a few questions?"

"That's about the only thing lawyers ever do is ask questions, as far as I can tell, and I think we should all object," Dennis said, and he gave everyone in the room another grin. Roscoe had told Mia that Dennis had an odd sense of humor. Maybe Roscoe didn't know the difference between odd and corny.

"That's part of our job," Diana said. "Asking questions."

"I guess," Dennis said. "I have a dentist appointment later."

"What time?" Diana asked, glancing at her wristwatch.

"You ain't got no dentist appointment," Lorene said, sounding resigned, as if they'd had this conversation many times.

"Then when is it?" Dennis asked.

"You don't have one," Lorene said.

"I was supposed to, because I'm having trouble with my enamel again." He turned to Mia. "Many people think the enamel on your teeth can repair itself, but that's not true. Once you've worn a spot away, it's gone for good. Then what happens is that spot becomes sensitive, so you don't brush it as good, and before you know it, you've got gingivitis, and then you get a cavity there, and so on. Periodontal disease. That's the fancy name for it. Tooth loss isn't pretty. Do you want recessed gums?"

Roscoe said, "Dennis, quit screwing around." He looked at Mia. "He's just screwing around."

"Dennis," Diana said, "tell me about the injury that required a tetanus shot."

"It wasn't a big deal," Dennis said. "I scraped my arm on a

rusty condenser housing. Didn't need stitches or anything like that."

"But you needed a tetanus shot," Diana said.

Dennis gave her a skeptical look. "That's what they told me, but when I got to that doctor's office, I could tell he wasn't a straight shooter."

"How so?"

"Dennis," Roscoe said, impatient, "just answer her questions without a lot—"

"I'd like to hear about that doctor," Diana said. It was important that she maintain control of the discussion. "What was your problem with the doctor?"

Dennis said, "None of his equipment was calibrated right, and he knew it, but he didn't care. Same with the rest of his staff. They probably pay the inspector to give them a passing grade. That's the way they usually do it. Am I supposed to trust a doctor like that?"

"Dennis," Roscoe sighed, giving up. He was shaking his head, defeated.

By now I'm sure all three of us had concluded that Dennis didn't have an odd sense of humor, he wasn't playing a prank, and nobody was using threats to make him participate in an insurance scam.

"Sucks that I didn't have much choice," Dennis said, "and it wasn't until later I figured out the shot was filled with toxins that damage nerve endings. That's what they're *designed* to do. I should've asked my dentist for a referral to a decent physician." Now Dennis turned to me and said, "My dentist calibrates all his own equipment, and he's been doing that for years. He's certified to meet the standards, so I know everything is safe, including the X-ray machine. X rays are at the exact right wavelength to affect your cerebral cortex if the machine isn't calibrated."

Dennis stopped talking and the room went quiet for several seconds.

Then Mia said, "Dennis, we appreciate you talking to us. I

think we have enough for now."

"You're going to help me, right?" Dennis said.

"I'm going to do my best," Mia said.

"That's why I picked you," he said. "You looked like someone I could count on."

Roscoe was frowning, puzzled. He didn't understand what they were talking about, which indicated he didn't know about the note Dennis had dropped for Mia.

Now Dennis stood, raised his arms, and walked out of the room.

Mia obviously had something to say, but she waited until we heard the door close at the end of the hallway.

"You people are ridiculous," Mia said, looking at Roscoe, then at Lorene.

"What?" Roscoe said.

"How on earth did you think this would work? Did you think Dennis could fool the experts? Or did you think you could somehow get through this without him having to see any doctors?"

"Lady, I got no idea what you're talking about," Lorene said.

"I'm talking about Dennis's illness," Mia said.

She waited. Roscoe and Lorene kept quiet. They wouldn't make eye contact with her now.

"What is it?" Mia said. "Schizophrenia? Or some other type of delusional disorder?"

Roscoe and Lorene continued looking at the carpet.

Mia said, "You want to tell us how the scam started?"

Another long pause.

Finally, Lorene said, "Y'all just need to leave."

Mia ignored her. "I'm guessing Dennis got the tetanus shot, and then he began to question what was in it. He probably went online and found all kinds of wacky conspiracy theories. There are a few people who've made claims similar to his. When we first heard about Dennis, we figured he was copying those people. But he wasn't. He truly believes the shot damaged his nervous system somehow. If I'm off target, just let me know."

"Shit," Roscoe said, dragging the word out, as if Mia were talking nonsense, but he didn't rebut what she was saying.

"Then it got interesting," Mia said. "And criminal. When Dennis began to walk like that—with his arms up—you probably asked him what the problem was, and he told you, and you ignored it for a while after that. Or you made fun of him, which is probably more in line with your character. Then you had an idea. A really stupid idea. You thought you could cash in on it."

By now I'm sure I had a smile on my face. Mia was slamming the lid closed on this case and nailing it shut. Her theory explained everything, including the note Dennis had dropped for her, and the fact that he didn't want the cops involved. Maybe he didn't trust any authority figures, other than his dentist. That included Roscoe and probably even his own sister. Who knew what kind of elaborate alternate reality Dennis Babcock had constructed for himself? Sad.

Mia said, "My heart breaks for Dennis, but for the two of you to take advantage of the situation—well, that's just truly horrible."

"You don't know what it's like," Lorene spat back, no longer attempting to maintain the charade.

"Then explain it to me," Mia said, softening her tone somewhat.

Lorene said, "I've had to take care of him since I was about fourteen, and there ain't no end in sight. You ever watch after a crazy person? It'll wear you out like you wouldn't believe. Full-time job, I guarantee. Anytime you wanna swap places with me, you just let me know." Now she was staring Mia in the face, using an indignant attitude to justify the scam she and Roscoe had attempted to carry out. *Look what his illness made me do! It's not my fault! I was desperate!*

"Is he on medication?" Mia asked.

"Yeah, but he won't take it," Lorene said. "Not for long,

anyway."

"What happens when he does take it?"

"He does okay for a while. Holds a job and whatnot. But then after a month or two, he stops, because he don't think he's sick. You understand that part? In his mind, he ain't sick, and he thinks we're all wrong and working against him. So then he'll pretend to take his meds, but it ain't long before I can tell he stopped."

"Plus, looking after Dennis means she can't work no more, either," Roscoe said. "We're dead broke now. Might lose the house. So, yeah, we did what we did. Fuck it. I'm a man and I'll do whatever I need to do to take care of my own."

Rationalizing their behavior.

"Besides," Lorene added, "if Dennis *thinks* the shot made him walk that way, how's that different from it really happening? Either way, he can't walk right, so what's the difference?"

Now the expression on Mia's face was one of painstaking forbearance. She slowly said, "Well, because, in reality, the shot doesn't cause that sort of neurological damage, and claiming that it does endangers other people who refuse to take the shot. They could *die* because of your scam. Surely you can understand how wrong that is."

Lorene sniffed, meaning *Whatever. That's just fancy talk.*

"Who are you people, anyway?" Roscoe asked. He wasn't the swiftest guy, but I gave him credit for understanding he'd been suckered.

"We're videographers who investigate insurance fraud," Mia said.

Roscoe grunted and popped a cigarette loose from a pack on the coffee table.

"So what now?" Lorene asked with the attitude of a teenager who thinks she is about to be unfairly punished.

"You realize you could be prosecuted for fraud?" Mia asked.

"Yeah, if you can prove it," Lorene said.

"Lorene," Roscoe said in an attempt to settle her down. I think he understood that they probably shouldn't antagonize us.

What neither of them knew was that Mia and I were wearing small video cameras, recording everything. On one hand, it would be tempting to provide the video to our client and let them decide whether to pursue criminal charges. On the other hand, a decent lawyer would probably be able to get the video tossed out of any type of legal proceeding, since we were recording inside the privacy of their home. Or they'd argue that the conversation was protected by attorney-client privilege, which might work, even though Diana/Adrienne wasn't actually an attorney. They *thought* Adrienne was an attorney, so that might be enough.

Then there was the issue of Dennis. Any punishment doled out to Lorene and Roscoe would be punishment for Dennis as well. What was best for him? His living conditions weren't ideal, but where would he go if Roscoe and Lorene ended up serving time? I'm sure these questions were running through Mia's mind.

"Here's what's going to happen next," she said. "And there will be no debate about this. Tomorrow morning, you will issue a statement to the *Austin American-Statesman* saying you no longer believe the tetanus shot caused any problems for Dennis, and you're no longer pursuing a lawsuit. You'll say that anyone who needs a tetanus shot should get one. If you're lucky—and I mean really lucky—that will be the end of it for you. I will give you the name and number of a reporter there you can call."

Roscoe and Lorene wore sour expressions, but they didn't object. They didn't have any choice.

I had no doubt our client would be thrilled with this result. Mia would call her after this meeting with news of the forthcoming announcement from Dennis Babcock's family. That way our client would know Mia was responsible for the resolution of the case. The client might be curious as to how

Mia pulled it off, but she'd have to be happy with a vague explanation.

Mia said, "You also need to promise me that you'll take care of Dennis as best you can, and that if you need any help, you'll call me. There are programs out there that can help you, but you can't expect them to fix everything. You have to take an active role yourself."

Roscoe and Lorene didn't respond. They had no interest in what Mia was saying. They were simply waiting for us to clear out of their house.

"Is he on SSI?" Mia asked. "Medicaid?"

"I forget the names of 'em," Lorene said.

"When was the last time he saw a doctor?" Mia asked.

Lorene shook her head, meaning she didn't remember.

"Within the last year?" Mia asked.

"I think late last year," Lorene said.

"Okay, then that's another condition I'm adding," Mia said. "Make an appointment for him as soon as possible. Talk to the doctor about the fact that Dennis won't stay on his meds. Sometimes they have suggestions that will work, or they'll try something else. But you can't just sit back and expect someone else to help him. You have to be an advocate for him. Will you do that?"

Both Lorene and Roscoe reluctantly nodded their heads.

And I was thinking, *Not a chance in hell.*

23

"You were amazing," I said thirty minutes later.

Mia and I were standing on her front porch, facing each other, about four feet between us. Diana had dropped us off a few minutes earlier in her Cadillac SUV, which was a believable vehicle for a reputable attorney.

"Thanks," Mia said. "It wasn't tough to figure out."

"But the way you handled it. And them. Perfect."

"I feel sorry for Dennis."

"Me, too."

"He deserves better than those two..."

She was struggling to find the right word, because she was too nice to label them as assholes or even pinheads. Finally she just let it go.

I started to say something, but Mia stepped forward and hugged me. I wrapped my arms around her. With her mouth near my ear, she said, "I'm sorry, Roy."

"I'm sorry, too."

"I've never been very good at saying it," she said.

I just held her.

"You had a right to be mad," she said.

In the past, with some of the other women I'd dated, I might've been inclined to feel vindication in a moment like this. I might not have voiced it, but I would've felt that I'd won a small victory by being "right." Not now, though. Not with Mia. All I felt was relief that we were putting the tension and the anger behind us. I didn't give a damn which one of us had "won" the argument.

"So did you," I said. "I was a jerk about it."

"Y'all get a room," a voice called.

It was Regina, who had noticed us while walking out to get her mail.

Mia giggled. I gave Regina a wave.

"That sounds like a good idea to me," Mia said in my ear, and she led me inside.

I was sleeping so soundly that when my phone issued an alert at 2:16 that morning, I didn't wake up. But Mia did. She grabbed my phone off the nightstand and looked at it. And she knew exactly what the alert meant, because she had used that same GPS tracking app many times.

When I did wake up, she said, "So you've got a tracker on his car?"

I was groggy. Still not understanding the situation. "What? Whose car?"

"Garlen's," she said, and my eyes popped open with sudden dread. She was propped on one elbow, still holding my phone. It was too dark in the room for me to make out the expression on her face.

My first inclination was to make a joke, but I resisted. Instead I said, "I do, yeah."

Then I waited. How would she respond? I figured she might be even angrier than she'd been two days ago. Surely disaster was forthcoming. I had crossed a line.

She said, "When?"

"Thursday afternoon."

"So right after we talked about him?" Her voice was neutral.

"A few hours later."

She didn't say anything for a long while. I think she was processing it—trying to decide just how large my transgression was.

"Is this the first alert you've received?" she asked.

"Yeah."

She punched the home button on my phone and brought up the screen again. Then she opened the tracking app and checked Garlen's recent movements.

"He drove west all the way to the end of Enfield, then took a left on Lake Austin Boulevard," she said.

Enfield Road, south of Mia's house, would've been just inside the three-hundred-yard range I'd set up for alerts.

There was one big question in my mind. Why was a newly sober man out and about in the middle of the night, specifically right after the bars had closed? I didn't need to say it out loud. Perhaps Garlen had fallen off the wagon. Mia was certainly wondering the same thing, and she was probably checking his earlier movements right now.

"Until twenty minutes ago," Mia said, "he was downtown—on Fifth Street. At one of those condo highrises. He'd been there since about seven this evening. Right now he's on MoPac, going north."

I knew that Garlen lived in Northwest Hills, so he was likely headed home. But why had he driven west on Enfield first? Had he been planning to drive past Mia's house, and then he changed his mind? Had he gotten distracted and missed a turn?

Mia set my phone down on the bedspread.

I reached out and clasped her hand, and she clasped back. Good sign.

"I want to forget about him for good," she said. "I don't want to talk about him. Don't want to think about him. Let's just pretend he doesn't exist, okay? And if he contacts me again, I will report the violation. Sound like a reasonable plan?"

Sounded perfect to me, so I nodded.

"You need to remove the tracker," she said.

"I will."

She put her head back on her pillow and cradled my hand

under her chin. In less than three minutes, she was asleep again. It took me considerably longer.

When I woke up the next morning, Mia was in the shower, so I grabbed my phone and checked on Garlen. He had continued home last night and hadn't moved since. Not surprising, considering it was Saturday. I would keep tabs on him more closely now, so I could figure out a good time to remove the tracker. I changed the settings to alert me the next time his car went anywhere. I also clicked a switch that would allow Mia to see the tracker from the app on her phone, in case Garlen came near her house again.

Then I lay quietly and thought about the Jeremy Sawyer case. I was at another standstill, with no idea how to proceed. I had followed every possible investigative trail I could think of, with very little to show for it.

I decided I would spend one more day working on the case. If I couldn't make additional progress, I would live with the fact that something bad happened on the boat that night, and I'd never know what it was. Neither would Heidi or her family.

Problem was, I had no idea what to do next. I couldn't force anyone involved to tell me what they were covering up. I couldn't badger Harvey or any of the other customers into remembering what had happened.

The shower shut off. Now I was picturing Mia in there toweling off. It was much more fun than thinking about the case. The more I thought about her, the more I realized that the case could wait for another hour or so.

"Need some help in there?" I called.

166 | BEN REHDER

I called Starlyn Kurtis again, got voicemail again, and left a message again. This one was much longer than the first.

"Hi, Starlyn. It's Roy Ballard. I left you a message two days ago about Jeremy Sawyer. What I'm about to say might make no sense to you at all, and if that's the case, you can completely ignore it. But I'm guessing you'll know exactly what I'm talking about. So here's the situation. I know that something happened on the party barge that nobody wants to talk about. I still don't know exactly what it was, but I will find out eventually. I always do, because I am very good at my job. At that point—if the truth has to come out against the will of the people who know what happened—well, that will not be a good thing. Much better if someone steps forward voluntarily and tells the story. I'm thinking that person should be you. I realize that various people are probably putting pressure on you to keep quiet, but you have to ask yourself if that's the best idea. What will happen if you don't come forward and I find out what happened? How will that affect your future? I've done a little research about you, and my understanding is that you are an intelligent woman. My advice is to use your brains and get a handle on this now, before it gets any worse. That could minimize the impact this situation has on your life, and on Anson's, too, if he was somehow involved. Give me a call and let's talk. I will do my best to help you."

I hung up. Eric Moss had promised to get me charged with harassment if I called her again, and now I'd done just that. Not that Moss could actually have me charged, because my calling Starlyn wasn't a crime. But it would be interesting to see how Moss might respond, assuming Starlyn told him about the call.

I remained seated on Mia's couch and enjoyed the peace and quiet. She had gone to see her hair stylist, for a trim and to get her roots "highlighted."

"Oh, you mean bleached?" I'd asked.

"No, no," she said. "We don't use that word. We say 'highlighted.'"

"Is there any bleach involved?" I asked. "Or any product that has a bleaching effect?"

"Don't make me smack you," she'd said.

I'd been tempted to ask for her help on this case, but she deserved a few days off after closing the Dennis Babcock case. She had already informed the client that the Babcock family would be contacting the media at noon today to reverse their opinion about tetanus shots. It would be interesting to see how much play that got on the news. I was guessing it would be very little. It was big news when a man claimed that a shot had basically crippled him, but recanting that claim wasn't nearly as interesting, was it?

I let my thoughts wander and created a mental list.

Adam "Meatball" Dudley.

Gilbert Holloway.

Eric Moss.

Dirk "Creek Guy" Crider.

Starlyn Kurtis.

Anson Byrd.

At least one, and probably more, of these people knew what happened on the boat. Harvey Selberg might know, too, but his memory had been obliterated by alcohol and he might never remember clearly. Anybody sober enough to have a memory of that night had already been questioned by deputies and investigators.

Whatever had happened, it hadn't been murder. Jeremy Sawyer had drowned. There was no dispute about that. So what did that leave? Had a crime been committed on the barge? If so, what kind of crime? If something had happened that wasn't a crime, what was it? Why cover it up? Jeremy Sawyer had flipped backwards over the railing of his own accord, so it appeared to me that nobody else was culpable in his death.

But if someone else had been partially culpable, who?

Anson Byrd immediately sprang to mind.

Of the six people on my mental list, he was, in my opinion, the one most likely to have done something that the rest of them were hiding. He was also the only one I hadn't talked to or tried to contact. Was it time to change that? Just like Starlyn Kurtis, he probably wouldn't accept or return my calls. Hell, it was often difficult to get perfectly innocent people to return calls.

But I placed a call anyway. Not to Anson Byrd, because I didn't have his number. I called Dirk Crider.

"Hey," he said with almost no enthusiasm, obviously recognizing my number.

"Isn't it a fantastic morning in Austin, Texas?" I said cheerfully.

"I guess."

"Need a little favor," I said.

"What?"

"Anson Byrd's number."

"I don't have it."

"I think you're mistaken," I said.

"I really don't. Me and Anson don't hang."

"Dirk, you're forgetting something."

"Huh?"

"You agreed to tell me the truth. And to answer all my questions. Plus, if push comes to shove, I can check your phone records and see if you're being straight with me. It's just that asking you for the number is a lot easier, and I always prefer the easy route. I'm basically lazy. It's one of my many shortcomings."

Accessing his phone records would be difficult if not impossible, but he wouldn't know that.

After a pause, he said, "I can probably get it."

He didn't want to admit he had lied.

"That would be dandy," I said. "And please tell your imaginary source I said thank you."

"Whatever."

Seven minutes later, he texted it to me.

24

I called the number and got voicemail, as expected. *Yo, it's Anson. I probably won't listen to your message, but you can leave one if you want.*

"Anson, my name is Roy Ballard. I've been calling Starlyn, but I'm guessing you know that. Time is running out. You really need to give me a call, and the sooner the better. That's all I have to say. You know what this is about."

I disconnected.

Empty threats. I had nothing.

I fixed myself some scrambled eggs and bacon, then made one more desperate phone call. This one went to Detective Ruelas. He surprised me by answering, but then I quickly understood why.

"Been getting yourself into all kinds of shit lately, from what I've heard," he said.

"Try not to sound so giddy about it," I said.

"Can't help myself. The thought of you in jail makes me smile."

"So does kicking puppies," I said. "But it ain't gonna happen."

"I don't know. Two against one."

He was referring to Gilbert Holloway and Meatball claiming I'd committed assault.

"Any idea where that stands?" I asked. "Has Holloway met with a detective yet?"

"You know I can't tell you that. Even if I could, I wouldn't."

"Did you catch the case yourself?"

"That I can tell you, and the answer is no. Unfortunately.

Woulda been the highlight of my career locking you up."

"Except that I'm innocent."

"I've never heard that before."

"Why would I punch the guy?" I asked.

"I can't think of any good reason, except, of course, the fact that you're an asshole."

"He's lying, and if you'd just figure out what happened on that boat, then we'd all know why."

"I already told your much smarter partner that it was a drowning. End of story."

"I'm not necessarily talking about the death of Jeremy Sawyer—at least not directly," I said. "I think something else happened out there, and they're trying to stop me from looking into it."

"Who is?"

"Gilbert Holloway and Eric Moss."

"Maybe you're just annoying the shit out of them."

"So as far as you're concerned, the case is closed?"

"Not closed, but inactive."

"What about Harvey Selberg? Why was he burglarized and assaulted?"

"Okay, smart guy. Are you saying you have evidence that ties the Selberg case to something that happened on the barge?"

"Seems like it would be."

"Brilliant. Seems like. It's real easy to come up with theories without any proof, isn't it? Hey, maybe Selberg knows where Amelia Earhart crashed, but somebody wants it covered up."

"Then give me a good reason why Holloway is trying to stop my investigation," I said.

"I love it when you use that word. Investigation. Like you know what you're doing."

"Don't duck the question. Why is Holloway trying to stop me?"

"You keep saying that, but you've got shit to back it up."

I thought about Dirk Crider and his confession. If I shared that with Ruelas, he'd know that my claims about Holloway were accurate. But I wasn't ready to give Dirk up just yet.

"The fact that Holloway fabricated a charge against me is evidence in itself," I said.

"Look," Ruelas said, plainly reaching the end of his rope. "If some other crime was committed out there, nobody saw it and there wasn't a victim. We talked to everyone on that boat, and we looked at hundreds of photos, and it was exactly what it appears to be—a drowning."

A text from Mia popped onto my screen. *Just saw an article about Dennis Babcock's retraction. Client is thrilled.*

I sent her a thumbs-up.

"Can you send me some of those other photos?" I asked.

"Because you'll find something we missed, right? You are a fucking piece of work."

"Obviously, my skills could never match those of the infamous Detective Ruelas," I said, "but what would it hurt to let me have a look?"

"Because—and try to keep up with me here—you are not an employee of the Travis County Sheriff's Office. Nor could you ever hope to be."

"That last part was just rude," I said. Then I said, "What if there *was* another crime, but the people who saw it didn't *know* it was a crime?"

"What the fuck're you talking about?"

Truth was, I didn't know. I was just brainstorming, as Mia and I did sometimes, but Ruelas wasn't the type to play along.

"Use your imagination," I said. "That's the thing wedged between your obstinacy and your preconceived notions."

He let out a long sigh. "I'm gonna share one more detail with you, because you're gonna find out eventually from Heidi, and because maybe, just maybe, it will shut you up about this case."

I said nothing, because I didn't want to risk him changing his mind about whatever was forthcoming.

He said, "This is all according to Starlyn Kurtis's attorney. What happened was, her boyfriend went to the bathroom, and while he was gone, Jeremy Sawyer started flirting with her again. He asked for a kiss on the cheek, and she thought, *Okay, what the hell—this guy is sweet and harmless.* So she goes to kiss him, but Jeremy got clever and turned his head at the last second, so she kissed him on the lips instead. She said it was funny because he tricked her. Not a big deal at all. Only problem was, Anson Byrd came back just in time to see it. He obviously wasn't happy about it, and when he came to talk to Jeremy about it, Jeremy flipped backward over the railing to get away. They didn't realize at the time that he never came out of the water, but fifteen or twenty minutes later, people started noticing he wasn't on the boat."

Finally we had the missing piece of the puzzle—and it was anything but satisfying. Like when a firecracker fizzles, but doesn't explode. Nobody had done anything illegal that night, and the crew on the boat certainly wasn't liable for what had happened.

Okay, but why would Gilbert Holloway claim I'd assaulted him? Why send a goon after me? Maybe it was a misguided attempt to protect Starlyn's reputation. Suppose, for instance, she wanted to run for office herself someday. Even years from now, her opponents could dig up media reports of the barge incident and use them against her. They'd paint it as something worse than it had been, twisting facts in an attempt to make Starlyn appear responsible for Jeremy's death. That was the way things went in politics today. So Holloway tried to cover it up. Maybe Eric Moss had paid him to do it. Maybe we'd never know all the details.

"When did you learn about this?" I asked.

"About thirty minutes ago. Starlyn's attorney called and said she wanted to revise her statement about what happened that night. The part about the kiss—she'd suddenly remembered that part."

"Right," I said. "Suddenly remembered."

"Funny how that works."

It wasn't lost on me that the attorney had called Ruelas not long after I'd left those voicemails for Starlyn and Anson—meaning my pressure on them appeared to have worked—but I was too dispirited to even gloat about it.

"Still doesn't mean she's telling us everything," I said. "Maybe Anson threatened Jeremy."

"Maybe, but the bottom line is, he didn't touch Jeremy Sawyer. Shitty situation, but that's what it is."

This all meshed with the photo Jayci had taken. Jeremy had flipped backward over the railing before Anson had gotten close enough to grab him.

"But you'll talk to Anson about it again, right?" I asked.

"I called and he refused to meet with me again. Said he's done talking about it."

I was reluctant to give up, even though the time had clearly come. "What about Harvey Selberg?" I asked.

"What about him?"

"I assume that case is still active."

"Of course it is."

"I still think it's tied in somehow," I said.

"Last time I'm gonna say this," Ruelas said. "Do you understand you gotta come up with evidence to back up your theories?"

"Isn't that your job, too?" I said, knowing he'd hang up on me, and he did.

I sat there for a moment, trying to process what I'd just learned.

Such a simple explanation. Made sense, too. Starlyn had been reluctant to tell the cops exactly what had happened, and Holloway had helped cover it up.

It all fit.

So why wasn't I buying it?

Before I could figure that out, I got an alert on my phone. Garlen's BMW was on the move.

25

At about that same time, Mia was getting a phone call from Roscoe. She was seated in a chair at her stylist's salon, the roots of her hair wrapped tightly in foil, waiting for the "highlights" to kick in.

"I saw the retraction online earlier," she said. "Thank you."

"That ain't why I'm calling," he said.

"What's up?"

"Lorene is all upset 'cause Dennis has gone missing."

"Since when?"

"This morning, after we talked to that lady newspaper reporter. Far as I'm concerned, it's good riddance. But Lorene won't have none of that. She wants to know he's okay."

"How do you know he's missing? Doesn't he sometimes leave the house on his own?"

"Well, sure," Roscoe said, "but he ain't answering his phone, and he won't text, either. Plus, a duffel bag is gone, along with some of his clothes."

Mia started to suggest that Roscoe should call the police, but she knew that wouldn't do much good. Dennis wouldn't be classified as a missing person because he had left voluntarily. Yes, he had a mental disorder, but so did thousands of other poor souls wandering the streets of our cities. As long as Dennis wasn't a danger to himself or others, he still had the right to make his own choices, including taking off without telling anyone where he was going.

"I'm sorry to hear that," Mia said, at the same time wondering how Dennis was carrying a duffel bag while walking with both arms straight up. After all, even though

Roscoe and Lorene had admitted their part of the fraud scheme, Dennis's delusion about the effect of the tetanus shot wasn't faked.

"That don't get me real far," Roscoe said.

"Pardon me?"

"You can say you're sorry and all, but what I need is help. Yesterday you said to call if we needed anything. So now I'm calling. Did you mean it for real, or was that just a line of bullshit?"

"No, of course I meant it. I'll help however I can. What would you like me to do?"

"Well, you proved you're pretty damn good at nosing around in people's lives, so why don't you find Dennis for us?"

Garlen's BMW stopped at a taco truck in south Austin, but before I could get there, it had moved on. He stopped at a dry cleaners, and then at a gelato shop, and then at a jewelry store. By then I'd been following him around for thirty minutes, waiting for my chance. Then he finally pulled into a Home Depot. Perfect. Even if you needed just one item at a Home Depot, it was almost impossible to get out of there in less than ten minutes. Hell, just locating the item could take longer than that.

I watched him walk inside, and then I gave it another full minute. Then I drove my Toyota closer to his BMW and parked a few slots away. Waited another minute. Stepped from the Toyota and strolled over to the BMW.

I dropped to my back and shimmied underneath the BMW—and immediately realized that something was wrong. The tracker wasn't where I had attached it. And I knew it hadn't fallen off the vehicle, because the app was still showing me the correct location. That meant the tracker was inside the car.

Then the situation got worse when a pair of shoes appeared about four feet from my head. Garlen's shoes, of course. Attached to Garlen's feet.

I worked my way out from underneath the car and stood up, facing him. He appeared fit and healthy, but that was the way he had appeared a few months back, when he'd been dating Mia and drinking heavily.

"Your tie rods look fine," I said. "But your idler arm has some play in it, and that could affect the handling before too long."

Garlen had his arms crossed and appeared pleased with himself.

"One of my tires felt a little wobbly yesterday, so I had it checked out," he said. "The guy spotted your little toy. I put it in my trunk and figured you'd show up before too long. Clever, huh?"

I said, "Nobody ever said you were a dimwit—except, of course, me."

"You always have an answer for everything," he said.

So I didn't answer.

"What you did was illegal," he said. "I should call the cops."

"Do it," I said. "I'll stand right here and wait. I'd love to hear you explain why you violated the protective order."

"She *allowed* me to come talk to her," he said.

"Doesn't matter," I said. "She can't give you approval to break the law. I'm sure you already know that, but you're the kind of guy who thinks the law is for other people. Just like sobriety."

"Well, that's really fucking low," he said. "I've gone fifty-three days without a drink."

"And yet your personality hasn't improved," I said.

"I'm trying to make a fresh start," he said. "From what I understand, you've needed a couple of those yourself."

He was trying to needle me, and it was working. I could feel my cheeks heating up. "True, but there's a slight difference. I've never stalked a woman who wants to be left alone. I've never tried to run an innocent person off the road. Plus, I can drink a beer or two, and then stop."

Honestly, I wasn't particularly proud of some of these comments—who says that sort of thing to a person with an addictive disease?—but I couldn't stop myself from saying them. That's how much I disliked this guy. I had a feeling that, even if he weren't an alcoholic, he would still be a jerk who caused problems for other people.

"Your problem," he said, "is that you're basically a mean guy."

"Give me the tracker," I said.

"Plus, you stick your nose where it doesn't belong," he said. "My relationship with Mia is none of your business."

Now I could barely restrain myself. I edged closer to him and he stepped backward.

"You don't *have* a relationship with her," I said. "Can't you get that through your head? It's over. If you really care for her, and if you're any kind of man, you'll leave her alone."

For a moment, his face bunched up and it looked as if he might cry. Or he was about to fly into a rage. Or possibly he had gas pains.

Then he said, "You're doing the same thing I used to do—rationalizing your manipulative behavior."

I laughed. "You're a therapist now?"

"Don't you see that you're trying to control her—to isolate her from other people—and coming up with lame excuses for why you're doing it?"

"There is only one person I don't want her to see, and that's you. Look, seriously, I wish you all the best in your recovery, and I hope you transform yourself into a totally different person, but in the meantime, I'm going to be right here, in your way, doing what I think is best for Mia."

"Oh, man, you don't even know, do you?"

He wanted me to ask "Know what?" So I didn't. He continued anyway.

"She told me she's not in love with you," he said. "But she

hasn't figured out how to tell you. You wormed your way into her life, and now she feels stuck."

I could feel my temper beginning to flare. He was lying. I knew it. That's what guys like him did. He was trying to plant seeds of doubt in my head, to erode my confidence. That meant it was time to end the conversation, or I would hear more of the same.

"I need the tracker," I said.

"Ha. Right. That takes a lot of gall."

"Give me the tracker."

"Not a chance. I'm keeping it. That's the price you pay for thinking you're some sort of slick investigator."

I took a deep breath. I was beginning to get tunnel vision—a sign that my anger was reaching a tipping point, and violence was almost inevitable. His face was *right there*, just waiting for me to smash it. Right now, with my judgment clouded, it seemed like such a reasonable solution. Who wouldn't do the same, right? He deserved it. He was asking for it. And it would feel so good. Reminded me of Gilbert Holloway grabbing me by the arm. Pushing his luck. What was up with these morons?

"Garlen," I said slowly. "If you don't give me the tracker, I will take your keys from you and get it myself. Your choice."

I meant it. I was done talking. If he showed any resistance or made any more comments, I was going to lose my shit. That would be bad for him in the short term, and likely even worse for me in the long term. I would do some serious damage, as long as nobody stopped me.

I could tell that he wanted to resist—to tell me to go to hell—but ultimately he didn't have the guts. Guys like Garlen and Gilbert Holloway never did.

He stepped to the rear of the BMW and popped the trunk.

"What kind of phone does Dennis have?" Mia asked.

"Just some cheap brand," Roscoe said. "Came with the plan."

"Does it have a find-my-phone feature built in?"

"A what?"

"Like GPS tracking, so you can find your phone if it's lost or stolen."

"Man, I got no idea."

Just great.

"What about social media?" Mia asked. Before Roscoe could ask what that was, she said, "Facebook, Instagram, Twitter—stuff like that. Does he use any of them?"

Of course, she had looked into that when we were first investigating him, but as far as she had been able to tell, Dennis had no social media presence. Still, he could've been using a screen name instead of his real name.

"Don't think so," Roscoe said.

"Okay, I want you to make a list of all the places he might go. Where would he hang out? Is there anyplace he talks about in particular that he'd like to visit? Friends, too. Write them down for me."

"He ain't got no friends," Roscoe said.

Which was sad as hell.

"Does he have any money?" Mia asked.

"No telling how much he might've squirrelled away over the years. I'd guess he's got at least a couple hundred."

"Does he have any credit cards?"

"Hell, no. Can you 'magine turning a guy like him loose with a credit card?"

"Where are you right now?" Mia asked.

"Driving around, looking for him—but it's real tempting to drive to Florida or California and never come back."

"Where's Lorene?"

"At home, waiting."

"How about I meet you at the house in two hours?"

"Fine," Roscoe said. "Although this sure as shit ain't how I wanted to spend my Saturday."

26

I couldn't help myself. The Jeremy Sawyer case was a dead horse—but I wanted to speak to Gilbert Holloway and Meatball to see if their accounts of the evening matched the new information provided by Starlyn Kurtis. Obviously, they knew about the kiss, because they were the ones trying to cover it up. Once I revealed that I knew about it, too, and that I'd be out of their lives as soon as they told me the story in their own words—well, who wouldn't jump all over an offer like that?

Also, I was hoping to make a deal with Holloway: if he would drop the assault charge against me, I wouldn't press charges against him or Dirk Crider for that little charade at the creek. Seemed fair to me.

So after I'd cooled off from my encounter with Garlen, I went back to my apartment, changed into some appropriate marina-wear, then hopped back into the Toyota and drove toward the lake. We were enjoying a break in the heat today. The high was supposed to be in the mid-80s, and right now I was enjoying driving with the windows down and some Tom Petty cranked.

I took Bee Caves Road west, turned right on Highway 71, then took another right on 620. Seven miles later, I took a left and went north on Hudson Bend Road. This road went straight up the middle of a fat thumb of land created by a horseshoe-shaped curve—the eponymous bend—right before the river reached Mansfield Dam, which formed the lake. Hudson Bend had been a busy and popular area for as long as I could remember, but in the past ten or twenty years, it had nearly grown to maximum density. I just didn't see how they'd be

182 | BEN REHDER

able to jam any more houses or businesses into this area—but I guess the developers would figure out a way.

I stopped at a convenience store for a Dr Pepper and I noticed that Mia had called earlier and left a voicemail. This is when I got the latest news about Dennis Babcock.

Hey, Roscoe called. Dennis is AWOL since earlier this morning. He took a bag and some clothes, so Lorene is pretty upset. Can you give me a call when you get a minute? I'm meeting with them in a couple of hours. She let out a sigh. Then she added, *Remember when I told them to call me if they needed any help? Don't let me do that in the future, okay?*

I contemplated calling her back right then to get the specifics, but I didn't want to tell her I was on my way to speak to Holloway. She'd say it was a bad idea and try to talk me out of it, and because she is almost always right about such things, I decided to call her back later.

After driving for several minutes on Hudson Bend Road, I took a right on a smaller road and began winding my way downhill to the marina. I'd checked the booking calendar for the Island Hopper online earlier and saw that it wasn't going out until a sunset cruise starting at six o'clock this evening. Which meant Holloway and Meatball would likely already be there, preparing the barge for another voyage. If they weren't, I'd wait until they showed.

I could have called first, but I wanted the element of surprise. I also realized that I would need to strike a somewhat conciliatory tone. Indicate that I understood their inclination to keep Starlyn out of this mess. She didn't do anything wrong. In fact, she was being nice, giving Jeremy an innocent kiss. Not her fault that Anson saw it and got mad. Not her fault that Jeremy flipped backwards over the railing and was never seen alive again.

The marina lot was fairly full, but I managed to find a parking spot with a view of the lake—and the Island Hopper— below. This time, I carefully checked the vehicles around me.

Didn't see anybody. So I grabbed my binoculars and focused on the party barge. Sure enough, I could see Meatball moving around on the lower deck, getting things in order. No sign of Holloway, which might be a good thing. Meatball would be less confrontational. Probably.

I took a deep breath, then opened the car door. Time to get this over with.

I reached the end of the long wooden pier and was now standing beside the Island Hopper. Meatball, who had been doing something in the storage area beneath the steps to the upper deck, came out and saw me waiting. He immediately pointed at me in an angry manner, obviously about to tell me to hit the road, but I spoke first.

"I come in peace," I said, raising my hands in surrender. "Promise. Everything's cool. But we need to talk. Just give me a few minutes. I know the real story about Starlyn. I know what really happened."

He lowered his arm slowly, but he was watching me suspiciously. Glaring a hole in me was more like it.

"She finally told the cops everything," I said. "And I believe her."

"Then why are you here?"

"Because I want to hear it from you. You or Gilbert."

"Why? What'd she say?"

"Well, that's the thing," I said. "If I tell you what she said, what's the use of me asking to hear your version of it?"

"I got no version of it. I didn't see anything."

I gave him the look that said I didn't believe him, but he just shrugged.

"Look," I said. "I understand your reluctance, but just give me the highlights—a quick recap—and you'll never see me again."

184 | BEN REHDER

"I told you, I didn't see anything."

"Come on, Meatball. Time to 'fess up."

"You calling me a liar?" he asked.

This was not going as smoothly as I had hoped it would.

"Well, you told me you didn't know anybody on board that night," I said. "In reality, you knew Starlyn, and so I'm guessing you knew Anson, too. Wasn't that a lie?"

"None of your damn business," Meatball said. "Who the hell are you, anyway? You're not a cop or anything. You're just some insurance guy that pokes his nose into everyone's shit."

"I have to say I've heard more poetic descriptions of my career choices," I said. "But in any case, why do I get the feeling I still don't know the full story?"

"I don't give a fuck about your feelings," Meatball said. "And if you don't bounce right now, I'm gonna kick your ass."

"Wait a sec," I said. "You're the kind of guy who says 'bounce'? I'm afraid I overestimated you."

"Bro," he said, taking a few steps toward me, "you really do like pushing your luck, don't you?"

Now we were less than eight feet from each other—me on the dock, him on the boat.

"I just want to know what happened," I said.

"You need to leave."

"I didn't know Jeremy Sawyer," I said. "But from what I understand, he was a great guy. Whatever happened on the boat, his family deserves to know the truth."

His expression changed, and I had a hard time reading it. Anger? Remorse? Guilt? Didn't matter. Either way, it was a tell. Starlyn's story of the kiss may or may not have been true, but something else happened that caused the cover-up. I was sure of it now.

I said, "I'm sure it's nerve-wracking to be in charge of the safety of so many people—especially a lot of young drunk people behaving like idiots. When you throw in all those laws and regulations, it's probably hard to make sure you do everything just right. The heat of the moment—people are panicking."

Meatball was a large man, but he seemed to be shrinking into himself. He was holding his sunglasses, but they slipped from his hand and landed softly on the carpeted deck. He bent to retrieve them, and that's when something peculiar happened.

I began to think about the carpet. The tan carpet. Just your basic water-resistant carpet that you find on boats, docks, and outdoor patios. And it was right then that I realized the carpet on the two decks wasn't identical. Here on the lower deck, the carpet was just plain tan. But the carpet on the upper deck was tan with a faint herringbone pattern to it. Such a small detail—and yet it told me so much. How had I missed it for so long?

I looked up and saw that Meatball was watching me. I should've turned and left. I had what I needed. But I wanted more. I wanted Meatball to confirm my new theory, and to come forward with his account of that night.

"The kiss wasn't the problem, was it?" I asked.

It appeared that Meatball wanted to talk, but he couldn't bring himself to do it.

"It had nothing to do with Anson Byrd being jealous," I said. "The problem was bigger than that."

Meatball's reaction—or lack of one—told me I was right. I paused again. Meatball remained silent.

"You'll have to tell the truth eventually," I said.

"I didn't see anything," Meatball said. He put his sunglasses on—no longer wanting to make eye contact.

"You sure?" I said. "Or are you just too scared of Gilbert Holloway and Eric Moss?"

"Dude," Meatball said, shaking his head.

He seemed right on the verge of coming clean—like he was torn between telling the truth or staying loyal.

But 'seemed' is the key word, because that wasn't what was actually happening. No, he was shaking his head for an entirely different reason—more like, *Oh you poor son of a bitch*—but before I could figure it out, I was hit from behind, hard, on the side of the head. My knees buckled and I fell forward, unable to stop myself as I fell into the gap between the boat and the dock.

27

I don't know if I lost consciousness or not, but I was suddenly aware that I had an up-close view of the carpet in question. Just tan, no herringbone pattern, which meant I was on the lower deck. I was lying on my belly, with my right cheek pressed flat on the deck, and my shoulders were killing me.

That's because I'd been hogtied, tightly, by someone who knew what he was doing. Made sense. Plenty of rope on a boat, and I'm sure Meatball had mastered a variety of effective knots.

I was soaking wet, with water still trickling from my hair and running down my face, indicating I hadn't been out of the water for long.

My head was hurting pretty badly, too, although not as much as I would have expected. Just a medium-sized headache at the moment.

A foot stepped over me. The foot was clad in a basic leather sandal, so I knew it wasn't Meatball. The other foot followed, and now I saw hairy calves, and he stepped further away, so I could see his khaki shorts and teal-colored polo shirt, and then his face. And his captain's hat.

Gilbert Holloway.

Then someone else stepped over and joined him.

Anson Byrd.

They both stood looking down at me. I realized now that the boat was moving.

"If you're not careful, your boat is going to get a bad reputation," I said.

"Shut up," Holloway said.

"Good point," I said.

Holloway looked away—checking the horizon. I assumed Meatball was at the helm.

Anson Byrd was still glaring at me.

"Nice to meet you, Anson. Pardon me if I don't shake."

"Fuck you."

"What an odd greeting."

"Eat shit."

"That's just rude," I said. "I thought we might be friends. Maybe play squash together."

"You ain't seen rude yet," he said.

"Or proper grammar," I said.

I could tell that he was seething, but he kept quiet.

The lower deck had a hip-high railing around the perimeter, with a running bench beneath that for passenger seating. Unfortunately, the area beneath the bench was used for storage, so I couldn't see through it. I had no idea where we were on the lake or whether any other boats were nearby. It also meant no passing boats would be able to see me.

Holloway was looking at me again, waiting patiently, and I figured I wouldn't like where we were going or why we were going there.

"I understand why you're trying to protect Starlyn," I said, "but you're only making it worse."

Anson said, "You really need to shut the—"

Holloway held a hand up and Anson went quiet. Holloway was much more composed than the previous time I'd encountered him. Like he was angry, but resolved.

I was fairly certain we were heading in a northward direction, based on the position of the sun. Lake Travis had an average depth of more than sixty feet when it was full, as it was now, and some places between Hudson Bend and Volente were more than two hundred feet deep. In the past few decades, at least nine people had disappeared into the lake and never been found. I tried to push that thought from my mind.

"Hey, can we go down the slide later?" I asked. "Maybe break out some of the water blasters? That would be fun."

Neither man replied.

"I have to say, the name Island Hopper just doesn't fit this boat. Surely I'm not the first person to point this out. The colors are all wrong. Too sedate."

I was acting calm. Cracking jokes. But inside I was a mess. Starting to panic. I tried to pull against the ropes, but there was absolutely no chance of breaking free.

"The cops will find my car at the marina," I said.

"We'll move it later," Holloway said. "Maybe drive it to Dallas or Houston. Or take it to the middle of nowhere and set it on fire."

"They'll track my phone," I said.

"I already turned it off and tossed it into the water," Holloway said.

Anson Byrd had a look of smug satisfaction on his face.

"Come on, guys," I said. "Think this through. It's almost impossible to get away with murder nowadays. Too much technology. Think they won't find surveillance cameras at the marina?"

Holloway laughed. "Funny you mention that. A lot of the boat owners have been bitching at the marina management to install a security system. Some of the boats got vandalized a few weeks ago after a frat party."

His phone emitted a tone, so he pulled it from a holster on his hip and checked the screen, apparently reading a text. Then he stepped over me again and walked to the other end of the boat. A few minutes later, I could hear him talking, but I couldn't make out the words.

The barge kept moving right along. Not fast—just the same kind of pace you'd expect on a leisurely outing.

"You shouldn't get messed up in this," I said to Anson.

"Wouldn't miss it for the world," he said. He was practically licking his lips.

"Really?"

"Paybacks are hell," he said.

"Payback for what?"

"Being a pain in the ass."

"You're ruining your future."

"Maybe so, but I'm gonna ruin yours first," he said.

"I have to admit I admire a clever retort," I said.

Now Meatball and Holloway were having a conversation behind me, but I still couldn't make out any words. They were intentionally keeping their voices low.

By this point, my shoulders were screaming, my thighs were cramping, and my neck was beginning to ache.

"Does Eric Moss know what y'all are doing?" I asked.

"Be quiet," Anson Byrd said.

"Could you flip me onto my side?"

"Nope."

"Loosen the rope a little?"

"Not a chance."

"I'm a sensible guy," I said. "No matter what happened that night, Starlyn wasn't responsible for Jeremy Sawyer's death. I can keep it to myself. Won't tell a soul."

Holloway came back. "What's he saying?"

"Trying to talk his way out of it," Anson Byrd said. Then, to me, he said, "They will never find you."

"How can you be sure?"

The pitch of the barge's motor dropped a little. We were slowing down.

Anson Byrd hadn't answered my question, so I said, "You're making things worse for Starlyn. When they find my—"

"They will never find you," Anson Byrd repeated.

"You're dreaming," I said. "They'll send divers down, and if that doesn't work, they've got underwater drones with sonar and HD cameras."

"It's a big fucking lake," Anson Byrd said. "And if they do find you, so what? They won't be able to tie it to us."

"They'll put pressure on all three of you," I said, "and one of you will eventually break. That's the way it always happens. One of you will take a sweet deal, and the other two will probably get the death penalty. Like Ben Franklin said, three people can keep a secret—if two of them are dead. Oh, hey, Eric Moss knows about this, too, doesn't he? So that makes four of you. And you don't think anyone will talk?"

Now the drone of the engine dropped even lower. We were idling.

Holloway walked behind me again and was gone for several minutes.

Then he came back and dropped an anchor on the deck directly in front of my face.

"Should've minded your own business," he said.

Mia was on her way over to Dennis Babcock's house, but she pulled over to call me. It went straight to voicemail.

She said, "Hey, I'm meeting with Roscoe and Lorene in a little bit, and I was hoping to talk to you beforehand. Did you get my voicemail earlier? Call me in the next thirty minutes if you can, okay?" Then she added, "This morning was nice, by the way. I'll see you later."

"Speaking of Moss," I said, "how much is he paying you to do this?"

Gilbert Holloway's expression changed just enough to give me an answer.

Anson Byrd tried to laugh it off. "Dude, you are so desperate."

"Oh, come on," I said. "Think about it. Moss is the only one who isn't here, and he probably wants me gone more than any of you. Plus, he's richer than hell. When you get caught, and you will, he's gonna say, 'Hey, I had no idea what those knuckleheads were doing.' Then he'll get the best lawyers money can buy—for himself, but not for you."

"Shut up," Anson said.

"And despite all that, y'all haven't asked him for a dime? Use your head, man."

Anson grabbed the anchor, which obviously wasn't for the barge. Too small. Something you'd use for a sailboat or a buoy. Probably weighed about thirty pounds. Mushroom shaped. It would certainly pull a body to the bottom of a lake—but would the body stay there? Considering that the bottom of this particular lake was littered with the remnants of old trees and other collected detritus, yeah, there was a good chance the anchor would get the job done. Anson began to remove the existing rope from the anchor and replace it with fresh new rope. Chain would be better, but I wasn't going to offer that little bit of advice.

I noticed that Gilbert Holloway hadn't moved. He was just standing there, possibly pondering what I'd said.

"Fifty grand would be nothing to Moss," I said. "Or even a hundred grand. Hell, ask for a quarter million and see what he says. The man is worth some serious cash. You're taking all the risk. What's he doing?"

Anson picked up the anchor like it was a toy and moved it closer to my feet. He began to tie it to the rope around my ankles. Holloway didn't move.

Anson looked at him. "He's just stalling."

"Yeah, but he's got a point."

"Seriously? Now you're gonna think about that?"

"Why not?"

Anson shook his head.

"You think he's going to be your father-in-law someday?" I asked. "He's not going to want you in Starlyn's life after this."

"You shut the hell up," Anson said.

"Can you imagine sitting around at Thanksgiving, having

this secret between you? A constant reminder of the worst thing he's ever done. Why would he subject himself to that?"

Anson Byrd said nothing. I was starting to get to him.

"Might as well get some money out of him instead," I said. Then I looked at Holloway. "And what about you? You're buying this boat from him, right? Bet he's financing it for you, huh? The least he can do is call that loan square."

Holloway's expression told me he was surprised I knew about his purchase of the Island Hopper.

"What's he gonna say?" I asked. "No? Fat chance. You've got the upper hand. How often does that happen when you're dealing with a guy like Moss? You'd be an idiot not to take advantage of it."

"He's just trying to buy himself some extra time," Anson Byrd said.

"Well, of course I am," I said. "Wouldn't you? But that doesn't make what I'm saying any less sensible. It'll take five extra minutes. Why not call him?"

I really didn't have much of a coherent plan at this point. I *was* stalling, because what was my alternative?

I waited, trying not to appear terrified.

"Come on, Gilbert," Anson Byrd said, getting more agitated. "We don't have time for this shit."

I said, "It'll take five minutes."

Byrd suddenly kicked at my face, but I managed to pull my head back, which brought renewed aches from my burning shoulders.

"Hey! Cool it!" Holloway barked.

"You let this kid tell you what to do?" I said to Gilbert. "He's the one who caused all the problems to start with."

Byrd said, "We need to—"

"Just be quiet for a minute and let me think," Holloway said.

"What's there to think about?"

"You don't think you deserve some money for this?" Holloway asked.

"Maybe," Byrd said. "But it's too late now."

"Why?"

Byrd just shook his head. He had no answer.

I realized I was holding my breath. I wanted more time. Even a few extra minutes might make the difference.

After a long pause, Holloway said, "Fuck it. I'm calling." Then he stepped around me again and walked to the other end of the boat for some privacy.

28

Mia called a third time and left another voicemail. "Hey, slacker, you got your phone turned off, or did you fall down a well? Give me a call, okay? Or shoot me a text if you're in the middle of something. I'll be meeting with Roscoe and Lorene in about an hour, but I just want to hear from you, so I know you're okay. Text me, call me, something. Please."

Fifteen minutes passed. We were waiting, and I was smart enough to keep my mouth shut. Every minute that ticked by was a minute in my favor.

Obviously, Holloway had not reached Eric Moss. He was waiting for a call back. Great news for me. I later learned that Moss—being what many people might call "a rich douchebag"—owned two homes: his primary residence here in Austin and an oceanfront cottage in San Diego. I was fortunate that Moss and his wife were, at that moment, on a plane bound for San Diego. I was even luckier that the plane had no Internet access. Moss was effectively out of touch until the plane landed.

Gilbert Holloway and Anson Byrd sat on the bench near me, mostly silent, but every now and then Byrd would say something, like, "We can't wait all day."

"Just a few minutes longer," Holloway would reply.

"You keep saying that."

"Because you keep opening your fucking mouth every five fucking minutes."

The bickering was fine with me.

Anson resorted to shifting around impatiently, but he didn't speak. Every now and then, Holloway would check his phone, looking for an incoming text or call that hadn't come yet.

Mia was less than a mile from Roscoe and Lorene's house when she remembered our conversation earlier that morning and had an unsettling idea. She pulled over and dialed my number yet again.

"Roy, seriously, maybe I'm overreacting, but now I'm starting to get worried. Did something happen with Garlen? Where are you? Give me a call. I'm going to blow off my meeting with Roscoe and Lorene for now. So...let me hear from you."

Her mind was beginning to race. *Did Garlen catch Roy snooping around his car? Did they get into another fight? It wouldn't be out of the question for Garlen to carry a gun.*

Then she remembered the tracker on Garlen's car. Was it still on there? Checking the data might provide some useful information. She opened the tracker app—and stared for a long moment at her screen, slightly confused. According to the map, the tracker was now located in the parking lot of the marina where the Island Hopper was docked. It threw her for a moment.

Did Roy go out to the marina again?

Confronting Gilbert Holloway again would've been a stupid idea—possibly even dangerous.

Is that why Roy isn't calling me back?

She had another useful tool that might provide an answer. She opened the Find My iPhone app. We both had each other's

Apple ID and password—for events just like this. She logged in with my password, saw a graphic of a compass calibrating, and then a map appeared, showing the Hudson Bend area. She noticed that my phone wasn't at the marina itself, but was instead in the middle of Lake Travis, and that it had been offline—either out of range of a tower or turned off—for one hour and seventeen minutes. That didn't make sense. Mia knew that area was well served by cell towers. Getting a signal wouldn't be a problem, even out on the water.

Would Roy turn his phone off if he were going to confront Holloway? No reason he should. He might mute it, but he wouldn't turn it off.

Should she call the cops? If she did that every time she was worried about me, it would be a weekly occurrence, and most of the calls would be false alarms.

She turned her car around and headed west.

Another thirty minutes passed with no conversation and no incoming calls or texts to Holloway's phone. My body had now gone so numb from being hogtied that it was actually more comfortable than before. Weird. I hoped I wasn't going to sustain any sort of long-term damage to my ligaments or cartilage.

My brain, on the other hand, was free to do its thing—and it did. I had another idea. A big one.

"No word from Moss, I guess?" I said. "Can't reach him?"

"Jesus Christ," Byrd said. "You seriously never stop talking, do you?"

"You're doing the right thing," I said to Holloway. "No reason he should get off so easy. In fact, I just came up with a great idea. Get ready to have your mind blown." I waited a beat, then said, "The four of us could blackmail the ever-loving crap out of him."

Neither man responded, but I didn't expect a congratulatory clap on the back. I had to sell the idea. Make them see the beauty of it.

"Think about it," I said. "Moss and the four of us are the only people who know the truth. What would he pay to keep us quiet? We've got him by the balls, guys. That's the bottom line."

I noticed that Anson Byrd stole a sideways glance at Holloway to check his reaction.

I said, "Plus, it stops you from committing murder, which, if you ask me, is a pretty good upside. See, then I'd have a great reason to keep my mouth shut, too. It's perfect, really."

I waited. Nobody was telling me to shut up now. I wondered what Meatball was doing. Probably staying at the helm, away from these two lunatics. Couldn't blame him.

I said, "Either of you know how much Eric Moss is worth? Because I do. It's probably a lot more than you think. A *lot* more."

Throwing out some bait. Seeing if either of them would bite.

Finally, Holloway said, "How much?"

"Based on my research—and I have access to a lot of good information—it's about thirty-seven million dollars."

It was a total lie—I had no idea what Eric Moss was worth—but it had the effect I wanted.

Holloway said, "Holy shit."

Anson Byrd looked at me with distrust.

"And he might have more tucked away somewhere," I said. "Most rich bastards do. To avoid paying taxes. If he had an offshore account somewhere, I would have no way of finding that out. That's the whole point. He could be worth millions more. Yet here you are, out on this boat, doing what? Ignoring the biggest opportunity of your life, that's what."

"No way he's worth that much," Byrd said.

"You can check it out yourself," I said, knowing he wouldn't. "Or cut me loose and I'll show you everything myself."

Both men were contemplating my suggestion—no question about it. Now Holloway turned to Anson Byrd with an expression that plainly said, *You in on this?*

Byrd opened his mouth, about to answer, but right then Meatball yelled a warning from behind the helm of the barge.

"Someone's coming!"

Reacting quickly, Anson Byrd grabbed the neck of my shirt and began to drag me along the carpeted deck, which stoked the fire in my joints again. My knees were going to have a serious case of carpet burn. I was tempted to yell, but if the person was too far away to hear me, my scream might only get me gagged. So I kept quiet.

We went past the captain's helm, with Meatball standing behind the wheel, trying to appear casual, and then Byrd pulled me into the enclosed storage area behind the helm. It was basically a closet, with built-in shelves, but it was roomier than I would have guessed. It shared a wall with the bathroom. Excuse me, the head.

I was still facedown.

Anson pulled a lock-blade knife from his cargo shorts and flicked it open with the ball of his thumb. Then he poked the point of the blade into the side of my neck, in the soft spot below my jaw. I knew the carotid artery was somewhere in that neighborhood. Wouldn't take much pressure for that blade to sink in deep.

"Just so you know, I'm cool with the blackmail idea," Byrd said. "But right now, you need to stay quiet. I'll cut you if I have to. Hear me?"

I grunted an affirmation.

Was he just saying that to keep me quiet? If so, pretty smart.

Now I could hear the engine of an approaching craft. Sounded like a jet ski.

"How's it going?" a woman's voice called cheerfully.

"Afternoon," Holloway answered.

"No passengers today?"

Oh, good Lord. That wasn't just some woman. Not by a long shot.

Earlier, when Mia had arrived at the marina, found my car, and still had not heard back from me, she'd acted quickly.

She rented a jet ski and headed out to find the Island Hopper. Big lake, but it was a big boat, too, and she'd spotted it in just a few minutes.

Now she had a plan.

It revolved around a single question. If she was wrong about the situation—meaning I was not being held on the Island Hopper against my will—how would the crew members react when she showed up?

How would most men react if Mia approached them? Almost sad to say how predictable the result was in most cases—which is why we so often used her as bait when trying to catch a fraudster. Most men would jump through hoops to please her, to help her out, to catch her eye, to believe for just a moment that they might have a shot with her. They would smile, be friendly, crack jokes, and put on the best show possible.

Unless they had a captive on board.

29

"That's the Island Hopper, right?" Mia asked.

She was wearing shorts and a tank top, rather than a swimsuit—because she hadn't planned to be on the lake—but it didn't raise any red flags with Holloway.

"Yes, ma'am," he said, sounding plenty composed.

Anson Byrd was straddling me, all hot and sweaty. Still, it would be easy to call out to Mia—to let her know I was in here—but I didn't want to put her at risk.

"And you're the captain?" Mia asked.

"That's right."

"Cool boat. How many people can you carry?"

I had no idea how she'd figured out where I was, but she was obviously playing an angle to see if I was on board and okay.

"About a hundred, but that's kind of tight," Holloway said. "Fifty to seventy-five is better."

"That would be perfect," Mia said. "My twin sister and I are looking for a place to celebrate our birthday next month."

I almost grinned. The imaginary twin sister was a great touch. The only thing better than a woman who looked like Mia was two of her.

"Well, you can book it through our website," Holloway said, still friendly, but trying to wrap up the conversation.

"Could I hop on board and take a look around?" Mia asked.

Brilliant tactic. Under normal circumstances, a man like Gilbert Holloway would welcome Mia on board with overwhelming enthusiasm. By the time she left, he'd be offering a major discount on her booking. Anything to get her and her friends on board for a party.

But these weren't normal circumstances for Holloway.

"Uh, right now?" he said.

"Sure. I can tie up. Just a quick peek."

She began to grab for a ladder on the side of the barge, as if preparing to come aboard.

"Sorry, no!" Holloway said sharply. "Now isn't a good time. I need to get back to the dock."

And that reaction—or overreaction—gave Mia the answer she needed.

So she said, "In that case, I'll take off, but Roy will be coming with me."

I couldn't see Holloway, but I'm sure he tried to appear confused. "I'm sorry, who?"

"We're not going to play it that way," Mia said. "Look behind me. See a black truck parked at Windy Point? A friend of mine is in that truck, watching us."

"I have no idea what you're talking about. Have you been drinking?"

"If Roy doesn't leave with me, my friend will call the cops," Mia said. "You already know there's a sheriff's boat that patrols this part of the lake. They'll be here in less than five minutes. Plus, there's this."

"Jesus!" Holloway said. "What the hell're you doing?" He managed to sound both fearful and indignant.

I could picture what she was doing. She was aiming a gun at him. That's the only thing that made sense. That changed the situation entirely—for better or worse would remain to be seen.

"Where's Roy?" Mia asked.

"I still don't know what—"

"Right here!" I yelled.

Anson Byrd poked the knife a little harder.

"You okay?" Mia called out.

"Not bad," I said. "Except for the knife at my throat."

Byrd increased the pressure again, and now I could feel a trickle of blood running down my skin.

"You get one warning," I said to Byrd. "If you don't remove that knife, I'll find you later and shove a cattle prod up your ass. I mean that literally."

He eased up, but just a little.

"Let him loose," Mia said to Holloway. "You've got ten seconds."

"Jeez, take it easy," Holloway said. "He came out here and started threatening me again. Trying to make me drop the charges against him. What was I supposed to do?"

It was just a lame excuse, but one that would be hard for me to dispute, since Meatball and Anson Byrd would back him up.

"So you brought him to the middle of the lake?" Mia said. "Why would you do that?"

"Just to scare him," Holloway said.

"Well, your fun is over," Mia said. "Let him go."

"You're a bossy little bitch, aren't you?" Holloway said. "Why don't you come up here and get him?" Daring her. Taunting her.

"I might," Mia said. "But if I do, I'm going to shoot you in the face first."

For about five seconds, Holloway didn't reply. I'm sure he was reluctant to let a woman force his hand—but he had no other options.

"Let him go," he finally called out.

"Fuck," Anson Byrd muttered. But he pulled the knife away from my neck and began to saw the rope behind my back.

"I didn't call the cops," Mia said, "because I wasn't sure you were even on the boat."

I could tell she was wired to the max from adrenaline.

"I understand. You did the right thing," I said, rubbing a

chafed spot on my wrist.

We were sitting in Mia's Mustang, parked outside a convenience store on Hudson Bend Road. She had followed me here, and I'd noticed that my hands had trembled on the wheel of the Toyota as I'd been driving. I'd pulled in here to settle my nerves, and because we'd needed to talk about what had just happened. I hadn't wanted to have that conversation at the marina.

She said, "There was also the possibility that you forced Holloway to take the barge out onto the lake, where you were going to extract information from him in ways that could land you in jail."

"Yeah, that sounds like me," I said.

Mia had already described how she had grown concerned earlier about my lack of communication, and how she'd located me using Find My iPhone.

And I'd recounted everything, too, starting with the abduction at the dock.

My body was still aching. After Anson Byrd had cut me loose, it had taken me a couple of minutes before I could stand up and walk on my own. I'd been in no shape to take a swing at anybody, but I'd come close anyway. Revenge would have to wait.

Mia said, "That part about just trying to scare you—think he meant it?"

"Hell, no. They were going to toss me over. You saved my life."

We talked further and agreed that calling 911 to report the abduction would be a waste of time—and it might actually work against me. Holloway would repeat the claim that I had come out to the marina and threatened him, and that would be used against me in the current assault case.

"I'm going to send you a bill for my phone," I'd said to Holloway on my way off the boat, which sounded pretty lame in hindsight.

Holloway had simply glared at me without responding.

He realized by now that I had the skills and the persistence to screw his world up in a major way.

And now I also had the knowledge.

"I know what happened on the boat that night," I said.

Mia looked at me. "Well, what? Tell me!"

I pulled out my back-up phone, which had been in the Toyota. "I need to show you something. This is big."

"I've heard that before."

"I bet you have."

I accessed my cloud storage and opened a folder of photos from the evening of the ill-fated cruise. I scrolled through them quickly, then stopped at a photo of Jayci taken in full sunlight on the upper deck.

"Who's that chicky?" Mia asked.

"Forget her. Look at the carpet."

"Okay. I see it. What, uh, am I looking for?"

"See that there is a herringbone pattern to it?"

"Yeah."

I flipped through some other photos from the upper deck. "And see that there is no place on the upper deck where the carpet doesn't have that pattern?"

"Yeah, okay."

Now I opened the key photo—the selfie of Jayci and her friend Cady. This was the one that had also captured Jeremy Sawyer in the background, flipping over the railing, with Anson Byrd nearby, and Starlyn Kurtis to the right of him.

"See the carpet here?"

"No pattern," Mia said. "So this photo must've been taken on the lower deck."

"Exactly. The carpets don't match. Makes sense, because the upper deck gets more sun, so the carpet up there probably wears out faster."

Mia hadn't studied the layout of the party barge as extensively as I had—it wasn't her case, so why would she?—and as a result, she wasn't connecting the dots.

I said, "We always thought Jeremy went overboard from

the upper deck, but this proves we were wrong. So was Harvey. He was too drunk to remember which deck they were on when it happened."

"Okay, but I don't see how any of this matters," Mia said.

I couldn't help taking a dramatic pause.

"See Starlyn over here? She's standing behind a little wall or something that is about chest high. When I first saw the photo, I thought she was standing behind the little bar on the upper deck. But she wasn't. She was standing behind the captain's helm."

Mia's eyes widened as she figured it out.

I said, "The problem—for her and Eric Moss and Gilbert Holloway—was that Starlyn was illegally driving the boat."

30

Detective Ruelas had seen the photograph before—Jayci had sent it to him—but now he looked at it on my iPad with a fresh eye. I waited patiently. The two of us were in an interview room at the sheriff's substation, which, coincidentally, was on Hudson Bend Road, a few miles south of the marina. It was now 4:30 on Saturday afternoon. Mia had rescheduled her appointment with Roscoe and Lorene and was on her way over there right now.

I didn't like the look on Ruelas's face, but that was nothing new. He was dressed casually—a red polo shirt, faded blue jeans, and some leather loafers. His day off. I had called him several hours after Mia had rescued me—after pondering my options. I'd narrowed it down to this one. Tell Ruelas. Dump it in his lap and wash my hands of it, basically.

Ruelas used his thumb and forefinger to zoom in on the photo. I had already explained the context once, but I couldn't help repeating myself.

"That little wall in front of Starlyn is actually—"

"Yeah, I get it," Ruelas said. "It's the helm."

"Yeah," I said.

"And you think this proves she was driving the boat."

"Well, if you look at some of the other photos, you can pretty much tell exactly where she was standing, which was right in front of the steering wheel. So she was driving. Probably not her first time, either. I'm guessing her attitude was, hey, it's no big deal, right? I mean, she's the owner's stepdaughter, so why couldn't she drive the boat now and then? Just on open water, though. Not docking it or anything tricky. She left that stuff to the captain. But even just steering it was illegal. She's not licensed."

Ruelas was shaking his head, and I realized he wasn't buying it.

"Even if she knew what she was doing," I said, "the liability—the legal exposure—was enormous. It's like a commercial pilot letting a passenger fly a plane. Maybe the risks aren't as great on a boat, but still, she wasn't qualified to captain the vessel. That's the point. That kind of thing could lead to a major lawsuit, and a man like Eric Moss has plenty to lose. Gilbert Holloway, too. That's what the cover-up has been about all along. To avoid a lawsuit."

"Not to shoot a hole in your brilliant work," Ruelas said, plainly enjoying the very idea, "but just because she was standing in front of the wheel, that doesn't mean she was driving the boat. Holloway could've been standing right beside her."

"Or he might not have been," I said. "But even if they were only kinda sorta pretending to let her steer, the liability is still there, if her hands were on the wheel. Moss's lawyers would cringe if they saw this. Scroll to the next photo and you'll see Starlyn wearing the captain's hat."

He frowned at me. "So what?"

I stared at him. He stared back.

"Oh, come on," I said.

"Come on with what?"

I took a breath. Why was Ruelas always so uncooperative? "Why do you think she was wearing it?"

"Because she looks cute in it?"

He wasn't stupid. Just obstinate.

I said, "Imagine you're the captain on a party barge. Turns out the owner's stepdaughter is gorgeous. She asks to steer the boat. What're you gonna do? Say no? I mean specifically *you*. What would *you* do?"

"I wouldn't be the captain on a party boat," Ruelas said. "I got better things to do."

He placed my iPad on the table and slid it toward me.

"You'd let her steer any time she was on the boat," I said, "and if she was being a flirt and took the hat off your head, you'd go home later with dirty thoughts and see if you could smell her shampoo on it. Or you'd put the cap on her head yourself. Either way, the captain's hat was on her head because she was steering the boat."

Ruelas let out a dismissive snort. "Can't believe I drove up here for this. Holloway might've been standing right fucking beside her, just out of the photo, maybe even with one hand on the wheel. This photo is basically worthless. Another one of your theories, with nothing to back it up. That might work in your world, but it doesn't work in mine."

It was time to lay all my cards on the table.

I said, "Eric Moss was willing to have me killed to shut me up. Three hours ago, they had me tied up on the Island Hopper, ready to drop me in the lake."

He gave me a skeptical look, so I told him the full story—every last detail—and I ended by saying, "Feel the bump on the back of my head." I leaned toward him. "Seriously, feel it."

I didn't think he would, but he did. The knot on my head was tender, but the blow hadn't broken the skin or caused any bleeding. I still didn't know who had blindsided me—Holloway or Byrd—but it didn't really matter at this point.

"You could have a career in phrenology," I said.

"You could have a career in getting your ass kicked," Ruelas said, leaning back. "Did you call it in?"

"Why would I? Holloway and his punks would simply say I was lying."

"Pretty funny that your partner had to save your ass again."

Which meant he believed my story. That was progress.

"Again?" I asked.

"Yeah, that's the way it usually works with you two. You fumble around in the dark while she actually gets shit done."

"I'm bringing you fresh information on this case. I was

hoping you'd do something with it."

"You wanna file a report about the abduction? Go for it."

He knew as well as I did that reporting the crime would likely create more legal headaches for me in regards to Holloway's assault charges. Ruelas also probably believed Holloway's claim that they were only trying to scare me, so he wasn't taking the incident seriously.

I said, "I would prefer that you talk to Starlyn about this photograph. Surely you can get a twenty-year-old girl to crack under your skillful interrogation."

"She's not a girl, she's a woman," he said, totally needling me. "And she's not talking anymore. None of them are. I already told you that."

"Then talk to her attorney. Tell him it's Starlyn's last chance to stop this thing from getting even worse for her than it already is."

He'd had enough of me telling him how to go about his work.

"At this point," he said slowly, "you'll be lucky if I don't charge you with interfering with an investigation."

"That would be great," I said. "At least you'd be making an arrest." Then, before he could respond, or perhaps punch me in the teeth, I added, "That was out of line. I apologize."

He said, "You should leave now, and it would be great if I didn't hear from you again for a long time."

On the way back to my apartment, I daydreamed about various ways to set things right with Gilbert Holloway, Anson Byrd, and Eric Moss. No doubt about it, they were going to pay for what they had done.

I don't know why, but I wasn't quite as angry with Meatball. He hadn't given me an egg-sized lump on my head. He hadn't tied me up—as far as I knew. He hadn't tried to kick me in the face, or taunted me, or taken great enthusiasm at the prospect of sinking me into the lake. On the other hand, he'd driven the boat, so he would need to atone for that.

I took a shower—to wash off all that panic-induced sweat—and when I got out, Mia had sent a text. *Still no Dennis.*

I sent one back. *What a menace.*

She replied with a sad face.

I tried to watch a college football game and decompress, but it didn't help much.

Finally, an hour later, I got a decent distraction: a call from Mia.

"Let me just say that these people would fit right in on an episode of Jerry Springer. It's like their IQ is just high enough that they can get through the day without injuring themselves."

I could tell from the ambient noise that she was talking to me hands-free in her Mustang.

I opened my mouth, but she had more to say. "Roscoe actually believes that smoking doesn't cause cancer. He says it's all a scam so the government can put a tax on cigarettes. And it's not just that he's willfully ignorant, it's that he's so damn obnoxious and condescending about it."

"So, uh, you're not enjoying your time together?" I asked.

"I have no idea what to do. Dennis could be anywhere. He might literally be halfway to Florida or California by now. I'm not sure what they expect me to do about it."

"You owe them nothing," I said.

She ignored that comment and instead said, "If you had a brother like Dennis, wouldn't you take some precautions against this sort of thing?"

The answer, of course, was yes. The same kinds of precautions Mia and I took with each other, such as the Find My iPhone app that had basically saved my life earlier in the day. If Dennis were my brother, I'd be in charge of his cell phone account and make sure that I could track his phone if it became necessary. He probably wouldn't like it, but he'd have to live with it just the same.

It was a rhetorical question on her part, so I said, "What's your plan?"

"Right now, I'm going to go home, have a glass of wine, and try to relax a little."

"You want any help?" I said.

"Sure. Meet me at my house. Oh, and bring some wine."

"I was talking about finding Dennis," I said. "But I like your idea better."

31

After I did everything in my power physically to reduce her stress and lower her frustration level, we both got a good night's sleep, and in the morning, she agreed to let me help find Dennis Babcock.

"Did they have any guesses as to where he might go?" I asked. "Favorite places? Strip bars? Crack houses? Book clubs?"

We were still in bed at 8:03 on Sunday morning. I'd been awake since 7:15, but Mia had been sleeping so deeply, I lay still until she finally woke at 7:52.

"According to Lorene, he doesn't have many friends," Mia said. "She said Dennis occasionally mentioned a guy named Ted, but she'd never met him before and didn't know where he lived. There's also the very real possibility that Ted doesn't exist."

"Except in Dennis's imagination?" I said.

"Right. As to where else he might go, they named a couple of restaurants in his neighborhood, but I checked both of those with no luck."

A cool front had blown in overnight, and I could tell from the muted light filtering through Mia's bedroom curtains that it was a cloudy morning. I'd noticed that the air conditioner hadn't kicked on since I'd been awake.

"Did he take his cell phone with him?" I asked.

"Yes, but he won't answer. Goes straight to voicemail."

"Does he have a debit card?"

"Yeah, but there's no way to know when and where he's using it. Lorene and Roscoe don't have access to his accounts."

I tried to remember some details from our early investigation into him. We hadn't been able to find a Facebook account for him, or any social media presence, for that matter. That was unusual for a person his age, and it would make our job all that much harder. But there was also the chance that he used a screen name instead of his real name.

I asked Mia about that possibility, and she said, "Lorene said he wasn't into all that."

"No Twitter? No Snapchat? Nothing?"

"As far as she knew."

"So what did he do with his free time? Any hobbies?"

It was odd how little we had learned about Dennis Babcock in the time we'd had him under surveillance. He didn't leave the house much. We didn't know if that was typical for him, or if he'd avoided going out in public after making the claim about the tetanus shot. It wasn't unusual for fraudsters to become hermits temporarily, especially if they were feigning some sort of physical impairment or disability. The less they went out, the lower the chance of getting caught in a moment of forgetfulness.

"He spent a lot of time online doing something—maybe forums or gaming or something like that," Mia said. "But his laptop was password protected. Lorene admitted she'd tried to snoop on it before."

The man had delusions of paranoia. Of course his laptop was password protected.

"He took the laptop with him?"

"Yep."

"Did Lorene or Roscoe ever come up with the brilliant idea of simply asking him what he did with his time all day?"

"You're talking about people who show more interest in his government check than they show in him."

"Good point. I'm going to repeat that you owe them nothing. They are both horrible people, from what I've seen."

"Yeah, but Dennis isn't," Mia said.

"Maybe he wants to be gone. Maybe it'll turn out to be the best thing for him."

"Oh, I agree. He needs to be in a better environment. But

right now, he's probably on the street, and since I promised to help…"

We lay in silence for several minutes.

"Is that rain?" Mia said.

"Sounds like it. Just a sprinkle."

But I knew she was picturing Dennis Babcock out there in the weather with nowhere to go. Then it began to rain harder.

"I just have no idea how to find him," Mia said.

It was frustrating that the police might be able to find Dennis fairly quickly—through cell phone tracking or debit card usage—if they had grounds to look for him. But Dennis's illness didn't strip him of the rights and autonomy every other adult enjoys. I couldn't help thinking that maybe it should.

"We'll figure something out," I said. "We always do. And until then, I'm going to stay right here, rubbing your thigh. And what a thigh it is. Oh, hey, here's another one just like it!"

Mia placed a hand over mine to stop the rubbing. Now wasn't the time, I guess.

"Okay, so we start with good old-fashioned canvassing," I said. "We visit every convenience store and restaurant within a mile of Dennis's house and ask if they've seen him."

"He should be memorable, since he'll still be holding his arms over his head," Mia said.

Which was true. Just because we had gotten Roscoe and Lorene to confess to their scam, that had no impact on Dennis's delusion that he'd been damaged by the tetanus shot.

"I wonder what makes something like that go away," I said. "I mean, eventually it will, right? He can't walk around like that forever. Maybe it just takes time. Or some other delusion has to take its place."

Mia sat up suddenly. "Those are great questions," she said, her mood totally different now. "And we should ask the person who probably knows more about Dennis than anybody else. Because they might also be able to help us figure out where he is."

"Uh, who are we talking about?" I said.

Her name was Dr. Caren Creech, and we had her on the phone less than an hour after Mia had her flash of brilliance. Creech was, of course, Dennis's psychiatrist.

Roscoe and Lorene hadn't been able to give us a name—surprise, surprise—so Mia had instructed them to check for a physician's name on one of Dennis's prescription bottles. After that, it was easy to find the doctor's website, and then a phone number, and then an after-hours phone number for use in the event of a crisis. We decided Dennis's disappearance counted as a crisis. Mia left a voicemail explaining the situation, and Creech called back in less than five minutes.

"I understand the reason for your concern," she said, "but we have no reason to think he's in any danger. Correct?"

"He's not taking his meds," Mia replied, using speakerphone so I could hear the conversation.

"I figured as much, but that alone isn't a reason for me to reveal any confidential information," Creech said. "And even if I did, I'm not sure if it would be helpful. I haven't seen Dennis for six weeks."

I was thinking, *Isn't that in itself confidential information?* But I kept my mouth shut.

"His sister is concerned about him," Mia said, "because he has never taken off like this before."

There was a pause on Creech's end, and I interpreted that pause to mean, *His sister is concerned? Really?*

Finally the doctor said, "You can ask questions, and if I can answer them, I will."

"Thank you," Mia said. "Have you heard from Dennis lately?"

"I have not."

"He hasn't tried to call you or anything like that?"

"Not that I'm aware of."

"Has he ever brought up the idea of just taking off

someday?"

"That I can't answer."

"Has he mentioned any friends that might take him in for a few days?"

"Sorry. Can't answer that, either."

"Do you think he might go to a homeless shelter—the Salvation Army? Places like that?"

"Seems like a decent guess, but honestly, I don't know if he'd go there or not. Maybe for a meal, but probably not to stay overnight."

"Do you have any other ideas where he might go? I'm talking local, even within walking distance from his house."

I got the sense that Creech felt that she was overstepping her boundaries, but that the circumstances called for it.

"There's a small library branch near the bus stop he uses. I know he hangs out there sometimes."

The branch was maybe five thousand square feet. Had a large service desk right up front, a media and technology room with maybe a dozen computers to the left, and, in the back, several rooms filled with…books. Imagine that. Real printed books, in this day and age. Who would've guessed?

I moved to a nearby table and took a seat. It wasn't busy, but there were enough people seated at tables and browsing at various racks and shelves that it took me a full minute to scan them all. No Dennis Babcock.

I did see two men I assumed were homeless. Yes, I was profiling. The men were unshaven, their hair unkempt, and their clothing hadn't seen a washing machine in some time. Ragged backpacks rested on the floor under their chairs. One of the men had his head on the table, plainly sleeping. Who could blame him? I didn't know where I'd go if I were homeless, but a library would look pretty good. My understanding was that many of the shelters allowed overnight habitation only—they didn't allow patrons to hang around in the daytime—so all those people had to go somewhere. Why not pick a safe, quiet place with a restroom and access to a variety of entertainment choices?

Earlier, on the drive over, Mia had said, "If we get lucky and find him there, I don't want to talk to him. I just want to call Roscoe and Lorene and tell them where he is. If we talk to him, or if he even sees us, he might take off again."

"Agreed. That's why I should go in alone."

"Wait, why? This is my mess and I should clean it up. I'll go in."

She meant it, too. She didn't see the flaw in that approach. So I said, "Think about it. Which one of us do you think Dennis Babcock is more likely to remember? Some random dude like me, or the potential supermodel?"

"Oh," she said, but she didn't argue the point.

Still, though, I needed to be as discreet as possible, and that's why I was wearing eyeglasses with a thick black frame—to change my appearance, even just a bit. I would be willing to wager I could walk right past Dennis Babcock without turning his head—if he were here, inside the library, which he probably wasn't.

I rose from the table and made my way to the rear left-hand room in the building. Judging by the colorful posters and other artwork on the wall and the toys in one corner, this was the children's section. Also, there were some children, so that was a clue. I glanced quickly down the three aisles of books. No Dennis.

I moved to the next room over, which was about twice as large as the children's room. The shelves here were closer together and taller, giving the room the feel of a maze. This appeared to be the fiction section. No Dennis browsing in the aisles. No Dennis sitting at either of the small tables at the rear of the room.

I exited the room and Dennis walked past me.

He didn't see me. Didn't even look my way. He was heading for the front door, carrying only a small duffel bag.

And he was walking normally.

32

I yanked my phone from my pocket and began recording video as quickly as possible, but by then, Dennis Babcock was already walking out the front door.

I followed, but not so closely that he would notice me. By the time I exited, he was fifteen yards away, crossing the parking lot toward the street. Fortunately, the light rain from earlier had stopped. I recorded for several seconds, then slipped my phone back into my pocket, still recording, so I would at least capture audio. By now, Mia would be recording from her SUV, which was parked about twenty yards away. She would have seen Dennis leave the library, arms down, and known what to do.

We had agreed not to approach him, but under these circumstances, I made a judgment call.

I walked faster, and when I got within five yards, I removed the eyeglasses and called out, "Hey, Dennis."

He stopped walking and turned to look at me. I saw recognition slowly dawn on his face. Then he grinned. "Oh. Hey."

"Good to see you again," I said, now close enough to extend a hand, which he shook.

"You're, uh, that guy," he said.

"That's me," I said. "That guy."

"What's going on?" he asked. He was still grinning. I interpreted this to mean he knew I'd seen him walking normally, and now we shared a little secret.

I laughed. "Maybe you should tell me."

"Uh, it's all good, you know?"

"Roscoe and Lorene are worried about you," I said. "But I'd say it's more likely they're worried about your disability check."

Now he really smiled. "Sounds about right."

"How do you put up with them?"

"It ain't easy. Roscoe especially."

"He's a world-class asshole, isn't he?"

"No doubt."

"Did he talk you into it?" I asked.

"Well…"

"Might as well tell me," I said. "Think of it this way. If the truth comes out, he might wind up in jail. Wouldn't that be nice?"

"You wanna know something?"

"What?"

"I'm way ahead of you on that."

"How so?"

He hesitated, then said, "It's a long story."

"I've got time," I said. "Hey, are you hungry? My partner Mia is parked right over there. Remember her? Why don't we all go somewhere and get a bite to eat?"

He chose pizza. Mr. Gatti's. We had a table in a quiet corner. I was worried he might be apprehensive, but instead he appeared relaxed and even enthusiastic about telling his story. I noticed right off that he was more focused on Mia than on me. Great. I'd also noticed that he had walked to Mia's SUV, and then into the restaurant, with his arms down. No more pretense.

"I stopped taking my meds a few days after I got the tetanus shot," he said, pausing after he'd eaten one slice of pepperoni pizza. "I know I shouldn't do that, but I hate the way they make me feel."

"How *do* they make you feel?" Mia asked, and I knew that the empathy in her voice was genuine.

"Like I'm not myself. They make me tired and slow. Like I'm numb. Would you want to feel that way all the time?"

"Absolutely not," Mia said. "And I'm really sorry there aren't better options for you."

The expression on Dennis's face was simultaneously heartwarming and heartbreaking. He appeared amazed that anyone would show such concern for his well-being.

He said, "Sometimes I just need to take a break from it, and the problem then is that my head starts filling up with all kinds of weird stuff. It's like I sort of know it's not true, but I can't stop thinking about it. It's hard to explain."

"But you're doing a good job," Mia said. "It's helping me to understand."

She was so good with him.

"Thanks," he said.

"Are you on your meds right now?"

He nodded. "I started again last week."

"When, specifically?"

"I think it was Wednesday."

"And you were also on your meds when you got the shot?"

He said, "Yeah, and I had been for several months, but getting that shot—or any shot—well, those things always freak me out a little, because you never know what's in them. How can I be sure there aren't a lot of chemicals and other crap in there?"

"I understand," Mia said.

"It's like getting a flu shot, which I would never do. Why risk it?"

I suspected that even when Dennis was medicated, there was a certain amount of paranoia and delusional thinking he had to deal with on a daily basis—and he might not recognize it for what it was.

"So," Mia said, "tell me about the days after the tetanus shot."

"Okay, I stopped taking my meds a couple days later. Or maybe it was the next day."

"Did you stop taking them *because* of getting the shot?" Mia asked.

"Not really, no. I just didn't want to take them anymore. I was feeling off. That's the best word for it. Off."

Dennis picked up another slice of pizza. Mia and I waited patiently while he took several bites.

"And what happened after that?" Mia asked.

"I started to think the shot had some bad stuff in it, and one morning when I woke up, I couldn't walk right. I was, like, all cramped up. I couldn't extend my arms and legs completely. I was convinced the shot had been designed to do that to me. Not everybody, just me, because someone at the place where they make the shot was after me. But then I figured out I could walk okay if I held my hands above my head. I was totally stoked that I'd figured out a solution, you know? I beat them."

I said, "Dennis, speaking of the flu shot, have you ever seen the video of the woman who claimed she couldn't walk right after getting one? And she also suddenly had a Scottish accent?"

His sly grin returned. "Yeah, and I know what you're thinking. I saw that and it put an idea in my head. Right?"

"I'd say it's a possibility. One time I saw a video of Tom Brady and I decided I could become a Hall of Fame NFL quarterback."

He looked at me for a minute, puzzled, before he realized I was kidding. Then he gestured at Mia with a sly look on his face and said, "I think she has a better chance of being Gisele."

I had to laugh. "Oh, man, you're right."

I held my hand over the table for a high five, and Dennis obliged with enthusiasm.

"That's very sweet," Mia said.

It was a good moment, and I'd say we'd earned Dennis's trust by this point.

"I'm curious about something," I said. "When you're on your meds, are you able to understand that some of the things you're thinking aren't right? They aren't real?"

Mia had explained to me a condition called "anosognosia," which prevented people with schizophrenia from recognizing their mental illness. Anosognosia was present in about half of schizophrenics, and it could be either partial or complete, meaning that those with the condition could have moments when they were aware of their illness, and other moments when they weren't.

"Sometimes," Dennis said. "Like when I lost my driver's license. I ran from the cops because I was thinking they were really assassins pretending to be cops, and they were trying to abduct me. So, yeah, it freaked me out and I ran. But later, on my meds, I knew they just wanted to write me a stupid speeding ticket."

I said, "Let me make sure I understand the timeline. You were on your meds when you got the tetanus shot, but you stopped taking them a few days after that, and then you started again on Wednesday of last week."

"Right."

I said, "So when you dropped the note for Mia in the parking lot last Sunday, that was legit. Not a prank or anything like that."

"Yeah."

"And the note was referring to Roscoe, right?" Mia asked.

"Yeah."

She said, "If you thought he was going to kill you, why didn't you get out of there or call somebody?"

"That's kind of complicated," Dennis said. "See, in my mind, Roscoe didn't know that I knew he was going to kill me, but if I took off, then he'd know. So it was better if I stayed, because then I'd be fooling him. I know it doesn't make sense, but as Dr. Creech says, I can't expect an irrational mind to make rational decisions. That's what she says to keep me on my meds."

"And once you were back on your meds, you no longer thought he was going to kill you?" I asked.

"Right."

"Okay, if you started your meds again on Wednesday, when we met with you and Roscoe and Lorene on Friday…"

He knew what I was getting at.

"Yeah, you caught me," he said, grinning again.

I grinned back. "So you suckered us? You were faking the walk and everything?"

"Yeah. Pretty good, huh? I've had practice."

"But why?" I said. "By then you knew Roscoe was trying to run a scam, right? You weren't planning to help him with that, were you?"

"Oh, no way. In fact, I told Roscoe I wasn't gonna take part in his stupid plan, because it was illegal, you know, and we'd get caught. He got all pissed off, and then you know what he did?"

"What?"

"He hid my meds from me."

Mia said, "What a son of a —" But she stopped herself.

"I had some more in a different bottle, though, and I stayed on them," Dennis said.

"But why didn't you tell anyone what he was doing?" I asked. "You could've told us on Friday."

"Because by then I'd come up with a plan."

"What kind of plan?" Mia asked.

He started to talk, but he giggled at his own thoughts. Then he said, "I figured if I played it just right—and told the right people what was going on—I might be able to get Roscoe busted. I hate him so much. I wish he was gone forever."

I nodded in agreement, then said. "Who are 'the right people'? Tell me more about the plan."

He had taken another bite of pizza, but when he was done chewing, he said, "Well, at first, I thought maybe I should just refuse to go along with the scam. But then Roscoe might not get in trouble, and I'd have to listen to him bitch all the time. So then I decided I needed to tell somebody, but I wasn't sure who to tell. I'm not a big fan of the cops, you know. But I looked around on the Internet and finally figured it out."

I was doing my best to remain patient, but I wanted him to get to the bottom line. "So then you did it? You reported it to someone?"

"Yeah, finally. I snuck out to the library yesterday so I could have some privacy, and then I wrote a long email explaining everything, and making sure to say that none of it was Lorene's idea, or mine, and then I sent it."

"When?" I asked. "Yesterday?"

"No, I was gonna do it yesterday, but I chickened out. So I stayed at a motel last night and went back to the library today."

"And this time you sent the email?" I asked.

"Yep. Right before you showed up."

"Who did you send it to?"

"That, uh, lawyer guy. I already forgot his name."

"A lawyer?" Mia asked. "Why to a lawyer?"

"No, not just a lawyer," Dennis said. "He's like the top lawyer guy for the state."

I said, "Are you talking about the Texas attorney general?"

"Yeah, that's him," Dennis said.

I laughed. "Oh, man. That's good."

"I wasn't sure who I should tell."

"No, that's a good start," I said. "A great start. I've got a couple more in mind, though, if you really want to shake things up. Might as well go big, right?"

33

And so the Dennis Babcock case finally drew to a close for us.

Of course, before we left the pizza joint, Mia and I encouraged Dennis to send a copy of his email—which was surprisingly cogent and well written—to the fraud unit in the Texas Department of Insurance, as well as to the manufacturer of the tetanus shot, their attorneys, and their insurance company.

In short, there was a good chance that Roscoe would face criminal charges. The only hold-up I could think of was the issue that started all of this: Dennis's illness. Would the TDI fraud unit, who would head the case, pursue charges when their star witness was a man with a tenuous grasp on reality? Possibly not. Sad, but true.

We had to caution Dennis that if any prosecutory action was taken against Roscoe, it would be a slow process. In the meantime, Roscoe would know what Dennis had done, and Dennis needed to prepare for that. In fact, if we'd found Dennis before he'd sent the email, Mia and I would've come up with some other way to remove Roscoe from Dennis's life. If we'd known everything Roscoe had done—like hiding Dennis's meds, which was a crime—we would've demanded that Roscoe clear out of the house within twenty-four hours or face charges for that. It was a moot point now, so we advised Dennis to find some other place to stay for a few days.

Then I called Roscoe, got voicemail, and left a message: "Roscoe, it's Roy Ballard. We found Dennis. He is fine and has been taking his meds. You, on the other hand, are not going to be fine. In fact, some bad things are going to be happening to you very soon. Because of that, I want you to know that I'm going to be in touch with Dennis on a regular basis, and if you do anything to him that crosses any lines, including verbal abuse, hiding his medication, or any other bullshit like that, I'll be there to make sure you don't do it again. Do you understand what I'm saying? It's important that you do. Leave Dennis alone or deal with me. If you have any questions, feel free to call me back. I'd be happy to come over there and explain things in greater detail. Have a nice day."

When I ended the call, Mia said, "I worry about him."

"Why on earth would you worry about Roscoe?" She knew I was kidding. I added, "Dennis will be fine. Roscoe's a bully, and now that Dennis has a support system around him, Roscoe won't have the guts to do anything."

We rode in silence for a moment.

I said, "If this were a movie, right now you'd say, 'I hope you're right.'"

Mia smiled, and it was the highlight of my day. "I hope you're right," she said.

The rain and clouds had cleared, and now it was a bright and sunny Sunday afternoon. The temperature was in the seventies. We drove the SUV to Mia's house and quickly decided we needed to decompress. So we jumped into Mia's Mustang and drove with no destination in mind. We wound our way up to 2222 and went west, and eventually we were skirting Lake Travis on Bullick Hollow Road.

"Sorry," Mia said. "I didn't intentionally come over here. I wasn't thinking."

"Don't worry about it. It's not like I'm emotionally scarred or anything, having been just moments from certain death."

She reached over from the driver's seat and placed a hand on my knee.

"I need to get a new phone," I said.

"You want to do that now?"

"Nah, I'll do it tomorrow."

The windows were down, and the breeze flowing through the car seemed like it could whisk away anyone's troubles or concerns. Didn't work for me, though. I began to stew. To ponder ways to pay Holloway and his punks back. I acknowledge that I have a temper, plus an impressive ability to hold a grudge, and sometimes my imagination takes me to some dark places, where I commit some atrocious acts.

I tried to derail my train of thought by turning and looking at Mia. That's a mood lifter, right there. Anytime. Anywhere. She'd pulled her long blond hair into a ponytail to stop it from whipping around in the wind.

"Think Dennis went home?" she asked.

"Don't know, but at some point, we have to let him stand on his own. He hasn't called, so I'm sure everything is fine."

He had the number for my back-up phone, and when I replaced my iPhone tomorrow, I'd let him know to use that number instead.

Mia turned right on FM 2769, then left on Anderson Mill Road. I hadn't been in this area in years. Not my neighborhood. Wrong side of the lake. She took another left on 1431, and we followed that curvy road through Jonestown, then Lago Vista, and all the way to Marble Falls, where we stopped for a piece of pie at the Blue Bonnet Café, which was packed with locals and tourists alike.

When we were done, we sat quietly, with no pressure to do anything except enjoy the moment. No cases. No clients. No ex-boyfriends.

"You're the most beautiful woman in the room," I said. "As usual."

Mia smiled bashfully and took my hand. She looked like she was just about to say something important when the waitress arrived with our check.

34

Six days passed and we didn't hear from Dennis Babcock. I was tempted to call him a few times, but I resisted. I assured Mia that this meant he was doing well.

I knew one of the investigators from the Texas Department of Insurance's fraud unit and she told me, off the record, that it appeared they would be taking action against Roscoe. Yes, it took them nearly a week simply to make that determination, but that's how it worked. You can't expect a large government organization to act swiftly.

I'd gotten myself a new iPhone, but it used the same number as the one in the lake, and late that afternoon, I got a call from Ruelas.

"Want to hear some depressing news?" he asked. "Holloway is dropping the charges against you."

I'd been wondering why I still hadn't heard from an investigator about that. Those investigators—or the experienced ones, at least—usually had an intuition for knowing which cases were a waste of time. Even on legit cases, it could take a backlogged investigator several weeks to make contact with a suspect.

"Guess you're crushed," I said.

He didn't come back with some bullshit remark, which was unusual. And he didn't hang up.

"You're wondering why he did that," I said. "He had no reason—except that I was no longer investigating the Jeremy Sawyer case. He hasn't seen me in a week and he figures that's all done, because I hit a dead end. I can't prove that Starlyn was driving the boat, so why poke the ant bed? Why give me a reason to keep going after him? Sound about right?"

"Here you go again with your theories."

"Look," I said. "I know we have our differences, and I guess we always will—and I apologize for that snide remark I made the other day—but if you think I'm wrong, just come right out and tell me." Silence. After a couple more seconds, I said, "That's good to know."

"It can't be theories, though," he said. "You've got to have evidence. And right now, you've got nothing."

"I'm going to take that as a challenge," I said.

Bold talk.

Empty talk, as it turned out.

Another four days passed and I was beginning to accept that there was going to be no further resolution of the case. I couldn't prove that Starlyn was driving the boat. I couldn't prove that I'd been abducted and had been on the verge of drowning at the bottom of Lake Travis.

So be it.

Then a client sent us a fresh case, and I had no choice but to move on.

The case was fairly simple and straightforward. A middle-aged couple had one son who'd received his driver's license about a year earlier, but they'd never added him to their coverage. Who could blame them? Covering a teenager could be outrageously expensive. Problem was, the insurance company suspected that the teen was regularly driving at least one of the covered vehicles. Why? Because the family's $90,000 Mercedes had been wrecked at 2:46 in the morning— late on a Saturday night or early Sunday morning, depending on how you looked at it. Estimated damage was $34,516.29.

Here's how it went. A woman living on a fairly busy but residential street was woken by the sound of a vehicle slamming into a light post. She went outside and found a damaged Mercedes, but no driver or any passengers. She called 911. A deputy arrived in seven minutes and searched the surrounding area for any injured persons. Came up empty. They found no blood in or around the vehicle.

The obvious conclusion was that the driver had been intoxicated or otherwise impaired and had fled the scene. Happened frequently. A quick license plate check provided the owner's name and an address less than a mile away. There, the deputy found two parents who had plainly been asleep, were not intoxicated, and did not appear injured in any way. The deputy explained the situation, and when he asked who had been driving the car, the parents—cooperative until that point—began to waffle.

"Are you sure it's our car?" the father asked.

"Absolutely. VIN number matches. You have children?" the deputy asked.

"A son," the father answered.

"He lives here with you?"

"Yeah."

"Where is he right now?"

"He spent the night with a friend."

"How did he get there?"

"The friend picked him up."

"So he was not driving your Mercedes?"

"That's exactly right," the father said.

"You understand that if your son was driving, he could be injured right now. On top of that, providing false information is a crime."

"I was driving the car," the father said.

"Sir," the deputy said, preparing to warn the father further.

"No, I *was*. I was disoriented after the crash, so I walked home. I was alone."

"You seem fine now."

"I know, right? I was more mentally shocked than anything. I wasn't actually hurt."

"You were mentally shocked, and that made you disoriented?"

"Exactly."

"Did you suffer any memory loss?"

"Uh, well, not that I know of."

The wife was lingering in the background, looking like she'd just smelled raw sewage. Not happy that the husband had chosen this route.

"Where did the crash occur?" the deputy asked.

"Pardon?"

"If you were driving, you can tell me where the crash occurred. Can't you?"

"But I was disoriented."

"You just said you had no memory loss."

"Obviously I was wrong. Have I committed a crime?"

"Leaving the scene is a class B misdemeanor," the deputy said.

"What, uh, is the penalty for—"

"Six months in jail and a fine up to two thousand dollars. Sure you want to stick with that story?"

"What I want to do," the father said, "is talk to my lawyer."

Our job, obviously, was to capture video of the son driving the mother's car, a Jaguar F-type convertible, or the dad's Chevrolet rental, and we'd get brownie points if we could document evidence of any injury the son might have received, which was unlikely now, because the crash had taken place nearly two weeks earlier.

In the meantime, the deputy had gone ahead with charges against the father for leaving the scene of the crash, but that probably wouldn't stick, because the father's lawyer would repeat the claim of disorientation, which would probably work. In other words, the father's dishonesty had paid off. So far.

Mia and I took turns keeping the kid under watch as discreetly as possible. On the first few days—weekdays—he rode to school with a friend who lived in the neighborhood, and after that, there was no need for us to watch him until school had gotten out.

Complicating matters was the fact that the family lived in a gated community in the suburbs west of Austin. Gated communities sucked for us. There were tricks we could use to get in and out for short visits, but setting up surveillance on a house for a full evening was out of the question. That meant we had to set up as close to the gate as possible and keep an eye out for the Jaguar or the rental. The road out of the neighborhood fed onto Loop 360, one of the main north-south thoroughfares in Austin. Fortunately, there was a strip center near that intersection that provided a good place to park and watch.

On Saturday, I was waiting in my van when the Jaguar passed with the top down. Mom driving, son in passenger seat. I followed as they went to the Domain, an upscale shopping center in the north part of town. They parked outside a shop called Aldo and the mother went inside. The kid stayed in the car and started messing with his phone. I found a spot across the street and down about twenty yards. Close, but these people were oblivious to anyone who wasn't standing directly in front of them.

I checked my phone and saw that Mia had sent a text. *Heidi called. Roscoe has been arrested. He admitted everything.*

Perfect. He probably wouldn't serve much time, but it would get him away from Dennis. In the meantime, Lorene could take the proper steps to evict him as a tenant, if that's what she wanted to do. She could also get a protective order if he hassled her or Dennis at all. I sent Mia a thumbs-up emoji.

The mother came out of Aldo and walked across the street to a store called Anthropologie. The kid was still looking at his phone.

I got out my Zeiss binoculars and took a closer look. Both Mia and I had studied him at every opportunity, but we'd seen no evidence of injury. Same thing now. If the kid had been driving the crashed Mercedes—and I think he was—he'd been damned lucky.

Eight minutes later, the mom came out of Anthropologie and continued walking north, out of sight from my vantage point.

Thirty minutes passed and the kid began to fidget. He got out of the car, crossed the road, and walked south, passing directly in front of my van. I looked down at my lap, but he didn't look in my direction.

Seven minutes later, the mom, carrying two shopping bags, returned to the car. She put the bags in the backseat, then took out her phone and did some typing. Sending a text. Asking the kid where he was. She got a reply, then got into the car, backed out, and drove south.

I gave it twenty seconds, then followed. She picked the kid up near Yogurt Planet. He had a cup in his hand. The mom said something as he climbed in. *Don't spill that sticky crap in my car.*

They went south on MoPac, then south on Loop 360.

My phone rang. I didn't recognize the number, so I let it go to voicemail.

The mother turned the Jaguar onto the street that fed into her neighborhood.

Disappointing. Another wasted stakeout.

Then the mom surprised me. Before they reached the gate into her neighborhood, she pulled to the curb in front of a small, modest home. While the kid waited in the car, the mom got out, retrieved the shopping bags from the backseat, and walked to the front door of the house.

A woman with gray hair answered. The mom said something, and then she held the bags out toward the woman. There was a moment of hesitation, which indicated that the woman hadn't expected it. Her face was in shadows, so I couldn't make out her expression. She took the bags, though, and after about a minute of conversation, the mom turned, walked back to her car, and drove away.

I stayed where I was, confused about what I had seen.

Directly across the street was a wooden utility pole that appeared to be brand new. So this was the site of the accident. The pole had been replaced afterward, and the woman in the house was the one who had called 911.

Why was the mom giving gifts to this woman? I had one pretty good guess.

I walked to the front door and knocked.

When the woman answered, I said, "Hi, there. My name is Roy Ballard, and you must be Sue."

I had her name from the case files.

"That's right."

"Sue, I investigate insurance fraud for a living, and we're about to have a conversation that could screw your life up pretty bad for the next few years. Lawyers, legal fees, and all that."

"I don't understand."

I smiled at her. "Let's not play around, okay? I'm on your side. If you're truthful, I promise I'll do everything I can to help you out of this mess. You probably won't even have to go to jail. The cops will probably overlook the false report. How does that sound?"

35

She went for it. Told me exactly what happened that night.

She heard the wreck. Grabbed a robe and went outside. There was the Mercedes, still smoking against the utility pole, and there was the kid, staggering around. Injured? No, drunk. Disappointing, but this was a good kid, in general. He mowed her lawns during the summer for ten bucks, which was surprising for a kid who plainly didn't need the money. He was smart and respectful. Polite. Hardworking. A kid with potential, unlike some of the brats you see nowadays. Made decent grades. Wanted to be a wildlife biologist.

Okay, yes, he made a mistake, but did he deserve to have it ruin his future? Could he get into the colleges he wanted if this crime was on his record?

The kid pleaded with her not to do anything. She was torn. And then she agreed.

The kid ran off into the night, in the opposite direction from his house.

Just seconds later, her next-door neighbor arrived on the scene. He ran straight to the Mercedes, saw that nobody was inside, then looked around, puzzled.

"What happened?" he asked.

"I don't really know. I came outside and, well, this is what I saw."

"The driver left?"

"I guess so."

He spotted the cell phone in her hand. "Have you called it in?"

"I was just about to do that."

"Well done," Mia said later. "Bravo."

"Thanks. I advised her to get a lawyer and let him steer her through it. The cops might still charge her for making a false statement, but I kind of doubt it."

"So where did the kid go after the wreck?"

It was Saturday evening and we were grabbing dinner at Trudy's Four Star between Oak Hill and Dripping Springs. We were each having a drink—a margarita for Mia, whiskey rocks for me—to celebrate the quick resolution of this case.

"That we still don't know," I said. "I'm guessing he went back to his friend's house—the one he'd left just a few minutes before the crash. He was probably too freaked out to face his parents, or he was worried about the cops showing up, or a combination of both. Sounds like he was pretty drunk—or maybe on something else—so he bailed on the situation entirely. Of course, he had to deal with it the next day. His parents made him apologize to the woman for putting her in such a difficult position."

"You've got to be kidding," Mia said. "If they were any sort of parents, they would've taken the kid down to APD headquarters and made him 'fess up."

"Yeah, they aren't going to win the Parents of the Year Award anytime soon, but at that point, after Sue had already lied to the police, they had to worry about getting her in trouble, too."

"Convenient excuse for protecting their son. They were so deeply concerned about Sue, they had to keep quiet. Otherwise, I'm sure they would've stepped right up and done the right thing."

"The fact that the father lied to the cops right off the bat does make you wonder about his integrity, doesn't it?" I said.

Mia shook her head, stymied that anyone would behave that way.

"What about the shopping bags?" she asked.

"The mother took it upon herself to buy Sue some nice thank-you gifts. Just a small token of appreciation for engaging in criminal conduct. It was a couple of blouses that probably cost two hundred dollars apiece."

"Crazy."

Our waiter arrived with our food. We'd both ordered the chicken flautas.

After he was gone, I said, "Hey, listen to this."

I took my phone out and played the voicemail I'd received while I was parked outside Sue's house.

The caller said, "Hey, there. Thought you might like to know I found your phone at the bottom of Lake Travis. Obviously, it's pretty much a useless piece of junk now, because, you know, it doesn't even power on, but if you want it back give me a call. This is Todd, by the way."

"Whoa, really?" Mia said as she dipped a flauta into some queso.

"And this is why we engrave our phone numbers on our phones," I said. "This guy owns one of the scuba outfits on the lake, and apparently there's this whole subculture of people who dive solely to look for lost stuff, like treasure hunters. Todd keeps a running total on his website of all the stuff his divers find. He said they've recovered something like sixty thousand dollars' worth of sunglasses alone. That's the leading category—sunglasses."

Mia suddenly had a grim look on her face.

"What?" I asked.

"Just makes me sad that they are able to find those things, but a body can completely disappear forever."

I hadn't thought of that. It was an unfortunate irony.

We ate in silence for a few minutes.

"What do they do with it all?" Mia asked.

"Some of it, like my phone, gets returned to the owner. But things like sunglasses or jewelry— usually, there's no way to identify the owner, so it's finder's keepers. According to Todd, some divers go just for the treasure hunting aspect of it. They spend all their time on the bottom."

"That's gotta be creepy," Mia said.

"I would guess so. Scuba and skydiving—two hobbies I have no interest in at all. I'll stick with full-contact shuffleboard."

Mia smiled, but I could tell that the thought of bodies in the lake had dampened her mood. Or was something else bothering her? We'd made up after the latest Garlen episode—after I'd acted like an ass—and things had been fine since then. Except something was slightly off. I think. Maybe I was seeing something that wasn't there.

I should've left well enough alone, but instead I said, "You okay?"

"Sure."

"You're a little quiet tonight."

God help me, but I couldn't help wondering if Garlen had made contact again. Would she tell me if he had? I wouldn't blame her if the answer was no. Or maybe she was still upset by my behavior, even though she'd accepted my apology. Or, worse case, maybe she'd reached the conclusion that we never should've started sleeping together.

"Just tired," she said.

More like she had something on her mind, but I let it go. It took a lot of self-discipline, but I didn't push it any further. She could tell from my expression that I was worried.

She reached across the table and held my hand. "Just tired," she said. "Promise."

As I lay awake later in my apartment, instead of thinking about Sue and her poor choice to lie for the neighbor kid, or ruminating about the unfinished feel of the Jeremy Sawyer case, or wondering whether Mia was having doubts about our relationship, I found myself thinking about my phone.

If you'd asked me what the odds were that my phone would ever turn up, I would've said a million to one. Even if I'd known exactly where Holloway and his punks had tossed my phone overboard, complete with GPS coordinates, I wouldn't have thought it possible that a scuba diver could go under and find it. You've got strong currents to consider, and poor visibility, and all kinds of debris and muck on the lake floor.

Despite all that, my phone had been found. Serendipitously, yes, but it had been found.

And that made me wonder about Harvey Selberg's phone. If it hadn't been crushed or burned or smashed with a hammer, was it possible that I might be able to find it? Where would I even start to look?

I tried to think like the burglar who'd entered Harvey's home and eventually assaulted him. Chances were good that the burglar was Anson Byrd or Adam "Meatball" Dudley or even Gilbert Holloway. Whoever it had been—one of the three—the person inside Harvey's home would've been nervous. Scared. Heart pounding. Palms sweating. Hands trembling. Praying for everything to go smoothly. Just get in and get out.

He got lucky and managed to find Harvey's phone in the dark. Decided to grab the wallet, too, as a red herring. Make it look like an authentic burglary. Smart.

He turned to leave, and the worst possible thing happened. The phone in his hand suddenly began blaring with AC/DC music.

He tried to hurry, but it was dark and he smashed into something, and now Harvey was waking up and coming after him. That's when panic set in. Which way was the back door? Why hadn't he brought a flashlight?

And now here came Harvey, yelling, probably telling him to get the fuck out, and the intruder had no choice but to hit Harvey with…something. Didn't matter what it was. Harvey didn't go down, so the intruder hit him again, harder, and now Harvey dropped to the floor. The intruder finally found his bearings and hustled out the door.

He ran down the street, back to his car, and took off, breathing so hard now that he thought he might be having some sort of medical crisis.

Time to destroy the phone. That was, after all, the reason for the burglary in the first place. But he didn't have much time, because right this minute, Harvey might be using an app to track his phone. He might even be in his car, following. Not likely, but possible. Or he might be calling 911, and if a cop happened to be nearby…

The intruder had to act fast. He needed to make sure the phone was ruined, but he couldn't afford to pull over and make himself conspicuous.

So what would he do?

I sat up in bed, thoughts coming quickly.

What was the quickest way to ruin a phone? Wait. Correction. What did most people *think* was the quickest way to ruin a phone?

Drop it into water. Just like Holloway and his crew had done with my phone.

A lake or river. Toilet or sink. Pond or aquarium. Swimming pool or bathtub. Even a glass of water.

Water was the big killer, wasn't it?

But after Todd had called about my phone, I'd done some research—more out of curiosity than anything else—and I'd learned that it was sometimes possible to salvage data from a phone that had been submerged in water for an extended time. You shouldn't expect the phone to operate properly again, but there were ways that you might be able to save your photos or videos, for instance. If all else failed, you could take the phone apart and, well, I hadn't read much further than that—just far enough to know that someone with knowledge might be able to recover data from the internal flash chip, or whatever it was called.

I got out of bed and went into the living room, where my laptop rested on the coffee table. It was 1:17 in the morning and now I was wide awake, letting my hopes rise, and wondering if I might actually be onto something.

I opened the maps application and entered Harvey Selberg's address. He lived in Manchaca, a suburb in far south Austin, in a small neighborhood called Bear Creek Park. Fortunately, there were only two roads in and out, and both of them connected to FM 1626. Pretty good guess that the intruder would've turned right to go north, back toward town. That being the case, they would've crossed Bear Creek in less than a minute after leaving the neighborhood.

Could it be that easy?

If I'd been the intruder, I would've done two things for certain. First, I would've powered the phone off immediately, to prevent pinging off cell towers. And because I'd be worried that a cop might already be coming south on FM 1626, responding to a burglary call, I would've tossed the phone out the window, over the railing, into Bear Creek. Done. Phone destroyed. Or, at a minimum, impossible to find.

Right?

Now I realized I was pacing the floor.

It was 1:26. Nine minutes had passed. It was going to be a long night.

36

It was still dark when I found a place to park near the intersection of FM 1626 and Brodie Lane. Just a wide paved spot next to the road. There wasn't a No Parking sign, so the van would probably be fine while I was gone.

But I had to wait. No use fumbling around in the dark.

And I was trying to keep my hopes in check, because this would likely be a reconnaissance mission only. If the water was too deep or too murky, I would have to contact a scuba diver—maybe Todd—and hire him to conduct a search for me.

Finally, the sky turned gray and birds began to sing.

I locked the van and walked southwest on FM 1626. The bridge over Bear Creek was about one hundred and fifty feet away. I crossed over to the east side of the road, because the intruder would've been driving north, and he would've tossed the phone out the passenger-side window. The east side.

When I got close to the creek, I climbed over the guardrail and made my way down a steep embankment, to the north bank of the creek. I liked what I was seeing.

Bear Creek wasn't much of a creek. It certainly didn't flow year-round, and it wasn't flowing steadily now, meaning much of the creek bed was dry. Still, there were standing pools of water here and there, probably made deeper and wider by the recent rains. If someone had tossed a phone from the road, I guessed there was a fifty percent chance it would've landed in water.

I simply stood in place for a moment and assessed the area further.

The banks were covered with tangled weeds and grasses,

some waist high, along with random pieces of tattered trash that had been floating in the water at some point. Fast-food sacks and paper cups. Beer cans. Crumpled cigarette packages.

It would take me several hours to comb this area thoroughly. Even then, I couldn't be sure I hadn't missed something. And if I didn't find the phone, I'd feel compelled to search on the other side of the bridge, just in case the intruder had swerved into the oncoming lane and thrown the phone with his left hand.

Might as well get started.

I took a step forward, felt something hard under my shoe, and looked down to see a black iPhone.

I stared at it for a long moment, hardly able to believe my good luck.

What should I do next?

If I'd found the phone in water, my choice would've been easier. But here, on dry ground, even though it had rained days earlier, there was a good chance fingerprints remained, especially on the underside. As disappointing as it was, that meant I had to call the cops.

Eventually.

Maybe this wasn't even Harvey Selberg's phone. No harm in checking, right? That wasn't the same thing as tampering with evidence. After all, I wouldn't want to waste an investigator's time. I was doing them a favor, really.

I had planned ahead—incredibly optimistic—and brought some latex gloves along, for exactly this kind of situation. I tugged them on, then squatted down and gently pinched the phone on both sides with my left hand. Then I used my right index finger to press and hold the power button.

One second.

Two.

And now I saw the Apple logo.

Sigh of relief. The rain hadn't killed the phone.

Didn't mean it was going to function properly, but at least it had power.

I waited as the phone booted up, which seemed to take much longer than normal, and I just knew a screen was going to pop up asking for a password. But no. The home screen appeared, tiled from top to bottom with app icons, and behind them, a Dallas Cowboys logo. A good sign. I remembered that Harvey Selberg had had a cluster of Cowboys balloons in his hospital room.

The Photos app was on the third row down and I touched it, knowing I might be smearing a fingerprint. So be it. The camera roll had three hundred and fifty-one items in it. Below that, the videos folder had sixty-one items in it. I opened it and immediately saw Harvey's face in one of the thumbnails from one of the videos.

Oh, man. This was it. Harvey's phone. I'd found it.

I scrolled down to the most recent video and the thumbnail was just blurry darkness. The time-length indicator showed that the video was one minute and fourteen seconds long. I felt like I was on the verge of something big—something secret—and I couldn't help looking around to make sure nobody was approaching. And, of course, I was alone on the creek bank. Cars passing above couldn't even see me down here.

I pressed the blurry thumbnail and opened the video. Then I hit play—and experienced one of the most rewarding, and depressing, moments of my career.

What I saw over the course of that video answered all my questions and told me exactly what had happened on the Island Hopper. It also left me feeling chilled.

I watched it three more times, wanting to make sure I could remember every detail. Finally I decided my memory alone wouldn't be good enough, so I texted the video to my phone. Then I deleted the text from Harvey's phone. While I was still in the Messages app, I checked Harvey's most recent texts, but all of them were sent prior to the cruise. Nothing useful.

I went back to the thumbnails and looked for other videos from the cruise, but there weren't any. I did find a handful of photos taken on the barge, but none of them offered any new information.

I quickly checked the list of recent calls, just in case the intruder had been dumb enough to phone anyone, but, same as with the texts, no calls had been made after the barge had departed the dock.

Last, I checked Harvey's list of contacts—to make sure there weren't any surprises. Imagine, for instance, if he had known Starlyn or Anson or Meatball before the cruise, despite saying he hadn't. At this point, with as many twists as this case had taken, I couldn't take anything for granted. I was relieved to find nothing unexpected or suspicious.

I powered the phone off and placed it back in the same spot where I'd found it.

Then I pulled my phone from my pocket. It was time to call Ruelas.

But I couldn't bring myself to complete the call.

I found myself thinking yet again of my experience on the barge, hogtied and, yes, I'll admit it, pretty damned terrified.

I wanted payback.

Now that I finally knew everything, I wanted to rub their faces in it. I wanted them all to know that this new evidence would support everything I'd been telling Ruelas and the deputies. I hadn't assaulted Gilbert Holloway. He'd made that up to stop me from poking around. Same reason he'd sent Dirk Crider after me. Now I wanted to gloat about my discovery. To taunt them. To make them realize that the video on Harvey's phone, combined with my testimony, was going to put them all in prison for attempting to murder me, plus a variety of other charges.

If I called Ruelas, I wouldn't have that opportunity. Not the way I wanted to do it.

I left Harvey's phone exactly where it was. For now.

Back in the van, I called Eric Moss's cell phone. He answered on the second ring.

"This is Roy Ballard," I said. "I'm on my way over to your house."

"You'll be trespassing," he said. "And I will alert the authorities."

"Are you home?"

"Don't come over here. Consider this your only warning."

"I have video of Starlyn driving the barge when Jeremy Sawyer jumped overboard."

That stopped him cold. A long silence followed.

"And it shows what happened afterward," I said. "I'm not fucking around anymore. Either we do this on my terms or I'll call the cops myself. I almost went that route anyway. I don't know Starlyn, but everyone says she's a nice girl. I figure one mistake shouldn't ruin her life. I bet you agree."

He was in a tight spot. He didn't want to acknowledge the possibility that a video of Starlyn at the helm of the barge might exist, especially considering that I was probably recording this call—which I was. But he also couldn't risk telling me to go to hell. He had to find out if I was bluffing or not.

"I suppose the only way I'm going to get you out of my life is to deal with this nonsense," Moss said. Bluffing me right back.

"I'll be there in thirty minutes," I said, and I disconnected before he could respond.

37

Moss's front gate was open when I arrived. I parked the van in the circular driveway in front. The place looked empty. Dead. No light showing through any windows.

Maybe coming here was a dumb idea, but if I didn't do something, there was a good chance Eric Moss would be the only person involved who wouldn't pay the price.

I rang the doorbell, the dog inside started barking, and I waited for one full minute. Then I rang it again. The dog was now yapping at me from the other side of the decorative glass inset in the door.

This was a power trip on Moss's part—making me wait.

The door eventually swung open, and there was Moss, appearing simultaneously contemptuous and dismissive.

"It's amazing," I said. "You're a rich guy with every possible advantage in the world, but you always look like you have a stick shoved up your ass."

His eyes narrowed in anger. It was tearing him up that someone could talk to him that way and he couldn't do anything about it. The dog turned and trotted away to some other part of the house. He'd met me last time, and now I was old news.

"What is it you were babbling about on the phone?" Moss asked. "Or did you simply come here to make a nuisance of yourself?"

"We can do this on the porch, if you want," I said, "but by the time we're done, you'll probably wish you were sitting down."

He shook his head, as if he were patiently dealing with a mental defective, but there was no masking the concern on his face. He stepped back and opened the door wider for me.

I stepped past him, into the foyer, then waited for him to lead the way into his office, where I sat in the same chair I'd occupied last time, and Moss took the chair behind his desk.

He stared at me expectantly.

"I have to give you credit," I said. "You appear fairly calm and confident. I guess the business world teaches you how to do that."

"If you came here to show me something, you'd better go ahead and show it. Otherwise, you are wasting my time." Now his tone was downright icy.

"See, like that," I said pointing at him. "You're still acting like you have the upper hand, even though, deep inside, you know you might very well be screwed. Not just you, but all your pals. And Starlyn. That's what really bothers you, huh? But if it doesn't, or if you think there's nothing to worry about, by all means, just say the word and I'll leave. Last thing I want to do is be a bother."

I waited—enjoying every second. I was going to break this man before I was done.

Finally he said, "Show me the video."

He said it with a sigh, but the sneer was almost gone from his voice.

I took my phone out and cued the video up to play. Then I handed it to Moss. No worries there. Moss was far too intelligent to think I hadn't backed it up. Destroying my phone, or refusing to return it, would be pointless.

Instead, he did what he knew he had to do. He watched the video.

I'd watched it enough times now that I knew what was happening at any given moment, even though I couldn't see the screen.

The video opened on Starlyn Kurtis, wearing the captain's hat, behind the helm, and Jeremy Sawyer was standing right next to her. Rock-solid evidence that she'd been driving the boat—and Holloway was nowhere to be seen.

I could hear Harvey narrating. "Friggin' hilarious. Dude's at it again. Every time the boyfriend goes for a beer, this guy hits on the babe."

Harvey was quite obviously amused—and drunk, considering the way he was slurring. Judging by the scale of the video, I had concluded earlier that Harvey was on the other side of the deck, maybe twenty feet away. Jeremy was talking to Starlyn, but the microphone didn't pick it up. His body language indicated that he was being playful. Laughing. Flirting. Making time with a beautiful woman. Starlyn, to her credit, was paying attention—at least partially—to captaining the barge.

Jeremy said something else, and then he tapped one finger against his left cheek. Starlyn said something back, laughing. Jeremy touched his cheek again, moving closer to her, and Starlyn responded the way he wanted—by leaning over to kiss him on that spot. When I'd watched the video the first time, I already knew what was coming, and Eric Moss likely did, too, assuming he'd heard the unvarnished truth from Starlyn. As she leaned in, Jeremy turned his head quickly and, as a result, she inadvertently kissed him directly on the lips.

Harvey, still narrating to himself, or perhaps to the audience who might later view the video online, said, "Whoa, man, that was smooth."

Jeremy laughed and pumped a fist. *Yeah! It worked!* Starlyn laughed, too, and she was shaking her head at getting tricked. It was innocent, and kind of cute, really. He'd fooled her, this kid that otherwise wouldn't have any chance with her at all. He knew it. She knew it. No harm was done. It was just a joke.

Then the expression on Starlyn's face changed. Time to straighten up. The party was over. Her boyfriend was coming.

Jeremy saw him coming, too, and his grin faded as he

began to back up. Then Anson Byrd—or his broad back, really—entered the frame, and he was moving quickly toward Jeremy.

"Oh, shit," Harvey said, giggling. "Dude's toast."

But before Anson Byrd reached him, Jeremy vaulted himself backward over the railing, and just as he did that, a flash went off. That was one of Jayci's friends, snapping the photo of Jayci and Cady—the photo that showed Jeremy in the background, going over the railing.

Starlyn showed concern right off the bat, attempting to slow the boat down, but she fumbled around, forgetting what she was doing. An inexperienced captain. She said something to Anson, either chastising him or asking for help. He gave a dismissive wave— *Don't worry about it. He'll be fine.* Then he stepped over to gently ease her aside and take control of the boat. She said something to him—something sharp, judging by the cloud of anger on her face—but he shook his head.

"Well, that escalated quickly," Harvey said to himself, not sounding particularly concerned about what he'd seen.

Then Anson looked around to see if anyone else had seen Jeremy jump—and his glare came to rest on Harvey. So Anson knew that it had been recorded. Harvey lowered his phone and the video ended abruptly. No way of knowing how strenuously Starlyn had continued to object after that. Maybe a lot. Maybe not at all.

Across the desk from me, Moss had a face of stone. But now he did the same thing I'd done—he watched the video several more times. There was no changing the outcome. They'd simply left Jeremy behind, and he'd drowned as a result.

Anson, Starlyn, and Harvey were apparently the only people who'd seen what had happened. The boat was moving and the sun had set, so anyone with any sense would've known that Jeremy was in danger. I guess Harvey had an excuse, being as drunk as he was. But Starlyn and Anson? Not only had they seen Jeremy go overboard, they'd made a conscious choice to leave him in the water.

Moss finished watching, and then he placed my phone flat on the desk and slid it toward me. My guess was that he had been thinking about this scenario—being confronted by the video, or even just an eyewitness—and he'd prepared accordingly. He had an excuse all teed up and ready to go.

"Jeremy Sawyer told a lot of people on the barge that he was a state champion swimmer," Moss said. "He'd been bragging about it all night. There was no reason for anyone to be concerned."

"Starlyn looked concerned to me," I said.

"She was angry and upset with Anson."

"Then why was she trying to stop the boat?"

"Not because she was concerned for Jeremy's safety. She wanted to apologize to him for Anson's behavior. The video proves it."

I chuckled. "Really?"

He stared at me.

"Literally nobody will believe that," I said. "But it's going to be fun watching you try to talk your way out of it with the sheriff's office. Everything you've done to cover it up is about to hit the fan."

I could've left then, but I couldn't resist goading him some more.

"You know what happens in a situation like this?" I said. "Everybody starts turning on each other, looking for any chance to work with the DA and strike a deal. Holloway, Meatball, even Anson—they're all going to point the finger at you. You are well and truly screwed."

He was drumming the desktop with his fingertips. Getting anxious. Looking for a solution.

"What is it you want?" he asked.

"I want you to admit that you asked Holloway to kill me."

"But it isn't true."

"Sure it is."

"I'll give you fifty thousand dollars," he said. "And another

254 | BEN REHDER

fifty thousand to Jeremy's family. So we can put this misunderstanding behind us."

"You could afford a hell of a lot more than that," I said, "but money isn't the issue."

"Starlyn wants to go into a life of public service—to help people."

"She can still do that."

"Not really. Her options will be limited if that video comes out. It will follow her around forever."

"She should've done the right thing," I said.

"One hundred thousand dollars," Moss said.

I said, "Jeremy's family will file a civil suit and get millions. You won't need that money anyway, because you'll be serving time. A long time."

His face was turning bright red as the anger built up inside him, but he didn't respond.

I said, "That's all I came to say, really. That you should enjoy your free time now, because it won't last long."

"Get out of my house," he said, his jaw clenched so tight it was a wonder he didn't crack a tooth.

"It's been a pleasure," I said. I rose from my chair and he followed me out of the office, toward the foyer. He was just a few feet behind me, and I was almost hoping he would try to jump me, but at the same time, I knew he wouldn't.

Just as I passed a credenza against the right-hand wall, almost to the front door, he said, "A quarter million."

I turned to face him. "For me?"

"For you. Same for Jeremy's family."

I could see the desperation in his face, and I'll admit I enjoyed it.

"That's tempting," I said, "but all things considered, I think it would be better if you'd go fuck yourself."

I grinned at him.

If you've ever seen the angry, frustrated face of a five-year-old not getting his way, you know exactly how Eric Moss looked right then.

Likewise, if you have a temper, as I do, you're familiar with the adrenaline rush that comes in moments like this, when the promise of violence becomes as irresistible as any drug.

He was close enough that I could see a slight twitch under his right eye.

"You know you want to do it," I said, with my voice low and in control. "But you don't have the guts. You pay other people to do your dirty work. In a situation like this, you're a coward."

He was right on the verge of acting.

"You'll never get another chance," I said. "You'll have to remember this moment every day in a cell, and the shame you'll feel will haunt you like—"

And he finally swung. Not a good swing, of course, because a man like Eric Moss had never had to learn how to throw a proper punch. No, instead, he drew back with his right fist, giving me plenty of time to prepare, and then came around with it in a big, sloppy loop.

I leaned backward and the punch missed.

Then I stepped forward and drove my right fist like a piston into his exposed right cheek. I connected hard and Moss let out a pained grunt. He surprised me by staying on his feet, but he was wobbly.

He lurched toward me, trying to wrap me up, but I shoved him backwards with my right hand, then drove a left hook into his rib cage. He doubled over, cradling his midsection, and I resisted the urge to throw an uppercut into the center of his face.

He was struggling to catch his breath, and now he placed his right hand on the credenza for support. He seemed to suddenly focus on the woven basket beside the lamp. He lifted the lid, reached inside, and came out with a dog leash, which he set aside. Then he reached in again and came out with something I recognized immediately—a telescoping steel baton about twelve inches in length when collapsed.

Something he used to protect his tiny dog from larger dogs.

I made a grab for it, but I was too slow, and with a flick of his wrist, Moss popped the baton open. That changed the situation considerably. One forceful swing of the baton could easily break a wrist bone—or crack a skull.

And that was apparently what Moss had in mind, because he took a big horizontal swipe at my forehead. I managed to duck under it, but I could feel the baton brush against the hair on the crown of my head.

Now I was wishing I *had* thrown that uppercut.

Moss came closer, backing me up against the door, and tried a vertical swing this time. I attempted to step to the side, but he caught me hard in the left shoulder, and I could feel my collarbone snap. Not only that, I could *hear* it, and Moss could, too.

The grin on his face was almost demonic. This was a man losing control.

I had my good arm up, ready to fend off the next blow, if possible. He feinted a swing, but didn't follow through, obviously enjoying the fact that he had the clear advantage. Blood was trickling from a cut on his cheekbone.

"Your offer still stand?" I asked. Always the jokester.

"You're a dead man," he said.

"I'll take that as a no," I said. "But I should also mention that—"

And I rushed him, fast and hard, hoping to catch him off guard. He swung again, but it was too late and I was too close. I drove my torso into him, wrapping him up as best I could in my injured state. He toppled backwards onto the tiled floor and I landed on top of him, feeling a jolt of pain in my shoulder.

He was growling like an animal, with one hand tearing at my shirt and one trying to rip at my face. My right arm was still fine, so I used it—but not my fist. I couldn't draw it back, because he was grabbing my sleeve.

Instead, I pulled my fist up toward my own face, then

came down hard with my elbow on the bridge of his nose. He grunted in pain and blood flowed from both nostrils. I repeated the same move, even harder this time, and his grip on my shirt began to loosen. One final blow from my elbow knocked him unconscious.

My breath was coming in ragged gasps and my heart was hammering. I rose off the floor and took a minute to gather my thoughts. Did I need to call 911? Possibly, but I could also wait for Moss to regain consciousness. What I couldn't do was leave until then—not after delivering three strong blows to the head.

The baton was on the floor beside him, so I rolled it further away with the sole of one foot. Didn't want to put my fingerprints on it, just in case. Then something caught my eye and I bent down for a closer look. Oh, man. The final piece of the puzzle had just fallen into place. The surface of the baton featured a diamond-shaped pattern.

Just like the pattern left on Harvey Selberg's forehead.

I called Ruelas.

38

In the coming days and weeks, most of what I predicted in Eric Moss's office came true.

Meatball turned on Gilbert Holloway, Eric Moss and Anson Byrd. Dirk Crider turned on Gilbert Holloway. Even Gilbert Holloway, in an effort to blame Eric Moss for everything, squealed like a rusty piece of boat equipment. I can't specify what type of equipment, because I still don't know that much about boats.

All three of them hired lawyers to press for the best possible deal from the district attorney, in return for giving truthful and complete testimony about, well, just about every damn thing that had happened since the dawning of the age of mankind. If any of them lied about anything, the deal was off. There was one detail, however, that Meatball and Holloway wouldn't budge on, and that was our little excursion on the barge. They continued to claim that they were merely trying to scare me—as ordered by Moss—but they had no plans to drop me overboard. I still didn't believe them, but there wasn't much I could do about it.

Starlyn Kurtis remained quiet, for the time being, protecting her stepdad, or possibly giving in to his coercion. Her lawyer wouldn't let anyone near her.

That left Anson Byrd. Problem was, instead of trying to strike a deal, he took off. Just got in his truck and disappeared. I figured they'd track him down quickly, because it is extremely difficult to run without getting caught, but days passed and he remained elusive. Had he fled the country? If he had, his only viable choice would've been Mexico, and he would've had to cross by foot. Even then, it wasn't as easy to remain undetected as it used to be. He would've had to show a passport, unless he managed to cross illegally.

Still, without any testimony from Eric Moss, Starlyn Kurtis, or Anson Byrd, the sheriff's investigators were able to put together a fairly detailed re-creation of what happened the night Jeremy Sawyer died, and in the days afterward.

It began, of course, with the incident recorded on Harvey's phone. Jeremy went over the railing. Starlyn tried to stop the boat, failed, and then gave in to Anson's urgings to just keep going. Possibly she was upset by that, or maybe Anson convinced her that Jeremy would be fine, because he was an accomplished swimmer.

Some time later, Jeremy's friend Randy started wondering where he was. He searched the barge from top to bottom, then began to get worried. He asked everybody to just shut up for a second and look for Jeremy. No luck. Jeremy was gone. The most telling thing—from the standpoint of a potential jury—was that Starlyn and Anson didn't step forward right then and reveal what had happened. If they'd truly thought he could swim to shore, why not speak up? But they kept quiet.

Except that they must've told everything to Eric Moss, because, just moments after the boat arrived back at the dock, but before the deputies arrived, Anson called Moss, as confirmed by cell phone records.

Moss would've realized that Starlyn and Anson had created a potentially catastrophic situation for themselves. The call lasted more than seven minutes, suggesting that there had been a lot of discussion. Moss wouldn't have been concerned as much for Anson—screw him—as he would've been for his stepdaughter.

I could imagine the questions he would've asked.

"Are you sure nobody else saw it happen?"

"The guy who was recording it—do you know his name?"

"Are the cops there yet?"

"Have you told anyone anything?"

Based on deputies' logs, we knew that the first deputy arrived at the dock about two minutes before the phone call between Anson and Moss ended. That was just enough time for the deputy to walk down from his unit and take control of the scene, telling everyone who had been on the barge to gather around and put their phones away, because almost everyone would've been texting or calling someone.

All of the partygoers were interviewed, including Harvey, who was driven home afterward by his girlfriend Amelia, because she was sober by then. Later interviews with Amelia revealed that she was angry with Harvey for drinking so much, so she went home instead of staying over.

Then came the intruder in Harvey's house—which happened at about 4:30 in the morning. The alarm on Harvey's phone went off, waking him up, and he realized somebody was in his house. He got up, went after them, and got smacked with an object that left a diamond-shaped pattern in the bruised flesh across his forehead.

But who was the intruder? Gilbert Holloway, Dirk Crider, and Meatball all claimed they'd had nothing to do with it, and that they knew nothing about it. Meatball and Holloway admitted that Starlyn Kurtis had driven the boat for a brief period that night, and on a handful of previous occasions, but never for more than a minute or two, and only when they were out on open water. Had they known that a video existed showing Starlyn at the helm? They both gave an emphatic no.

However, Holloway did say that Eric Moss had called him at about 2:00 that morning and asked for a copy of the passenger manifest. Holloway thought that was weird. Why would Moss want that? Holloway said he'd already given a copy to the investigators, but Moss wanted a copy, too. Well, he was the boss, so Holloway emailed a photo of it to him. The manifest contained the name of every passenger on board. Oh, and the address. How convenient.

It was no leap of deductive reasoning to think Moss asked for the manifest so he could have Harvey Selberg's address.

And then he decided to protect his stepdaughter by making sure Harvey's recording never reached the cops. He went to Harvey's—carrying his steel baton, just in case—and stole the phone. The trick would be proving it all.

Fortunately, two days after my brawl with Eric Moss, forensic technicians processed Selberg's phone and found Moss's fingerprints. I can't tell you how happy that made me. The prints, coupled with the unique bruise pattern from the baton, were enough probable cause for the sheriff's department to secure an arrest warrant. Moss, accompanied by his attorney, turned himself in the next day and quickly bonded out. Of course, he refused to submit to an interview by investigators. Why would he?

Was Moss alone when he entered Harvey Selberg's home, or did he have an accomplice? My guess was that Anson Byrd had tagged along. Maybe he drove while Moss entered the house, or vice versa. Moss's fingerprints could've been on Selberg's phone either way. Conveniently enough, both Moss's and Byrd's phones failed to ping off any cell towers from about 3:32 a.m. until 5:17 a.m. Well, duh. They'd turned their phones off. Some people would say that was smart, but it would've been smarter to leave the phones at home, still turned on and pinging off the closest tower, which they could claim was proof they hadn't been anywhere near Harvey's house.

And what about Starlyn? What would happen to her? Technically, the sheriff's department might have been able to charge her with something, but it would be difficult to make it stick. Picture it from a juror's standpoint: Some guy willingly jumped off a boat, and this same guy had bragged about being a champion swimmer. Couldn't Jeremy have jumped with the express intent of swimming to shore? How far was it? A hundred yards? Two hundred? Not a big deal for a young, experienced swimmer. That's what a defense attorney would say.

For now, I simply had to have faith that the judicial

system would deal Moss the punishment he deserved, and that his wealth wouldn't allow him to avoid a guilty verdict. That possibility caused me to daydream about various ways I might extract some measure of revenge. Many of the ways were violent, and none of them were legal. I realize it isn't healthy to harbor this kind of animosity, but when I've tried to push such thoughts from my mind, I've failed.

The most rewarding aspect of having found Harvey Selberg's phone and determining what had happened to Jeremy was the closure I'd given his family. I'd met with them a few days earlier and they'd told me how healing it had been to learn the facts. Yes, they were still angry and grief-stricken, but the largest questions had been answered, and that provided a tremendous amount of relief.

That left just one mystery—at least, for me—and her name was Mia.

She called me one afternoon after everything had settled down and said, "Hey, I know I've been acting a little weird lately—"

"Just acting?" I said.

"It's because we need to talk."

"Yeah?" I said. "Everything okay?"

"I think so."

None of these words were comforting.

"What's going on?" I asked.

"Let's talk in person," she said. "How about if I come over in thirty minutes?"

It was a long thirty minutes, during which I convinced myself I knew what she had on her mind.

She was going to break up with me. What else could it possibly be? That's what "we need to talk" always meant. Who didn't know that?

She hadn't been willing to tell me she loved me, because she didn't. But it was better that way. I wouldn't want her to lie to me.

Now we needed to sit down like adults and see where we go from here. Would we be able to maintain our partnership? I would want to try. Would she? I couldn't imagine what my days would be like if Mia was suddenly out of my life. I knew that I would—

I heard a knock on my door.

Honestly, I didn't really want to open the door, but I did, and the expression on her face confirmed everything. I saw nothing but anxiety and worry.

"Hey," I said.

"Hey."

"You okay?" I said. "Never mind. I need to stop asking you that. Come on in."

She walked past me, without pausing for a kiss, and now I was wondering if I'd ever get to kiss her again. The very thought made me want to cry.

We sat on the couch facing each other.

"How's your shoulder?" she asked.

"Not bad. I haven't taken a painkiller in three days. It's healing up."

"Good."

She wasn't meeting my eyes.

I said, "Okay, now that we've gotten the small talk out of the way, you might as well do it."

She tried to laugh. "That obvious, huh?"

I had nothing clever to say.

She said, "Honestly, when you first told me—what you said at the creek bank—I didn't see that coming. I mean, I suspected you felt that way, but it still surprised me. Maybe it shouldn't have, but it did."

"I had to get it out," I said. "I couldn't go on any longer without telling you. I'm sorry if it made you—"

"No, Roy, I'm glad you told me. If I didn't make that clear, that's my fault. But…"

"Yeah, I know," I said. "I pressured you. What choice did you have? I know how you are—how big your heart is—and I should've known you wouldn't want to hurt me, even though you—"

"Roy, stop. I need to say something, and it's hard enough."

"Okay." I braced myself.

Mia said, "You know I don't like to rush into things—I'm not an impulsive person—but I can't remember ever feeling so right about someone. So sure. And that's why I came over here to…God, I'm nervous. I'll just say it. You wanna get married?"

Want to know when Ben Rehder's
next novel will be released?

Subscribe to his email list at:
www.benrehder.com.

Have you discovered Ben Rehder's
Blanco County Mysteries?

Turn the page for an excerpt from
BUCK FEVER

BUCK FEVER

CHAPTER 1

BY THE TIME Red O'Brien finished his thirteenth beer, he could hardly see through his rifle scope. Worse yet, his partner, Billy Don Craddock, was doing a lousy job with the spotlight.

"Dammit, Billy Don, we ain't hunting raccoons," Red barked. "Get that light out of the trees and shine it out in the pastures where it will do me some good."

Billy Don mumbled something unintelligible, kicked some empty beer cans around on the floorboard of Red's old Ford truck, and then belched loudly from way down deep in his three-hundred-pound frame. That was his standard rebuttal anytime Red got a little short with him. The spotlight, meanwhile, continued to illuminate the canopy of a forty-foot Spanish oak.

Red cussed him again and pulled the rifle back in the window. Every time they went on one of these poaching excursions, Red had no idea how he managed to get a clean shot. After all, poaching white-tailed deer was serious business. It called for stealth and grace, wits and guile. It had been apparent to Red for years that Billy Don came up short in all of these departments.

"Turn that friggin' light off and hand me a beer," Red said.

"Don't know what we're doing out here on a night like this anyhow," Billy Don replied as he dug into the ice chest for two fresh Keystones. "Moon ain't up yet. All the big ones will be bedded down till it rises. Any moron knows that."

Red started to say that Billy Don was an excellent reference for gauging what a moron may or may not know. But he thought better of it, being that Billy Don weighed roughly twice what Red did. Not to mention that Billy Don had quite a quick temper after his first twelve-pack.

"Billy Don, let me ask you something. Someone walked into your bedroom shining a light as bright as the sun in your face, what's the first thing you'd do?"

"Guess I'd wag my pecker at 'em," Billy Don said, smiling. He considered himself quite glib.

"Okay," Red said patiently, "then what's the second thing you'd do?"

"I'd get up and see what the hell's going on."

"Damn right!" Red said triumphantly. "Don't matter if the bucks are bedded down or not. Just roust 'em with that light and we'll get a shot. But remember, we won't find any deer up in the treetops."

Billy Don gave a short snort in reply.

Red popped the top on his new beer, revved the Ford, and started on a slow crawl down the quiet county road. Billy Don grabbed the spotlight and leaned out the window, putting some serious strain on the buttons of his overalls, as he shined the light back over the hood of the Ford to Red's left. They had gone about half a mile when Billy Don stirred.

"Over there!"

Red stomped the brakes, causing his Keystone to spill and run down into his crotch. He didn't even notice. Billy Don was spotlighting an oat field a hundred yards away, where two dozen deer grazed. Among them, one of the largest white-tailed bucks either of them had ever seen. "Fuck me nekkid," Red whispered.

"Jesus, Red! Look at that monster."

Red clumsily stuck the .270 Winchester out the window, banging the door frame and the rearview mirror in the process. The deer didn't even look their way. Red raised the rifle and tried to sight in on the trophy buck, but the deer had other things in mind.

While all the other deer were grazing in place, the buck was loping around the oat field in fits and starts, running in circles. He bounced, he jumped, he spun. Red and Billy Don had never seen such peculiar behavior.

"Somethin's wrong with that deer," Billy Don said, using his keen knowledge of animal behavioral patterns.

"Bastard won't hold still! Keep the light on him!" Red said.

"I've got him. Just shoot. Shoot!"

Red was about to risk a wild shot when the buck finally seemed to calm down. Rather than skipping around, it was now walking fast, with its nose low to the ground. The buck approached a large doe partially obscured behind a small cedar tree and, with little ceremony, began to mount her.

Billy Don giggled, the kind of laugh you'd expect from a schoolgirl, not a flannel-clad six-foot-six cedar-chopper. "Why, I do believe it's true love."

Red sensed his chance, took a deep breath, and squeezed the trigger. The rifle bellowed as orange flame leapt out of the muzzle and licked the night, and then all was quiet.

The buck, and the doe of his affections, crumpled to the ground while the other deer scattered into the brush. Seconds passed. And then, to the chagrin of the drunken poachers, the huge buck climbed to his hooves, snorted twice, and took off. The doe remained on the ground.

"Dammit, Red! You missed."

"No way! It was a lung shot. I bet it went all the way through. Grab your wirecutters."

Knowing that a wounded deer can run several hundred yards or more, both men staggered out of the truck, cut their way through the eight-foot deerproof fence, and proceeded over to the oat field.

Each man had a flashlight and was looking feverishly for traces of blood, when they heard a noise.

"What the hell was that?" Billy Don asked.

"Shhh."

Then another sound. A moaning, from the wounded doe lying on the ground.

Billy Don was spooked. "That's weird, Red. Let's get outta here."

Red shined his light on the wounded animal twenty yards

268 | BEN REHDER

away. "Hold on a second. What the hell's wrong with its hide? It looks all loose and…" He was about to approach the deer when they both heard something they'd never forget.

The doe clearly said, "Help me."

Without saying a word, both men scrambled back toward the fence. For the first time in his life, Billy Don Craddock actually outran somebody.

Seconds later, the man in the crudely tailored deer costume could hear the tires squealing as the truck sped away.

~ ~ ~

Just as Red and Billy Don were sprinting like boot-clad track stars, a powerful man was in the middle of a phone call. Unfortunately for the man, Roy Swank, it was hard to judge his importance by looking at him. In fact, he looked a lot like your average pond frog. Round, squat body. Large, glassy eyes. Bulbous lips in front of a thick tongue. And, of course, the neck—or rather, the lack of one. It was as if his head sat directly on his sloping shoulders. His voice was his best feature, deep and charismatic.

Roy Swank had relocated to a large ranch southwest of Johnson City, Texas, five years ago, after a successful (although intentionally anonymous) career lobbying legislators in Austin. The locals who knew or cared what a lobbyist was never really figured out what Swank lobbied for. Few people ever had, because Swank was the type of lobbyist who always conducted business in the shadows of a back room, rarely putting anything down on paper. But he and the entities he represented had the kind of resources and resourcefulness that could sway votes or help introduce new legislation. So when the rumors spread about Swank's retirement, the entire state political system took notice—although there were as many people relieved as disappointed.

After lengthy consideration (his past had to be weighed carefully—life in a county full of political enemies might be rather difficult), Swank purchased a ten-thousand-acre ranch one hour west of Austin. Swank was actually planning on semi-retirement; the ranch was a successful cattle operation and he intended to maintain its sizable herd of Red Brangus. He had even kept the former owner on as foreman for a time.

But without the busy schedule of his previous career, Swank became restless. That is, until he rediscovered one of the great passions he enjoyed as a young adult: deer hunting. The hunting bug bit, and it bit hard. He spent the first summer on his new ranch building deer blinds, clearing brush in prime hunting areas, distributing automatic corn and protein feeders, and planting food plots such as oats and rye. It paid off the following season, as Swank harvested a beautiful twelve-point buck with a twenty-two-inch spread that tallied 133 Boone & Crockett points, the scoring standard for judging trophy bucks. Not nearly as large as the world-renowned bucks in South Texas, but a very respectable deer for the Hill Country. Several of his closest associates joined him on the ranch and had comparable success.

Swank, never one to do anything in moderation, decided that his ranch could become one of the most successful hunting operations in Texas. By importing some key breeding stock from South Texas and Mexico, and then following proper game-management techniques, Swank set out to develop a herd of whitetails as large and robust—and with the same jaw-dropping trophy antlers—as their southern brethren.

He had phenomenal success. After all, money was no object, and the laws and restrictions that regulated game importation and relocation melted away under Swank's political clout. After four seasons, not only was his ranch (the Circle S) known throughout the state for trophy deer, he had actually started a lucrative business exporting deer to other ranches around the nation.

Swank was tucked away obliviously in his four-thousand-square-foot ranch house, on the phone to one of his most valued customers, at the same moment Red O'Brien blasted unsuccessfully at a large buck in Swank's remote southern pasture.

"They went out on the trailer today," Swank said in his rich timbre. He was sitting at a large mahogany desk in an immense den. A fire burned in the huge limestone fireplace, despite the warm weather. He cradled the phone with his shoulder as he reached across the desk, grabbed a bottle of expensive scotch and poured himself another glass. "Four of them. But the one you'll be especially interested in is the ten-pointer," Swank said as he went on to describe the "magnificent beast."

Swank grunted a few times, nodding. "Good. Yes, good." Then he hung up. Swank had a habit of never saying good-bye.

By the time he finished his conversation, a man who sounded just like Red O'Brien had already made an anonymous call to 911.

~ ~ ~ ~ ~ ~

ABOUT THE AUTHOR

Ben Rehder lives with his wife near Austin, Texas, where he was born and raised. His novels have made best-of-the-year lists in *Publishers Weekly, Library Journal, Kirkus Reviews*, and *Field & Stream. Buck Fever* was a finalist for the Edgar Award, and *Get Busy Dying* was a finalist for the Shamus Award. For more information, visit www.benrehder.com.

OTHER NOVELS BY BEN REHDER

Buck Fever
Bone Dry
Flat Crazy
Guilt Trip
Gun Shy
Holy Moly
The Chicken Hanger
The Driving Lesson
Gone The Next
Hog Heaven
Get Busy Dying
Stag Party
Bum Steer
If I Had A Nickel
Point Taken

For more information, go to
www.benrehder.com

Made in the USA
Coppell, TX
05 December 2023

25389719R00154